TO KILL A JUDGE

PAUL NELSON

BooksForABuck.com

2010

Paul Nelson

Published by
BooksForABuck.com
ISBN: 978-1-60215-130-7

Dedication

Pat Nelson 1923 - 2010

This book is dedicated to Gema. You taught me how to live, love and respect each person for the individual they are. As a young, widowed mother of three while working two or three jobs at a time, you still pounded away on an old typewriter and found time for us kids. I'm sure I inherited my love of books and writing from you and so I dedicate this one to you.

I love you, Mom.

REVELATIONS, 6:8 "And behold a pale horse: and the name of him who sat on it was death, and Hell followed with him."

To Kill a Judge

CHAPTER ONE

Sighting down the barrel, Matthew squinted into the scope, through the crosshairs onto the front door where he was certain the Judge would shortly appear; she always did. 7:10 AM. The door would open at exactly 7:15 AM. and she would come out on the porch in her white terry-cloth robe, bend over and pick up her morning newspaper.

He ignored his racing pulse, focusing on his duties. Refusing to allow the wrong questions to enter his mind, concentrating only on the necessities of marksmanship. Still, his mind wandered, so he deliberated on what he was doing and how he had gotten to this point.

He adjusted his scope, a Bausch & Lomb Elite 4200 with a 6X36 Matte: an expensive one and very precise. His rifle of choice, a Ruger semi-automatic 22 with a single 15 round clip. Carrying no spare clips was natural for him. Just as with his last five victims, he brought only what was necessary to the crime scene. The one full clip he had was loaded with Stinger 22 long-rifle hollow point bullets. In reality, he knew that one bullet should be more than enough for his purpose.

Come on, Judge! Come and get it. I've waited ten years for this moment. Your time has come.

Inside his head was a cacophony of sound, a tremendous roaring, as if he were standing in a cave under a giant waterfall. Having waited far too long to be put off by imaginary noises, he shook his head hoping to clear it and quiet the distractions.

Concentrate. Only a few moments to go. Almost there.

All in all, Dr. Matthew Hightower was a man of many talents. During the last ten years his talents had been honed, refined and conditioned by a searing hatred. His entire being had focused on revenging the wrongs six individuals had heaped upon him. Five were now disposed of. Only one victim remained.

Uncharacteristically and totally against his will, his mind wandered to Marilyn and the girls. What would they think if they knew that he was a murderer? What kind of husband could kill a Judge? What kind of father could kill an unarmed woman in cold blood? They knew nothing of his other victims. What if the unthinkable happened and he got caught? No 18 years this time. Nope, this was old sparky, straight up.

My God, Matt, get your act together! She'll be out in a moment. Feel the fire in your guts. Put it out! There's no other way! For God's sake, get a grip!

Blinking the sweat from his eyes, he looked at his watch. 7:12 AM.

He focused on the mailbox under which the newspaper lay in the curled up arms of the black wrought iron holder. The rifle sights were perfectly set; he had tweaked them himself, dead on target at 100 yards. Perched, about 10 feet off the ground in a seated position with a solid limb in front for a gun prop, he was situated almost exactly 100 yards from the Judge's porch. It was a clear shot from the perch to the Judge.

Cold and bruised from sitting on the hard bark of the limb, his ass hurt severely and his legs were totally numb from lack of circulation; still, he did not shift his position. No telltale motion would give him away before he completed his deadly task.

7:15 AM. Judge Alice Dana opened her door. As she did every morning, she stopped to smell the fresh air, breathing it in deeply as she looked around, absorbing the peace and tranquility of the country area she had chosen for her home.

No longer feeling the pain and numbness of his long wait, Matt blinked the sweat from his eyes for the last time. All visions of Marilyn and the girls receded into the recesses of his mind to allow total focus on the job at hand. Shutting down all questions and concentrating, his finger began to take up slack on the trigger. He took a deep breath, let out half of it, and gently squeezed. Through the scope he centered the crosshairs on a space at the top of her nose, precisely between Judge Dana's unsuspecting eyes.

* * * *

"Will the defendant please rise."

Rising to his feet, Matt was flanked on both sides by his attorneys.

God, I hope she's seen through this farce.

Looking at Matt and his attorneys, Judge Alice Dana focused her eyes on the defendant, Matthew Hightower and pronounced: "It is the decision of this court that you be sentenced to eighteen years in the Florida Penal System, said prison time to be followed by five years probation."

Gasping for air, Matt felt like he had been kicked in the chest by a bull elephant. *Eighteen years! Dear God, I'll be an old man and Marilyn will be a white haired old woman! Eighteen years!*

His bowels turned to water and it took every ounce of mental and physical strength he could muster to keep from spewing brown liquid down his pants, right in the courtroom. Even his concentration on his urethra and sphincter muscles did not prevent a few drops of urine from staining his shorts and darkening the front of his blue trousers. Legs filled with jelly refused to hold him steady and he leaned against Sam as his pulse raced and sweat began running profusely down his face and armpits. His mind swirled in a fog of confusion. What had brought him to this?

* * * *

Growing up as a country boy and raised in the woods of north Florida, Matthew Hightower always knew he would leave the country life some day. He felt destined for bigger and better things.

Matt's mother, Flora, stood five feet eight inches tall, and was pleasantly plump. Flora often mused that all of the world's problems, and especially the problems of her own family, could be solved with a lot of love and a good meal. Matt was her first and only child and from the moment he was born she called him 'her little angel', and saw too it that her angel had plenty of time to practice earning his wings at the local Catholic Church.

Matt enjoyed being an altar boy—he could see his mother beam with pride every Sunday as he recited flawless Latin in response to the priest's intonations. Besides, by being a good altar boy, he got to skip a lot of classes to assist the priest at weddings and funerals. Being a little angel had its moments.

His father, Cecil, was a slim but muscular man six foot two inches in height, with black wavy hair, gray eyes that twinkled when he looked at his wife and son, and a bright shining smile that constantly fought to be seen. A farmer by choice, he worked from sunup to sundown growing his crops and raising a small herd of Angus cattle. As a living, it was hard work and Cecil enjoyed it far more than did his only son. A patient and personable man, Cecil spent a lot of time with Matt, imparting on him knowledge of the woods, wildlife and the farming industry of North Florida.

Matt loved and respected his parents but he had no intention of following in his father's footsteps. It was not the work that bothered Matt. In fact, he liked the hard labor and the feeling he got when he really had to use his muscles. It was just that Matt was ambitious and personable with a lust for life that would not allow him to settle for a farmer's existence. After talking to the parish priest, Matt sat down with his parents one evening about six months before high school was out.

"Mom, dad, I've got something to tell you and it isn't easy," Matt began. "I've been doing a lot of thinking and I even discussed it with Father Dan. I want to join the Navy and see the world while I'm still young enough to enjoy it."

Dreading their response, Matt waited for his parents to speak.

Flora went first, and there was moisture in her eyes as she said, "I guess I've always known that you weren't one for farming. I had hoped that you would like to try college out first, but you're so much like your father that I can see in your eyes you've already made your mind up."

She paused, eyes brimming with tears and Cecil spoke.

"Son, I knew as much as your mom did that you're no farmer. You are a good worker and a good man and I believe you will make us proud whatever you do. I think I speak for us both when I wish you the best, even though it will break your momma's heart when you go. I'm sure I'll miss you too." His dad reached out, grabbed Matt by the neck and then hugged him.

Instantly, all three of them were hugging and crying and Matt experienced joint feelings of relief and sadness. These two people were the rock of his existence and he really loved them both. He would miss them every bit as much as they missed him.

Upon graduation at age eighteen, Matt signed up with the local Navy recruiter to set out to see the world. Although both parents knew it was coming, it was still a shock. Three days later, it was time. After tearful goodbyes, Matt's father gave him two one hundred dollar bills and his mother insisted he take two large slices of his favorite, pecan pie, and a very manly sterling silver St. Christopher medal and chain to protect him in his travels.

By now he had acquired his maximum body height of six feet one inch but he had yet to fill out, weighing in at a measly one-hundred-seventy pounds, albeit, with no fat; only lean mass adorned his rugged, farm boy frame. Striking good looks complemented his thick, wavy black hair and a fine set of even white teeth sat waiting to flash in a quick and ready smile. Accentuating his slate gray eyes, his face was handsome and intelligent looking which would serve him well with the ladies for the rest of his life.

The first stop on his new journey placed him at boot camp in San Diego, California. Although his aptitude test's showed Matt qualified for almost any enlisted job placement, it had only taken him a few short weeks to realize that the medical personnel received preferred treatment, so he signed up to become a Navy corpsman.

Following boot camp he went directly to enlisted medical training at the main camp educational facility, still at San Diego Naval Base. Co-ed classes allowed Matt to become involved with a cute redhead and experience his first major crush. Earlier encounters with a limited number of small town country girls hadn't prepared him for Sally. Although the same age as he, Sally was a far more experienced sexual partner than Matt. With her home in Los Angeles, weekends soon became a tropical fantasy come true; the drive itself became a test of extended foreplay often culminating in a rush indoors to strip and tumble into her massive king-sized waterbed. Afterward, in a much more relaxed state, they would share drinks while skinny-dipping in the pool until arousal once again took over. Sometimes they made it back to bed, sometimes the side of the pool or a convenient lounge chair sufficed. Those were weekends that most men could only dream of.

Reality set in soon enough though, and before their affair could lead to bigger and better things, they received orders to different stations. Elated with his placement at the head of his class, Matt was nonetheless upset that his orders would separate him from Sally at this point in their relationship. Assigned to a post on the attack aircraft carrier, USS Hancock, CVA 19, which was stationed out of Alameda, California, he could only fret about Sally's assignment to a hospital ship based in Norfolk, Virginia.

After only three letters, the long distance affair ended. Sally had discovered a new playmate and Matt was devastated for all of 24 hours.

Recovering from the hangover following his "Dear John" party, Matt realized that he had never really loved Sally, only the pleasure of her body and companionship. He also discovered a sympathetic friend, Judy, who had suffered the same basic fate in her last romance and, over the next couple of years, he found several other sympathetic female friends with whom to share time. It was a glorious time of awakening, full of fun, excitement, love and learning.

Truly enjoying his assignment time on the Hancock, Matt was at first relegated to the lowliest jobs: bed pans, bed sores, eye cleaning, ear washings and cleaning up messes made by sick sailors. All the jobs that no one wanted were assigned to him as the lowest non-rated enlisted man in the sick bay. He attacked each chore with calmness and efficiency no matter how nasty it appeared and was promoted to corpsman/seaman in six months. One year later he was corpsman 3rd class.

Shortly after his promotion, Matt was called to Captain's quarters to meet with his CO, Captain Kroger. After being ushered into the Captains lounge, a very nervous Matt sat waiting for his Commanding Officer to appear.

"Attention on deck" called out the boson mate assigned to CO quarters.

Jumping up so fast that his white hat fell to the floor, Matt almost forgot that sailors did not salute indoors and uncovered and instead, he stood rigidly as his ship's Captain walked in.

"At ease, Petty officer Hightower. Pick up your cover and have a seat," Captain Kroger said with a suppressed smile.

Still having no idea why he was here and feeling both silly and concerned, Matt did as he was told, picking up his white hat or cover as it was called and sat back on the couch albeit very stiffly as he awaited information as to why he'd been summoned to this almost forbidden place for enlisted men.

Not keeping him waiting the Captain began.

"Petty officer Hightower, I called you here because the Navy has seen fit to initiate a program that I believe has merit. After consulting with your superiors, I believe you are the corpsman from this ship's allotment to fill the billet. If you are interested in becoming a medical doctor, the Navy is willing to help you follow that career."

It seemed that the Navy was willing to take several young men to educate and make doctors out of if they appeared as career-oriented qualified candidates from the corpsman ranks. The offer was four years at Bethesda working a day shift in the Navy at Bethesda Hospital and full time in college. That would be followed by two years at med school and a final year on active duty at a naval medical hospital, whereupon he would finish with an MD and lieutenant's bars.

Matt jumped at the chance, and a week later was enrolled at Bethesda. At age 26, he became Lieutenant Matthew Hightower, MD. With his commission as an officer came a transfer to the U.S. Naval Air Station, Pensacola Florida.

Then came Marilyn.

Matt loved the sandy, white beaches of the Florida gulf coast and spent as much time as he could on them, soaking in the warm sun's rays and flirting with the numerous young ladies who lined the waterfront every weekend. His good looks contributed to his seemingly good fortune with the other sex and he was thoroughly enjoying himself when he ran into the future mother of his children, Marilyn.

Strolling down the beach with the waves gently lapping at his feet, Matt was watching a seine boat surrounding a school of mullet about fifty yards off shore. As the men began to drag the net in and force the fish into the pocket in the center, the men themselves began backing up onto the beach. Matt was joined by several other onlookers, all focused on the scene before them. Backing away to allow the fishermen more room, Matt accidentally bumped into a girl he had not noticed before.

"I'm sorry," he said. "I didn't see you."

"No problem," she answered. "I didn't see you either."

Matt suddenly found himself stating into the most beautiful blue eyes he had ever seen. For the first time he could remember, he was at a total loss for words and he continued to stand there, just looking. Finally realizing how foolish he must look, Matt managed to stammer out a few words.

"My, my name is Matthew Hightower, Lieutenant Matthew Hightower."

You idiot! Why did you say that! Now she must think you are not only a fool but an arrogant one at that!

"Why, pleased to meet you, lieutenant. My name is Marilyn Joyce. I'm from Fort Walden." She hesitated. "And you must be one of those jet pilots stationed at the Naval Air Base." She was smiling a crooked little smile that melted him and drew him even further into those beautiful eyes.

Right then, Matt couldn't have told anyone what type bathing suit she was wearing, or even what color. As the Italians say, he was 'thunderstruck'.

Dummy, dummy, dummy! You really set yourself up for that one. Now you can tell her you're only a lowly doctor, not a fancy jet pilot. Dummy, dummy, dummy!

"No, I'm a doctor. I just examine those pilots, I don't fly the planes. Look, I think I got off on the wrong foot and I'm sorry. Can we start over?"

Matt was almost pleading now, worried that she would get away and he would never see her again. All he knew was that somehow she was the most appealing woman he had ever met and he wanted to get to know her. For the first time in years, sex was the furthest thing from his mind.

Her eyes twinkled and she continued to gaze directly into his. "Sure. Would you prefer that I call you Matthew, Matt or lieutenant?"

Sensing that she was being playful but honest, Matt said, "Matt will do just fine, Marilyn."

* * * *

They spent the rest of the day together, wandering up and down the beach, sitting in the sand and then taking a dip in the Gulf to rinse the sand off, all the while talking occasionally, touching. One time, Matt offered her his hand to help her up off the sand. When she stood up, she landed against him and they both stood there, looking, smiling and smelling the clean warm scent of each other.

Only too soon, the sun was setting and they both realized it was time to go. Their cars were parked within a block of each other and, after going to pick up her blanket and towel from where they were lying in the sand, Matt escorted Marilyn to her car. They were unusually silent, both feeling as though something fantastic had happened, something they did not want to let go. As she reached into the car and pulled out her cover-up shirt, Marilyn turned and looked straight into Matt's eyes and they both melted into each other's arms.

Their first kiss was loving and tender and seemed to last forever, only ending when they both felt like coming up for air.

"Wow." Marilyn said,

"Wow back to you." Matt never took his eyes off of her.

They stood, holding hands and totally content to just allow the feeling of togetherness to engulf them, neither one wanting to come back to reality.

Finally Matt said, "May I see you again, soon?"

"Would tomorrow afternoon, four o'clock be soon enough?" she replied.

"Right here?" He asked.

"I'll be here." Marilyn turned to get into her car.

Matt stood watching until she disappeared and reality finally set in. He began mentally kicking himself. *What a dummy. I never got her address or even a phone number.*

Later, when he climbed into his bed, he could still smell her clean aroma and taste the sweetness of her kiss. It took him two hours to fall asleep, and Marilyn was in his dreams all night long.

Matt was almost fifteen minutes late when he arrived back at the beach. Marilyn was already there wearing a different bathing suit and looking more beautiful then before. Taking a deep breath, Matt's piercing gaze almost dissected her until she became uncomfortable and complained.

"Do I look that bad?" She followed with a mocking smile that brought him back to reality.

"Anything but." He replied, finally regaining some of his normal poise." Actually, you're the most beautiful girl on the beach."

"And how would you know, Mr. Lieutenant. You only just got here and certainly have not surveyed the entire beach yet."

"Don't need to," he retorted. "You're already everything I consider beautiful and perfection needs neither comparisons nor improvements."

"Well, at least the cat has let go of your tongue since yesterday, Matt."

As they bantered about they both unconsciously moved closer and soon they were standing face to face, only inches apart.

"I missed you." Matt said in a now husky voice.

"It seems silly, but I missed you too," Marilyn replied.

As they stood here, rapt and beginning to lean even closer for the kiss they both knew was coming, a seagull suddenly swooped down beside them, grabbed a left-behind french fry in his beak and emitted an ear piercing shriek as he took back to the air, almost hitting Marilyn's legs in the process.

"Wow!" Matt cried in appreciation. "A perfect touch and go." Obviously referring to carrier flight practice.

The spell was broken and they clasped each other's hands and moved down to the beach at a comfortable stroll.

They spent the rest of the afternoon talking and getting to know one another, each becoming more infatuated with the other and neither trying to hide that fact. At dusk, they moved to a secluded spot among some sand dunes about a mile from where they were parked and sat on the towels, watching the sun go down.

"It looks like the sun is sinking right into the ocean," Matt said in a husky, contented voice.

"I'm sorry," she replied. "I really wasn't looking at the sun just then."

As Matt turned his head to look at her he felt her warm, sweet breath on his face. They were only inches apart and she was braced with one hand on the towel, leaning into him.

Dropping down on his left elbow, Matt put his right arm gently over her and scooted his body close to hers.

No words were spoken as they embraced, their bodies stretching out lengthways on the towels. Their kisses were soft and probing at first, but soon became more demanding as each of them fed off the desire of the other.

"God, you taste good," Matt whispered as he momentarily removed his mouth from hers, bending his neck to allow him room to kiss her neck and shoulders.

"Whatever you do, don't stop. Don't ever stop," Marilyn rasped, her voice becoming more hoarse and rushed as she plunged headlong into the flames of desire that were consuming them both.

They both almost ripped each others bathing suits off, so impassioned that they were trying to kiss and smell, touch and taste fondle and couple, all at the same time. Neither one of them was a virgin, but neither of them had ever had a moment like now as Matt entered her for the first time.

"Oh my God, I love you," Matt panted as he rode wave after wave of the all-consuming fire of his passion.

"Love me, Matt. Love me now and love me forever as I am loving you," Marilyn groaned back, too full of him and her own excitement to do more than shoot the words out in a rapid fire blurt of phrases.

Wrapping their arms and entwining their legs around each other, together they closed their eyes and rushed headlong into the climax of their endeavors as she met stab after stab of Matt's hungry sex with her own, equally hungry thrusts.

"Oooh, oooh, ooooooooooh God" Marilyn cried out as she could hang on no longer and surrendered to her body's final throes.

A prolonged grunt was Matt's only verbal response as he was totally transfixed with a combination of love and lust until his body could no longer restrain its natural explosion.

CHAPTER TWO

Monday, 3:00 PM

Lilly, Matt's secretary, buzzed him on his intercom. He was in his office, going over the blueprints for the design of his next clinic.

"Doctor Hightower, there are some men here to see you. They are from the State Attorney's office and there are several policemen with them."

What the hell?

Matt opened the door to his office to see for himself what was going on.

"Doctor Matthew Hightower?" The man asking the question looked about 30 years old. He stood about 5 foot 8 inches tall, had dark hair, black eyes, a pockmarked face and was wearing a blatant sneer on his countenance.

Matt nodded. "Yes, I am Doctor Hightower."

"Dr. Hightower, I'm Rupert Shimdugger from the State Attorney's office. I have a warrant for your arrest. Will you come with me, please?"

"Are you out of your mind? I'm a doctor. I haven't done anything. This must be some sort of sick joke. I have patients in this office. How dare you come in here like this?"

His face flaming red, Matt's voice quivered as it rose higher and louder with each sentence.

"Doctor Hightower, I assure you this is no joke. Put your hands behind you, please."

Dear God, this is crazy!

As Matt placed his hands behind his back, Shimdugger swiftly and expertly snapped the cuffs tightly in place, binding his arms and filling him with incomprehensible fear.

"You have the right to remain silent. If you give up that right, anything you say can and will be used against you in a court of law. You have the right to an attorney. If you cannot afford one, one will be appointed to you by the court."

"Do you understand your rights as I have explained them to you, doctor?"

My God!! These people are serious!

"I want my attorney," Matt finally spoke. "This is outrageous.

As reality set in, Matt knew he needed help and Sam was the only one he could think of who might understand and help.

"Lilly, get Sam Rosen on the phone, right now! I don't know what the hell is going on, but tell him these idiots have handcuffed me!"

Looking at Shimdugger, Matt asked: "Where are you taking me?"

"Well, first you will go to central booking. That is at the county jail facility on Orient Road. You will remain there until your arraignment. I'm sure your attorney will tell you all about it when he gets there. Now let's go."

The patients in Matt's office watched in horror, stunned as he was paraded through his own waiting room and out the front door of his clinic.

One of the other doctors in Matt's office ran up to Shimdugger and boldly questioned what was happening, only to be told to stand back and shut up or he would be arrested for interfering with an officer of the law in the performance of his duties.

Outside the clinic, three news crews from the local TV networks were rolling film and rushing forward with microphones. Obviously alerted in advance, this would be prime time news for tonight.

In response to their numerous questions, Matt merely kept repeating, "I don't know, I don't know."

Shimdugger, however, obviously relished the attention. With Doctor Hightower in hand, he stopped for a minute and addressed the cameras.

"This arrest is the result of an investigation conducted over the last eight months by my office in cooperation with the Tampa Police Department and the Hillsborough County Sheriff's office. Although I am not prepared to make a statement now, I will have one ready for you at my office in the Courthouse Annex at 5:00 PM. Now, if you will please excuse us…"

With that, Shimdugger bent Matt over and shoved him into the waiting vehicle.

Slamming the door shut, Shimdugger smiled as the police car pulled away with Matt in the back seat, badly shaken and confused.

* * * *

Just as Shimdugger had promised, Matt was booked into the Hillsborough County jail on Orient Road. Even though it was a new facility, it smelled and felt like what it was: a warehouse for the dregs of society.

As soon as Matt was in the booking area, the jailor took his shoes, belt, tie, gold chain and everything in his pockets. He was really startled when they also took his watch. When they confiscated his billfold they counted out his money in front of him, $368.42 with his pocket change added. A receipt for his money and all his belongings was placed in his pocket and then he was given a pair of flat canvas shoes. With his new shoes on, he was waved over to a section of chairs and told to wait until he heard his name called.

Looking around the room, he noted that it was a large place with at least fifty people sitting around in the cheap, classless colored, mock-leather easy chairs. Several of the women were obviously hookers and most of them seemed to know each other, as well as many of the male prisoners. Although the hookers were a mixed bunch, primarily black and white with a few Hispanics thrown in, the rest of the population was black and male.

Although raised in the south, race had never really played a role in Matt's life as neither his family nor friends were prejudiced. Now, however, for the first time in his life, Matt was focusing on race. He was scared and felt as if he was suddenly thrust into the role of being a minority of one.

Along one far wall was a bank of cells for people who did not wish to behave. One of those prisoners was banging his head against the glass. From the sound of the banging and the lack of shattering, Matt knew it must be a very strong type of Plexiglas. As a doctor, he also knew the prisoner must have had a very hard head. Further down the same wall was a row of phones with signs designating them as available for collect calls only. Long lines of people stood waiting in front of each phone; some of them obviously coming down off drug induced highs and in serious need of a fix.

Matt quickly realized there was a system at work in documenting the prisoners. First one was called for the initial paperwork: name, address occupation, next of kin, etc. Then sit. Next, off to see a nurse for a health history, medical or medicinal requirements, etc. Then sit. Then photos, fingerprints, weight and height and on and on. Each time a person finished with one interview, he or she was sent to sit in an area of different colored chairs to await being called by the next deputy in line.

Finger printing was the final call-up, and from there Matt was sent to the central seating area. Cheap vinyl chairs and couches filled the large area. Three TV sets played cartoons and animal shows.

Nothing too challenging for the novitiates.

Off to his right Matt took notice. A large man appearing to be in his early twenties was playing with himself while fooling around with a small, hooker. Obviously aroused, the man's head was literally glossy with the small bits of sweat shining off the ebony sheen of his shaved head. He kept reaching over to the girl, patting her breast and running his hand up under her short blossomy skirt. The pale whiteness of her skin was even more vivid when contrasted with the darkness of his huge hand as it slid over and in between her small thighs. With only a T shirt and sweat pants, it was obvious that there was nothing else to contain his ever-growing erection. She continued to push his hand away while he continued to stroke himself, totally unconcerned with anyone else who may be watching.

By now, things were surreal to Matt. It was as if he were watching everyone, himself included, from high above. He was only an observer, none of this was really happening to him.

Two and a half hours later he was called up to the front and then taken into a visitation room. It was a small room, cut in half with a desktop and Plexiglas dividing each section. A door at either end of the room provided access from each side. A round hole covered with metal mesh was fitted in the center of the glass so that sound would carry through. Matt's attorney, Sam Rosen, and another man Matt dimly recognized were waiting on the other side of the desk. There were two chairs on the visitor's side, one on Matt's side.

"Matt, I got here as soon as I could." Sam began. "After I called the State Attorney's office and talked with that prick, Shimdugger, I realized that this was way over my head. I'm not a criminal defense lawyer."

Turning to the man on his right, Sam said, "This is Bernie Cohen, one of the best criminal defense lawyers in the state. Bernie, meet Matthew Hightower; Doctor Matthew Hightower to be exact."

"Glad to meet you, Doctor Hightower, although I'm sure we both wish it was a meeting under different circumstances. How are they treating you so far?"

"OK I guess. This whole thing is a complete shock to me. So far, no one has beaten me with a rubber hose or anything," Matt said with a forced smile.

"Yes, well—"

"When do I get out? Matt interrupted. "And, what the hell is going on, anyway? This is crazy. I'm no criminal. There has to be a mistake. How soon can you get me out?"

"Easy Doc. One question at a time. First, you will have to stay here overnight. You've been booked in and can't be released until arraignment. Normally this is pre-arranged and no stay is necessary with someone of your stature in the community. However, Shimdugger wanted to make some press on this one. Must be considering running for State Attorney next election," Bernie said.

"Tomorrow morning you will be called up in front of Judge Hendry. He will set the bond for your release. We will ask for you to be ROR'd, released on your own recognizance, but with the number of counts you are charged with, I doubt he will go for that. This means you better be ready to come up with some money."

"After the bond is set you will be brought back here to wait until the bondsman gets here and posts the bond. Then you will be free to go home. You with me so far, Doc?"

Dazed, as if in a dream, Matt nodded. Then he asked, "How much is all this going to cost me?"

"At this point I'm not sure of the bond amount. With 150 counts of trafficking in narcotics we'll be lucky to get you out with a $1,000,000 bond. That will cost you $100,000 cash and a note against property to secure the remainder."

"My fees are $50,000 now and another $250,000 within thirty days. Are you going to be able to take care of all this?"

$400,000! Almost half a million dollars. For drug trafficking! I know nothing about illegal drugs!

"This is crazy," Matt said. "I don't do illegal drugs! I don't sell them! I have nothing whatsoever to do with illegal drugs! Something is terribly wrong. I can come up with the money, although it will hurt, but I don't understand any of this."

"Doc, it's not about illegal drugs. It's trafficking in narcotics. Legal narcotics, illegal prescriptions," Bernie said. "Shimdugger is tight lipped about all this right now, but between his press conference tonight and my contacts in his office, I will know a lot more tomorrow."

Matt looked at Sam. "Sam, please get hold of Jessie Lord, my bookkeeper. Ask him to write a check to Bernie for $50,000. I'll have to countersign it, so just bring it with you to the hearing in the morning. You will be there, won't you?"

"Sure Matt. I'll be there. You know I will help you any way I can."

"Also, have him cut you a blank check on our Nation's line of credit account. I'll fill it in and sign it when the Judge sets the bond amount."

"You may have to work fast on that, Matt. It's been my experience that when charges like this are filed, credit dries up in a hurry." Bernie said.

Looking at Sam, Matt said, "Have him find out what is available, and if there is not enough, I can get the rest from our money market accounts. Those are in my and Marilyn's names. If it is necessary to use them, have him get the paperwork for my signature and have it standing by."

"I'll take care of it for you," Sam promised.

Bernie spoke up. "You will be able to make collect calls tonight, so you can call your wife. It's much easier to make calls once you get to your pod. Here in this facility the cells are all in pods, with access to phones for several hours each evening. Be careful on the phone. Do not say *anything* on the phone that you wouldn't want repeated to the Judge."

"From now on, you say nothing to anyone about this case. I mean *anyone*, and I mean *nothing*! Unless I am with you, keep your mouth shut about this case or anything pertaining to your practice. At this point and until this is all over, I will do all the talking. It is very important that you follow me on this. You understand?"

"That's why I'm hiring you, Counselor. I understand."

"As I explained earlier, you will be in a pod of cells; usually two men to a cell. The temptation to talk, to ask questions, to deny guilt, etc., all of that becomes overwhelming at times. You must not give in to these temptations. Some of the worst outcomes I have ever experienced occurred when a cellmate of a client turned state's evidence and repeated what he was told in the cell. Usually, it is embellished to impress the state in order to elicit a better deal. I don't want to see that happen in this case. Shimdugger is already salivating and you can bet he or his investigator will interrogate anyone who has contact with you. Mum is the word. OK?"

"Yes. OK. God, this is all foreign to me. Like a dream. I keep expecting to wake up and it will be over. I keep thinking this must be happening to someone else, not me. Surely, not me." Matt was looking down, shaking his head. His eyes were moist.

"Keep the faith, Doc. We haven't seen their hole cards yet," Bernie said.

"Is there anything else I can do for you?" Sam asked.

"Not that I can think of," Matt replied. "Just please tell Marilyn that I'm OK and I'll call her tonight."

"All right, I'll see you in the morning."

As they all stood up, Matt automatically raised his hand as if to shake hands. Then he realized, he couldn't shake hands through the Plexiglas.

When Bernie and Sam walked out, Matt was still standing there, looking at his unshaken hand, wondering what the hell was wrong, and feeling more scared then he had ever felt in his life.

* * * *

Five minutes later, a deputy took Matt back to the main booking area where he was forced to strip naked and submit to a full search. Although Matt had viewed and palpated many naked bodies in his practice, he had never felt so degraded as when the guards had him lift his testicles, cough, turn around and bend over and 'spread his cheeks' for them. Finally, he was issued a pair of boxer shorts, T shirt and a blue jump suit. He was given another receipt for his clothes and fitted with a plastic bracelet, much like the ones used in hospitals, with his name and number easily readable through the clear surface.

Matt was then escorted in handcuffs down a long corridor to the entrance of another corridor marked 'A'. From there he and the two guards proceeded to the end where three sets of solid steel, double locked double doors marked the pod areas where he was taken through the double doors on the left into a large, open two-story room. Both the upstairs and downstairs walls were lined with doors. Two seating areas were arranged downstairs, each with its own TV set. The top floor had a railed walkway around it and was completely visible from the first floor. Matt noticed large metal mirrors spaced around so that every cell door and every inch of space could be seen from the guard station just inside the entrance. TV cameras placed several different views in front of the guard at all times.

To his left, Matt saw a courtyard outside a pair of large glass doors. The courtyard was surrounded by walls and the pod entrance, with no access to any outer areas. Even the top of the courtyard was covered with heavy wire mesh, filtering any light that came in from the sky. A single basketball net hung against the far wall and he saw that the entire courtyard was about a third the size of a regular basketball court.

Looking back inside, Matt spotted several tables and chairs scattered about, apparently for card playing, games or just talking. To his right was a built-in desk with a raised shelf around it, kind of like a breakfast bar in a kitchen. This was the guard station with the TV screens, phones, supply cabinets and other paraphernalia necessary for the officer to do his job. Several switches, which apparently controlled the individual doors, as well as master switches for each floor, were visible at the rear of the station.

Turned over to the cell guard at the desk by the admitting officer, Matt was given a full jail allowance.

"Inmate Hightower, you are now responsible for your gear."

As Matt collected them, the guard counted out and handed him his gear, along with a strong lecture.

"You have here, one bed roll, one tooth brush, one tooth paste, one towel and a roll of shit paper. Keep your eyes on them. They will not be replaced if you loose them. Now, in addition to all these goodies, you need to know I will not tolerate unnecessary noise for any reason. Noise will get you in lots of trouble; understand, inmate?"

Nodding his head, Matt listened as the guard continued.

"I am aware that you are a doctor and I hope that you get through this in good shape, but while you are in here, as I just said, you are an inmate. Do I make myself clear?"

"Yes."

"I also expect you to listen to and obey orders from myself and the other guards as well. Once again, do you understand?"

Nodding again, Matt drew a response from the guard.

"This place is only as rough as you make it, unlike the State Prison System. Politeness and an answer instead of a nod will take you a lot farther than disrespect. You are assigned to room number fourteen, a bottom cell and you have the honor of getting the lower bunk for the rest of your stay in our lovely inn. Your room door locks are electronically controlled by me and I open them after each count. Your door will remain open until I send you back to your room for the next count. If you manage to close the door during the open period, it will remain locked. If and only if you can prove it was shut by accident and not your fault, I might open it for you; if I feel like it and have time."

It was essentially Matt's responsibility to ensure the cell remained open and to be careful about the lock.

Taking his issue, Matt went to his room. A dreary place, it had a toilet with no lid or seat, just the stainless steel rim of the bowl. A small desk with a wooden chair stood against the right wall. Two bunks stuck out of the far wall, solid steel with a thin, filthy mattress on each. A skinny, flat, lumpy pillow also sat on each bunk, looking as filthy as the mattress.

If this is such a new facility, were did they get these obviously old and filthy beddings?

Apparently he had no roommates, so Matt placed his bedroll on the top bunk and began making up the lower bunk.

Home sweet home. God, what a thought!

* * * *

Matt called Marilyn that night about 9:00 PM. They were limited to a 15-minute call, and she cried the whole time. "It was in all the newscasts," she sobbed. "Everyone has called. Even your mother called from north Florida. You made the headlines there too. She kept repeating the nasty things this man, Shimdugger had said about you. He had said that you were using your medical license as a front to enable you to sell narcotics. She said it was horrible."

"The girls were so upset that when their friends kept calling, they all unplugged their phones from the walls."

Jenny, Carol, Eileen and Rachel without phones? Matt could hardly believe it. All four girls had their own phones and virtually lived on them. Jenny was 16 now, and very pretty. Actually, all the girls were very pretty. Rachel was the youngest at nine. Matt had been so upset with what was happening minute by minute that he hadn't even thought about what this must be doing to the girls.

Marilyn put each of the girls on the phone before she and Matt were cut off. They were all scared. They had all seen and heard Shimdugger. Rachel had only been able to sob "Daddy I love you"... sniffles and then, "Come home now... now daddy, pleeeease!"

Mind reeling as he tried to console his little girl, Matt could only wonder what drove a man like Shimdugger. Matt was beginning to truly hate the man, even though he had only met him one time.

Tossing and turning that night, Matt vividly remembered the birth of his first daughter. Jenny was born at three fifteen in the morning, a late delivery that almost inspired a cesarean section. Marilyn was a real trooper, suffering in labor for over 15 hours before finally giving birth. Matt had been there the whole time. He had watched her sweat and even attempted to kiss it away at first, marveling at her ability to handle pain and feeling almost nauseous himself when it was apparent that she was suffering in the extreme. Recognizing that he was too involved, he allowed her attending physician to call the shots, but Matt monitored him closely. Not more than fifteen seconds after her head first appeared, the squirmy, slimy little Jenny was whisked away. He'd touched her only when she was cleansed and placed on Marilyn's chest.

"My God" he whispered.

She was beautiful. As Matt gazed at the mother and child, he could only wonder at the marvel of creation and how lucky a man he was to have a beautiful wife he truly loved, and a beautiful baby girl that represented the culmination of that love.

Brushing back a few strands of Marilyn's hair from her face, Matt spoke in a low and loving tone, "She is every bit as beautiful as her mother. Nothing could be more perfect. God, how much I love you both."

As he slowly leaned over to kiss them both, the beauty of his dream was shattered. Shimdugger's pockmarked sneering face loomed over the placid reminiscence. He appeared demonic.

Alone in his cold cell, Matt's sweat soaked body shook with a combination of fear and anger. As his shaking finally began to abate, his fear was replaced with disgust and hate for his tormentor.

* * * *

Breakfast was at 4:30 the next morning and fifteen minutes later, Matt was issued an orange jumpsuit and cuffed and shackled for the van ride to the courthouse.

Seated in the van with several other prisoners, at least one of whom had a serious gas problem, Matt had his hands and feet bound together in chains and secured to an anchored center chain; he couldn't even cover his nose to help ward off the foul odor.

Arriving at a back entrance to the courthouse, all the prisoners were whisked into a holding cell prior to going into their assigned courtroom. From there, Matt was taken into his courtroom and lined up against the wall on a wooden bench. Still cuffed and shackled, he had not been allowed to shave or brush his hair.

Packed with people, cameras and reporters the courtroom air was awash with whispers and movement noises, but no one was talking out loud.

God, I look like shit! How did I ever get into this mess?

Marilyn was sitting with the girls on a bench about three rows back. Tears were rolling down her cheeks, but otherwise she appeared to be holding up well. The girls seemed listless, but OK.

Before Matt could signal to them, Judge Hendry entered the room from behind the judge's bench, and the bailiff called out, "All rise."

When everyone had been seated, Judge Hendry ran his eyes over the courtroom and then down the docket sheet. Matt was the fifth one listed to be called. The judge stopped at Matt's name, looked over at him and called out, "Who represents the State in the matter of State vs. Matthew Hightower?"

"Right here, Your Honor. Rupert Shimdugger, Assistant State Attorney." Already in the area reserved for attorneys, on the right side of the courtroom, to the left of the judge, Shimdugger was answering as he stood up.

"Counsel for the defense?" The Judge intoned.

"Yes, Your Honor. Bernie Cohen for the defendant, Doctor Matthew Hightower; and with me is Sam Rosen, co-counsel.

"Mr. Shimdugger. Is there a reason why Doctor Hightower was not given the opportunity to turn himself in for this hearing in the usual method involving professionals with clean records and strong ties within the community?" Judge Hendry obviously disliked the circus-like atmosphere in his courtroom.

"Your Honor, with the extensive number of charges against Dr. Hightower, it was felt that he could present an unacceptable escape risk if left free to roam prior to his arraignment." Shimdugger looked uncomfortable with both the question and his own answer.

"Did you discuss this with the Judge who signed the arrest warrant?"

"No, Your Honor."

"Did you discuss it with your superiors?"

"Yes, Your Honor. I was told it was my call to make. In the interest of public safety, I decided to play it by the book."

Judge Hendry rolled his eyes. "Doctor Hightower, please come forward and join your counsel at the counsel table. Bailiff, I think it is safe to remove the handcuffs and shackles from the doctor."

Barely masking his contempt, the judge glared at Shimdugger. "In the matter of State Vs. Hightower, what say the State?"

Rupert Shimdugger presented a "True Bill of Indictment for 156 counts of Trafficking In Narcotics against Matt", 52 of which were 2nd degree felonies and 104 of which were 3rd degree felonies.

"How does the defendant plead?" the Judge asked.

"Not guilty, Your Honor," Bernie answered for Matt.

"Does the defendant request bail?"

"Yes, Your Honor. Dr. Hightower is an honorable man with extensive ties to the community and to the state of Florida as well. Except for the time Dr. Hightower spent in the service of his country as an enlisted man and officer in the United States Navy, Dr. Hightower has spent all of his life in Florida. He is married, and has four beautiful children with whom he resides in this city. Besides his home, Dr. Hightower has extensive holdings in the Tampa community. He, along with his wife, Marilyn, is the sole owner of his corporation, which lists among its assets five medical clinics valued at several million dollars. He is a member of the North Tampa Country Club, the Florida and Tampa Medical Associations, is on the board of all the accredited hospitals in the Bay area and is active in numerous community groups."

"In his entire life, Dr. Hightower has never been arrested, much less convicted of anything. At age 46, his criminal history consists of two traffic tickets. He constitutes no threat to anyone. He is absolutely not guilty of these charges and has only one interest at this time which is to fight for his good name and reputation and beat these trumped up charges which the State has so far kept as closely guarded as possible. We ask that Doctor Hightower be released on his own recognizance."

"Thank you Counselor. Mr. Shimdugger, what says the State?"

"Your Honor, we oppose any bail of any amount. I realize that this is not a capitol case, but these charges carry over 1200 years of prison time if served consecutively. That is surely enough to cause a man to want to run. Coupled with Dr. Hightower's obvious financial prowess that represents an easy case for a real flight risk. Realizing that the law provides that some bail must be set in non capitol cases, and that this is such a case, the State requests the court to set bail at $15,000,000."

"Your Honor! That is absolutely preposterous!" Bernie was out of his seat and red in the face, looking for all the world as if Shimdugger had slapped him. "This is still a free country and one is presumed innocent until and unless he is proven guilty, in spite of what Mr. Shimdugger either believes or just plain wants; for whatever reasons. The law does not just provide that bail be allowed, as Mr. Shimdugger suggests; it provides that *reasonable* bail be set. It also provides that in considering the reasonableness of bail, the court take into consideration all the circumstances, including ties to the community, character, past history of the defendant, as well as all the other things we have alluded to this morning."

Cutting off Bernie, Judge Hendry spoke up, "The court does not need to hear any more. Bail is set at $500,000."

"Mr. Cohen, normally I would allow your client to leave with you and report to jail to set up his bond on his own. However, since he is already in an orange uniform, I'm afraid that if I let him go with you, some deputy might believe he had escaped and then all hell would break loose. How long will it take your client to arrange his bond?"

"Your Honor, a bondsman is standing by. We can have the bond in one hour."

"Very well then. Bailiff, see to it that Doctor Hightower is returned immediately to Orient Road for processing out on bond. I do not want him sitting here all morning waiting for no good reason. This case is already off on the wrong foot."

"Yes, Your Honor. I'll take care of it myself, right now."

Matt threw Marilyn and the girls a kiss, shook hands with his lawyers and was led away by the bailiff.

Shimdugger frowned, not at all pleased with the less than friendly look the judge had thrown his way while giving the bailiff his orders.

* * * *

Three hours later, Sam was driving him back to his office where Matt's Mercedes was parked. On the way, Sam filled him in.

"Matt, Bernie found out that these charges apparently stemmed from information given by a patient of yours, Geno Geraldi. This guy has been under investigation for over three years. Although he has ties to the Mafia and some major racketeers in the Tampa Bay area, the State has never been able to catch him red-handed. The State's break came when they caught him bribing a county commissioner. Further investigation showed at least two other commissioners, possibly more, have been selling favors to Geraldi for years."

"Shimdugger also connected him to buying off people in the licensing divisions of both the City and County, apparently this is where you come in."

"When they finally put a case together on him, Geno offered to finger a prominent, big named professional if they would cut him a deal. He pled to a five year deal."

Turning his head to momentarily look at Matt, Sam asked,

"Guess who the prominent, big name professional is?"

Feeling like he had been looking in from the outside of someone else's life, Matt shook his head.

"This can't be real. I never sold or bought anything from Geno. He was a patient, nothing more."

"Geno claims he put in the fix for you with the zoning board and others, and, in return, you supplied him with all those prescriptions."

"156 times?" Matt asked incredulously.

"No, that's where the State did some creative thinking. It would have been hard to prove any intent on your part to tie the prescriptions to the zoning violations. But Geno had copies of all the scripts. Obviously they were far above the normal sized prescriptions for these drugs. With the amounts, backed by testimony from Geno, intent is not necessary. Geno said he never took any of the drugs for himself, he only passed them along, and you knew it. Under the statute, the proof requirements are satisfied based on the number of prescriptions and the amounts of each one. The State does not need to prove anything else."

"The pharmacies backed up Geno's copies with their own records. Once they had the back up, the State came after you. You are a big fish for Shimdugger. You're his ticket to fame and fortune. That's about the size of it." Sam finished speaking just as he pulled into Matt's parking lot.

"Call me if I can do anything else. I would suggest that you have some one else come into the business with you, in case it becomes necessary. Marilyn cannot run it by herself."

"Take care, my friend." Sam extended his hand as Matt stepped out of the car.

They shook hands and Matt stood in the driveway and watched as Sam drove away. Then, shaking his head, he slipped into his office through his personal door.

Once in his own office, Matt opened his outer door to call to Lilly. However, the second he opened his door, Lilly jumped up from her desk so fast that her knees crashed into her desk drawer, knocking her back into her seat and almost causing her to fall over backward.

"Matt, I mean Doctor Hightower! You almost scared me to death!" With a catch in her voice she jumped up a second time, stepping into him and hugging him while she laughed and cried all at once. "I was so worried. That mean man, Shimdugger, and all those nasty things he said. But it's over now? It is over now, isn't it?" Lilly's eyes pleaded for assurance behind her sheen of tears.

"No, Lilly. It's not over, but it is under control, at least for now," Matt responded.

'Would you please ask Jessie to come into my office? And you can tell the rest of the staff the immediate crisis is over."

"Yes sir. Also, I've got a stack of messages for you. I made three piles. One is the press and the kooks. One is friends and well-wishers and the other one is business. In the business stack, I put the most important ones on top. I'll get Jessie."

Ducking back into his office, Matt took his seat in his overstuffed desk chair, and glanced at the message stacks. On the very top of the business stack was a note to respond to a 'rather urgent' call from Cal Henson at Nations Bank."

Damn. It's started already.

* * * *

In response to Lilly's call, Jessie came in and took a seat in front of Matt's desk. Shaking hands with Matt, Jessie said, "Good to see you back, Doc."

Even though Jessie had brought both of the ledgers with him, Matt knew it wasn't really necessary; he knew from experience that Jessie could give him any figure in either book, with the date included, right off the top of his head.

"How's our cash flow?" Matt asked.

"The $100,000 was no problem. We had enough in the general account to cover it and still leave more than enough for our operations. The additional $200,000 will have to come out of our money market account. That will draw it down to a little over $150,000."

"What about our credit line? It was half a million."

"I think you'd better call Cal about that. There may be a problem with the line of credit account."

"Damn. If we draw our money market account down below $150,000 the bank cuts our interest rate substantially. Plus, that is our primary backup for business funds."

Matt buzzed Lilly. "See if you can get Cal Henson on the phone for me, please."

"Yes sir," she said.

"Also, get me one coffee, when you can please. How bout you, Jessie?"

"No thanks, Doc."

"Coming right up."

Less than a minute later, Lilly spoke through the intercom, "Cal is on line 2."

Grabbing the phone, Matt said, "Hello Cal. How are you?"

"I'm OK Doc. The real question is, how are you?"

"Well, I'm sure a lot better now than I was two hours ago. I see you left a message for me?"

"Yeah, well, look, I don't know an easy way to put this, Doc. At eight AM this morning the board met and voted to rescind your line of credit until you get this matter resolved. I argued against it, but the vote was almost unanimous."

"Just like that, huh?" Matt said.

"The argument was that even though your operation is profitable, it is leveraged to the max. As long as you are at the helm, it will make money, but no one knows what will happen if you aren't there. You are your business, Doc.

"Right now we hold four mortgages on your clinics and one on your house. The board won't go for any more credit until this matter is straightened out. I'm sorry."

"OK, Cal. I know it's not your fault. I'll get back to you later." Matt hung up the phone without waiting for a reply.

"Bankers," Matt said to no one in particular. "When you don't need em, they beg you to borrow their money. But when you really need em, they're nowhere to be found.

"Well, I don't see any other options at this point. I've got to have legal counsel and he has to be paid. Cut a check on the money market account and take care of Bernie Cohen."

"I'll have it on your desk in a few minutes, Dr. Hightower," Jessie said. "However, there is something else we have to talk about."

"I think I know where you're headed, Jessie. But let's wait until I talk some more with Bernie before we try to sort out the future. OK?"

"Sure Doc, but let's not wait too long. If I don't miss my guess, some of the troops will be getting restless very shortly."

"Yeah, thanks Jessie. Let me know as soon as you think anyone is jumping ship. I really don't need any more surprises."

"No problem. I'll keep my eyes open," Jessie replied as he gathered his ledgers and left the room.

Matt buzzed Lilly. "Call Bernie Cohen and tell him I'll have the rest of his fee this afternoon. Set up a meeting between us and also see if Sam can be there. I need to know what the hell is happening."

"Yes sir," said Lilly. Can I get you any more coffee once I get him on the line?"

"Please, that would be nice," Matt said.

* * * *

The following Monday, Matt met with Bernie at his office which was located downtown about three blocks from the courthouse. It was 2:00 PM, almost exactly one week after Matt had been arrested and it was the first time Bernie had met with Matt since Matt gave him the fee. Sam was also present and they waited for Bernie to speak.

"Doctor Hightower, this morning I received copies represented to me as everything the State has on you at this point. I don't mind telling you that I am not at all happy with what they have. Let me give you the facts."

"If you, as an MD, prescribe medication that is to be sold from one person to another, or is to be used by anyone other than the named recipient on the prescription, that is a crime. If it is for the use of narcotics, illegally, then it is a felony. The degree of the felony depends upon the type of drug and the amount of the prescription."

"Geno Geraldi has sworn under oath that you and he had a thing going. He would keep your building plans moving forward on any of your clinics and, in return, you would supply him with narcotics, which he could resell at a huge profit. He claims that you were aware of why he got the drugs and that you had even asked him to spread the prescriptions around between non-affiliated drug stores so that the extreme dosages would not be noticed. He says you even supplied him with a handwritten list of various pharmacies that were isolated enough that no questions would be asked."

Damn him!! I gave him a list all right, but all the rest is a bucket of lies!

Bernie continued. "Geno made photocopies of all the scripts and, after he used them, he wrote in the dates and pharmacies on his copies. He also has the original pharmacy list, on your letterhead notepaper, in what he claims is your handwriting.

"Under Florida law, if convicted, 54 of these prescriptions each constitute a separate charge of trafficking in narcotics as a felony in the second degree. The remaining 102 of them constitute separate third degree felonies of trafficking in narcotics. The combined penalties equate

31

to over 1200 years of prison time if run consecutively. That's the bad news.

"The good news is somewhat better.

"First, is you. Doctor Matthew Hightower. Outstanding citizen, no prior criminal activity, prominent physician, veteran of the armed services, family man, etc., etc. This is your first offense.

"Second is a thing called the sentencing guidelines. Sentencing guidelines are an effort by the legislature to give uniformity to court sentences across the state. Judges must follow the guidelines unless something particularly heinous has occurred to enable them to go outside the guidelines. That is not a factor in your case. Your sentencing guidelines are air tight, with a maximum of 20 years versus a minimum of 12. Your medium is 16 years.

"Third is that currently, under the statutes, you receive a third off your sentence automatically. As soon as the judge sentences you, one third is gone. As soon as you get to prison, you begin to earn time off for good behavior. This is 20 days a month, or effectively, another third of your sentence. Worst-case scenario, if the judge sentences you to 18 years, max, what you actually serve is six.

"Now, a lot can happen between today and the final decision. Shimdugger can play hardball and force us to go to trial, which means lots of publicity and a major feather in his cap. This would take six to nine months. However, with all the evidence the State has, it would probably make the court more sympathetic to you and less with the State. Remember that they only have to prove that you wrote the prescriptions and that the prescriptions were not for use by the person named on them. I got to tell you, with the size of the doses and the list of pharmacies in your handwriting, it would be like shooting fish in a barrel for the State.

"The other option is to go for a plea bargain. We would try to get the State to back off the maximum penalty and go for a guilty plea coupled with a lighter sentence. The court would probably back a reduced sentence, for all the reasons I stated earlier. Shimdugger has allowed some flexibility in the past and he may be receptive to something now. I'll feel him out and see where he is headed. If we elect to plea bargain, you'll have to co-operate with them.

"Any questions at this point?" Bernie asked Matt.

"Only about a thousand of them, Counselor," Matt answered. "Are you really telling me that I am going to prison? I mean, I never did anything illegal in my life. Nothing that would qualify me for prison! Good God! That place is full of thieves, rapists, murderers, perverts whatever. I don't belong in a place like that. I mean, the language; the people; this is crazy!"

"Easy, Doc. I'm not telling you that you *have* to go to prison. Not yet. But it is a very distinct possibility. Now, why don't you tell me about your relationship with this Geno character?"

Matt sat there talking for the next 45 minutes, going over any and everything he could think of regarding Geno Geraldi. He left nothing out while Bernie took notes the entire time as Matt recalled his dealings with the man who was set on ruining his life.

Geno was huge, almost 400 pounds, and he downed drugs the way most people eat popcorn. However, even with his enormous appetite for drugs, Matt was sure that Geno wasn't personally using all of the prescriptions he gave him. Matt had written Geno so many prescriptions for narcotics that he insisted that Geno use three different drug stores to fill them.

Matt was worried. This was getting out of hand.

Geno had been his patient for almost three years. That morning, Geno had surprised Matt by saying: "Doc. I hear through the grapevine that you are having trouble getting zoning permits to build your new clinic over on North Florida Avenue."

How the hell did he find out about that? Better yet, where is he going with this conversation?

"Well, yes," Matt said. "It may be that I'll have to look elsewhere for my next clinic. Shame though. I really want that location."

"Oh, I wouldn't worry about it anymore, Doc. You see, that's what friends are for. You wait and see. By Friday everything will work out."

"That would be really great." Matt said. "How much would it cost me to have someone look into it?"

"Doc! You hurt my feelings. You gonna insult me with talk about money? I told you, this is a favor between friends."

Wow! He really looks upset.

Quickly Matt said: "I'm sorry. I did not quite understand. Well, if you are able to do something to help I would really appreciate it."

"That's more like it, Doc. And don't you ever doubt that Geno can do something about it. Now, about those pills you gave me last time."

Ten minutes later Geno was out of the office with a massive prescription in his hand.

Friday morning at 10:30 Matt had received a phone call from the county clerk's office.

"Doctor Hightower? This is Rachel Eckerd from the clerk's office. I hope I am not disturbing you?"

"No, Mrs. Eckerd, that's quite all right. What can I do for you?"

"Well, sir, I just wanted you to know that your zoning request was approved last night for that clinic you want to build off North Florida Avenue. Also, all the permits you submitted were approved this morning, even the one for the parking lot runoff to be diverted into the smaller drainage area. It appears to me that you are ready to get your contractors out to work."

"Mrs. Eckerd, I don't know how to thank you for the call. You made my morning, that's for sure."

"Just doing my job, Doc. Glad I could be of help. Have a nice day."

"A very nice day, now. Thank you again, goodbye."

* * * *

When Matt finished, Bernie asked him, "Doc, did you charge Geno for his office visits?"

"Yes, at first," Matt replied. "But after the zoning thing he did not pay up. We sent him a couple bills but when they were ignored I told Jessie, my bookkeeper, to just forget it. I have half a dozen or so patients that I don't charge. Like most doctors I have friends who fall into this category. I just placed Geno on that list."

"Bad move, Doc. Shimdugger will just use that to confirm the illegality of the relationship."

Sam spoke up. "In a plea bargain, if the State agrees, can the court approve a sentence below the guidelines?"

"Yes, it certainly may. The Judge has to give a written reason for the departure if it is over 25 percent less than the guidelines, but it can be done. That may well be our best bet."

"Tell me," Matt asked Bernie, "How much time do I have before all this comes to a head?"

"I'd say we are looking at three to six months. There's really no justification for lengthy discovery. The prescriptions are there; the zoning and planning schedules are there. Only one witness counts other than character witnesses. No, I doubt the State or the court will agree to a lengthy discovery process."

"Our judge is Alice Dana. She isn't a bad Judge to have. She has a reputation of being lenient, but much of that is directed toward youthful minorities. It does get her into trouble with the press sometimes. Having said this, it is still far too early to get a read on her in this case yet."

"Honest opinion, Counselor; am I going to have to go to prison? And, if so, how long?"

"Yes, in all probability you will. I hope for no more than 18 to 24 months," Bernie replied.

For this I paid a quarter million dollars? I should have been a lawyer instead of a doctor.

"I have a meeting with Shimdugger in two weeks," Bernie said. "I should be able to get a feel for what is going down by then. Meanwhile, I'll set Geno's deposition. Let's see how strong his story really is. I'll call you in the interim if anything comes up, Doc."

Bernie stood up and offered his hand to Matt.

"Well, at least I know where I stand, sort of," said Matt as he took Bernie's outstretched hand. "Now I've got some plans to make myself."

* * * *

It was 6:30 PM, and Matt was the only one left in his office. After everyone else had gone home, Matt did some serious thinking. Pouring himself a drink, Glenlivet, an excellent single malt scotch, Matt added two cubes of ice and took a sip. Instead of becoming relaxed as intended, Matt was almost panicked as the enormity of his situation hit him.

Prison! I'll be a convicted felon! What about Marilyn, the family? What will the girls have to face in school? What will they tell their friends? What can I tell my friends? What can I say to the girls? To Marilyn?

Every night, when possible, Matt sat in the den with the girls as Marilyn prepared supper, listening to their accounts of their day. Rachel invariably sat on his lap, with Eileen right next to him, snuggling up to him as he gently caressed her hair. All four girls always greeted him with a hug and a kiss before settling down and then squealed with delight when Marilyn announced dinner was ready. Marilyn, his rock, his love, his life.

My God, what have I ever done to hurt them or myself this badly? No matter how many prescriptions I gave Geno, I never deserved this. What can I tell them?

* * * *

Two weeks later, on his way to Bernie Cohen's office, Matt's business was falling apart. His cash flow was dragging. Patients afraid of being left in a lurch were finding other doctors to handle their problems. All seven of his clinic doctors were looking elsewhere. Several other doctors and hospitals had called Matt to find out the qualifications of his various employees.

Something would have to change, and soon.

Walking into Bernie's office, Matt noticed a new computer system. *Probably paid for by yours truly.*

Trying not to be bitter, Matt followed the secretary into the conference room that was already set up for the deposition, with a large silver coffee trolley rolled out and filled with confections, donuts and coffee. Through the large picture windows across the room, Matt could see straight down to the courthouse.

Bernie came in and they both helped themselves to coffee and donuts and then sat down at a massive, deeply reflective mahogany conference table. Bernie began. "I took Geno's deposition on Friday. He did not budge. He makes a good witness. Swears that you knew all along that he was selling the drugs you prescribed for him. Claims it was a flat-out payment to him to keep him providing you with favorable zoning decisions."

"He openly admits that the State has offered to go easy on him if he testifies against you, but claims that has no bearing on the truth of his statements. Typical ratting out on his part, but he pulls it off well."

"Shimdugger says he is willing to consider going for a lesser than guideline sentence and that he might consider 18 to 24 months."

"How much time would I actually serve on a 24 month sentence?" Matt interrupted.

"About one year, maybe a little less, depending upon how soon you began earning gain time," Bernie replied.

"Can we beat this thing if we go to court?" Matt asked.

"With the evidence the State has, along with the sworn testimony of Geno, even if Geno died, the State would have a winning case against you."

"In other words, we lose no matter what," Matt said.

"Our primary goal right now is to get you the best deal we can to give you the least amount of prison time possible. If we can get Shimdugger to recommend it, the Judge will probably buy it," Bernie said.

"So, how do we do that?"

"Shimdugger wants to take your statement, under oath. He says that cooperation will go a long way to ameliorate your sentence."

"He is also ready to set a trial date or a sentence hearing date, one or the other."

"How can we have a sentencing hearing date if I am pleading not guilty?"

"We can't. You would have to change your plea to guilty."

"How soon do we have to do all this?"

"Shimdugger wants your statement next week. We don't have to do it, of course. But if we agree, it will pretty well eliminate any chance of a trial. At that point we should be able to agree on a sentencing date."

"What do you recommend?"

"I don't really know Shimdugger. I've never dealt with him on anything serious before. I don't think he has ever had a case with this much notoriety before. He appears to be honest and seems willing to work with us. After all, you have an impeccable record up until now.

"I recommend we go for a plea. We work with Shimdugger; make him a friend, or at least less of an enemy. We also put together a lot of support in the community on your behalf. We will need a letter: lots of letters, in support of you. At the hearing we will have a dozen prominent citizens giving statements on your behalf.

"That's my recommendation," Bernie said.

"Set up the meeting," Matt said as he stood to leave.

* * * *

Rupert Shimdugger looked at Matt's outstretched hand and slowly extended his own to accept the handshake. It was with an obvious effort that he did so.

Matt almost winced. He had performed this seemingly automatic effort under instructions from Bernie. He would never make the same mistake again.

They all faced each other over a large, cheap conference table in a nondescript, small room in the State Attorney's office complex. A court reporter was standing by a little away from the table. Matt and Bernie were on one side of the table with Shimdugger and his investigator, Mickey, on the other.

"Doctor Hightower. I am sure that your attorney told you the reason for this meeting. I want to take your sworn statement, under oath just as if it were in court, as to the events leading up to your arrest."

"You understand that this is purely a voluntary meeting on your part. You do not have to answer any of my questions if you choose not to. You also understand that I am seeking to have you incarcerated for the crimes that I believe you have committed against the State of Florida. I am seeking prison time. At least 18 to 24 months in the state penal system. I am offering you no guarantees at all, but your cooperation in the investigation will be used by me to help me in my final recommendation to the Judge in a plea to the court, or in my agreement with any plea bargain we might arrive at.

"Do you understand everything I just said?" Shimdugger concluded.

Damn. This guy sounds slippery as an eel!

"Yes." Matt answered, keeping his thoughts to himself.

"Do you wish to proceed with the statement?"

"Yes," Matt said again.

"Very well. Madam court reporter, will you swear in the witness, please?"

"Raise your right hand, please. Do you solemnly swear that the testimony you are about to offer will be the truth, the whole truth and nothing but the truth, so help you God?"

"I do." Matt said.

Shimdugger began with getting Matt's name and essential facts, address, phone, etc., on the record. He then continued.

"Are you making this statement in a voluntary manner, of your own free will?"

"Yes."

"Has anyone promised you anything in return for your making this statement?"

"No."

"You realize that anything you say in this statement may be used against you in a court of law?"

"Yes."

"Do you know a man named Geno Geraldi?"

"Yes."

"How did you come to meet Mr. Geraldi?"

For the next 45 minutes Matt recounted, in detail, his relationship with Geno. He denied hiring him to intercede with the planning counsel or the zoning board, but admitted prescribing all the narcotics. He also admitted to authorship of the list of pharmacies and conceded it was done to lessen the chance of suspicion over the amounts of the prescriptions.

Halfway through the session Matt wished he had taken off his suit jacket when he had started. It had seemed cool then. By the end of the statement, he was sweating profusely and was so wet under the coat that he would have been too embarrassed to take it off.

Afterward, on the way back to Bernie's office, Matt asked, "Well, how did it go?"

Bernie and Shimdugger had met alone for about 15 minutes following the session and he and Matt had not talked about it yet.

"I'm not entirely sure. He produced a list of five or six people and asked me what I knew about them. I never heard of them and I told him so. He agreed to ask his secretary to fax me a copy of the list this afternoon. I remember one of them, Rose Santella. Do you know who she is?" he asked Matt.

Matt felt as if he had been kicked.

"She is a woman with a lot of problems; a real psycho. I spent five or six visits with her before I knew she was nuts. She has a fixation on doctors. Wants to have a baby by one. She is a fatal attraction type of woman. Once she latches on, it's hard to get her gone.

"I never had an affair with her. In fact, I wound up threatening her on several occasions with police action. She filed a complaint with the FMA, The Florida Medical Association, but after a brief investigation, they threw it out. What the hell has she got to do with this?"

"I don't know, but it's quite obvious she won't be coming in as a character witness on your behalf," Bernie responded.

* * * *

Later that afternoon Matt received a duplicate of the fax that Shimdugger sent to Bernie. The list was six people long and each one of the names represented someone who had filed a complaint against him with the FMA. All had been investigated and all had been thrown out.

Two of them had gone further and filed malpractice actions, but these too had been dismissed without any payments or admissions against Matt.

"What can Shimdugger do with these people?" Matt asked Bernie over the phone.

"Undoubtedly, he plans to use them to lessen your appeal as a good person. By the way, just before you called I got a call from Judge Dana's office. She set the pre-trial conference for a week from tomorrow."

"What does that mean?"

"Well, since we no longer have an option concerning trial, it means we will use that time to change your plea to guilty and get a sentencing date set."

Matt took a deep breath, and squeezed the phone tightly.

So soon! So very, very soon!

Shaking his head as if coming up from under water, Matt asked, "How much time will I have after that?"

"I can't answer that yet. A lot will depend on all of our calendars. I'll let you know as soon as I have some idea."

"Do I have to attend?"

"Yes, you must. Besides, it may be good to let the judge see that you are not the monster the State may have led her to believe."

"I'll be there with my best suit and tie then."

"Good. Be here in my office at 10:00 AM and we'll walk over together."

* * * *

Judge Dana looked older than Matt knew she was. Her age was actually in the early forties, but she looked as if she were in her mid fifties. She had short, straight hair; no makeup and a serious, no-nonsense face. Even when she smiled at the attorneys, she maintained a steady aloofness that seemed to say, "Make no mistake. I am in charge."

Matt was worried. This didn't look like such a friendly judge to him.

"Good morning, gentlemen," Judge Dana began. "Are we ready to proceed?"

"Yes, Your Honor," Bernie and Shimdugger replied in unison.

"This is the court ordered Pre-Trial Conference in The State of Florida versus Matthew Hightower, Case Number 93-1871-CV."

"Gentlemen, I ask that you identify yourselves to the court reporter. Counsel for the State?"

"Rupert Shimdugger, Counsel for the State, Your Honor."

"Bernie Cohen, representing Doctor Matthew Hightower, Your Honor."

"Well gentlemen, it looks like the party is ready to start. Anyone wish to volunteer?"

"Your Honor, I believe the defense has something to discuss that should go first." Shimdugger said.

"Counsel?" Judge Dana looked at Bernie.

"Yes, Your Honor. The Defendant wishes to change his plea to guilty. We are currently negotiating with the State concerning the terms of his sentence. The State has agreed not to oppose a continuation of the Defendant's bond through the sentencing hearing."

"Doctor Hightower, step up to the microphone," Judge Dana commanded.

Feeling much like an eighteenth century criminal stepping up to the chopping block to face the hooded executioner, Matt did as he was told.

"Doctor Hightower, do you now wish to change your plea to guilty?"

"Yes, Your Honor."

"Has anyone made you any promises in connection with this plea? Any promises at all?"

"No, Your Honor."

"You are entering this guilty plea of your own free will, voluntarily, and under no threats or coercion of any kind?"

"Yes, Your Honor."

"Counsel, please approach the bench."

Bernie and Rupert Shimdugger moved up to the bench and Matt could hear them conferring about a date for sentencing that agreed with all their calendars. It was almost surreal, Matt thought. *They are up there nonchalantly picking a time to send me to prison.*

He wanted to puke.

Finally the date was set. Matthew Hightower had six weeks of freedom left.

As the attorneys went back to their seats, Judge Dana thanked them, dismissing and sending everyone on their way. Once outside, on the way back to Bernie's' office, Bernie said, "I told Shimdugger we would be asking for 30 to 60 days post-sentencing for you to remain free on bond in order for you to clear up your finances once you know for sure how much time you will have to serve. He said he would probably have no problem with that. I then asked him for a time for us to nail down the plea bargain and he agreed to meet with me next Thursday."

"Try to get him to 12 months or less," Matt said.

"Obviously, I want to get you as little time as possible, but I don't think I can get him below 18 months," Bernie replied.

* * * *

"Six years!!" Matt screamed. "What happened to 18 months?"

"That was exactly my reaction," Bernie said. "He completely broadsided me with that one."

"I don't understand," Matt said. "I haven't done anything to deserve six years in prison."

"Doc, he wants another statement. Wants to verify some things he says he missed the first time."

"What the fuck for? Why the hell should I give him any more? He's already stabbed me in the back from the first time. Why in God's name should I give the bastard another shot at me?"

"Because we have nothing definite yet, Doc. We need to make friends. Show him what a nice guy you really are. He could still come back to the 18 to 24 month range."

"I trust you to work this out, Bernie. It goes against my grain, but go ahead and set it, if you think it will do some good."

"Be here at 1:30 PM next Wednesday, Doc. I'll see you then. Keep the faith." With that, Bernie hung up the phone.

Keep the faith! Shit! In five weeks I'm going to be sentenced to six years in prison and all he can say is keep the faith? This can't be happening. I've got to wake up and find this is all a bad dream.

* * * *

Matt found buyers for two of the clinics. He had hoped to sell them all in a group, but had no such luck. He also knew that the newest clinic, his flagship clinic, would sell with no problems. That left him only two others for which he needed to find new owners. He was happy that, so far, he had been able to sell them without having to resort to bargain basement prices. Once the word got out about his sentencing, all his leverage would be lost.

He had also found a doctor to sub-lease his Mercedes. He would use a rental car for the last month. He hoped, as Bernie promised, he'd have two more months after that, but he was taking no chances. Since the State had backed down on their original estimate, Matt had begun to think only in terms of the worst. Bernie assured him he would have at least 30 more days, but Matt was making plans anyway.

If he got six years, he would actually serve about two in prison. Marilyn and the girls would have enough in savings to get through that much time in their present home without too many lifestyle changes. Any longer, though, and their lifestyles would have to change, maybe even drastically. Matt had really begun to resent Shimdugger for his deceitful tactics.

Doctor Matthew Hightower had only begun to brush the surface of his feelings for Shimdugger.

* * * *

"All right, Dr. Hightower. Please take a seat."

As planned, on Wednesday Matt was back for his second statement. It seemed to him to be no more than a re-hash of the same questions and Bernie could see nothing new either.

Two hours after the statement, Bernie called Matt. "Shimdugger says ten years is the least he will go on a plea bargain."

"Ten years?" Matt was so mad he was shaking. "What the hell happened to six years, or for that matter, 18 months? What happened to making friends and all that bullshit? What in God's name is going on?"

"I know it sounds bad," Bernie said. "We can either take what he is willing to give, or we can plea straight up to the Judge and let her decide the prison sentence. Those are the only two choices we have at this point."

"My God, my God! I can't believe this," Matt cried. "I can't accept ten years from Shimdugger. He's nothing more than a lying, conning weasel. Real scum! No! I won't accept ten years from that scumbag!"

"OK. then. Get me something to work with." Bernie said. "They are doing a pre-sentence investigation right now. The man in charge of your case is Ralph Johnson. I need letters on your behalf, lots of letters sent to him. Then I need half dozen good, well known, solid citizens to come to the hearing and speak on your behalf. We have four weeks to get it all together."

Bernie gave Matt the address and phone number of Ralph Johnson and a few pointers on the type people he expected Matt to bring to the hearing.

Once he had hung up, Matt buzzed Jessie. "Jessie, come here for a moment, please."

"Sure, Doc. Right away."

As Jessie sat down, Matt asked, "When can we close on the first two clinics?"

"I should have that ready in the next week or so." Jessie replied. "I also have an offer on the Mason Drive clinic. It's a bare bones offer, but I think it will get better."

"Thank God." Matt said. "What about the Bush Boulevard clinic?"

"Two or three nibbles. Nothing solid yet."

"OK, Jessie. Now, who all wants this place?"

Jessie knew how badly Matt hated to bring up the sale of his newest clinic. Matt had originally planned and told Jessie, to try to lease it out for two years to coincide with his expected sentence. Obviously, for him to talk about selling the clinic, something had happened: something very, very bad.

"Well, the University of South Florida wants it. But they take forever with their boards, voting, etc. Two hospitals want it, especially University Community Hospital. Then there are the ones who fought us the most on zoning. They would use it as a satellite on their own operation. Finally, there are three or four medical groups that are interested. It can be sold pretty quickly, just as soon as you give me the word."

"OK," Matt said. We've got four weeks to get it all finished. Let's get a move on. If we can get them all moved, and we get enough for them, I can give final bonuses for everyone. Do the best you can."

"I'll let you know as each one firms up." Jessie said.

After Jessie left, Lilly poked her head in Matt's office. "Got a moment, boss?"

"For you, always." Matt said.

Lilly sat down in front of Matt's desk.

"I know this isn't an easy time for you and if there is anything I can do to help, you know you can count on me."

Matt nodded, waiting for her to go on with what was obviously painful.

"I've had an offer from Doctor Cervantes' office. His lifetime secretary is retiring next month and he has offered me her job. I like him, and I need to keep working. I told him that I would not leave you. However, if you are not going to be here, I need to know."

Lilly was looking down at her hands now, big tears streaming down her cheeks, her last sentence almost a whisper.

"Lilly, Lilly. You're such a dear friend. You *are* the best secretary a man ever had. I'll tell you, because I know you won't repeat it; I am going to be sent to prison."

Lilly gasped and then began sobbing out loud, too upset to speak.

Matt walked around his desk and pulled her up into his arms. Holding her close, he let her cry for a few moments. Then, as her sobbing subsided, he told her.

"Go when you have to. I have four weeks. If I am lucky, maybe a month after that. However, I hope to sell this place and the others before that."

"I'll tell Dr. Cervantes that I will be free in six weeks. Thank you, Matt; Doctor. I am so, so sorry. It isn't fair. It just isn't right. For the next six weeks I'll be here every day for as long as you need me."

"Thank you, Lilly. I appreciate that."

* * * *

The week before his hearing Matt picked up his morning paper and Judge Alice Dana was front-page news. She had refused to send a 12-year-old black youth to prison, even though he was a serious repeat offender with over 30 grand theft auto convictions. In this most recent episode, the State had tried him as an adult on grand theft auto, armed robbery, fleeing arrest and possession of a deadly weapon. The jury had come back with a guilty verdict in less than half an hour, and the minimum sentence for his crimes was 15 years. Judge Dana had thrown out the guidelines, and instead, she had given him two years house arrest.

The paper blasted away at her, claiming she did not deserve to be in office. She was said to be too soft on criminals and the editorials were urging the public to replace her with a "real judge" who would follow the law and put criminals where they belonged, behind bars.

Matt read the various articles with a keen interest. They inspired hope in him. Surely, if this kid had been as bad as the paper claimed then Matt should get a break to. *I'm not a bad person. I'm not a bank robber. I've never pointed a gun at anyone.*

For the first time in months, Matt felt a surge of real hope.

* * * *

"All rise," the bailiff intoned. "Court is now in session; the Honorable Judge Alice Dana presiding."

As soon as the Judge entered and took her seat, he continued: "Please be seated."

"Madam Clerk, would you sound the docket?" Judge Dana said.

"This is the sentencing hearing in the case of The State of Florida versus Matthew Hightower, case number 93…"

As the clerk droned on, Matt looked around. He was seated at a counsel table with Bernie. Across the way was another table where Rupert Shimdugger sat with an assistant.

Behind him, the courtroom was packed. Matt's family and several friends were there, along with several members of the press. There were others, too: onlookers and various lawyers who were in the vicinity and wanted to see what would go down.

"Gentlemen, before I pronounce sentence, does the State have anything to present to the Court?"

"Yes, Your Honor. The State has five witnesses who wish to be heard."

"Very well Mr. Shimdugger, call your first witness."

Shimdugger presented all five witnesses, all former patients of Matt's and all of whom suggested that Matt was a disgrace to the medical profession. They all wanted him thrown under the jail, for life if possible. Bernie crossed them only enough to ascertain that in each case, the Florida Medical Association had thrown out their complaint after an investigation. Their prejudice was palpable.

After the last one spoke, Shimdugger gave an impassioned speech, imploring the Judge to throw the book at Matt for the good of the community and the medical profession. He reiterated all 156 charges and embellished Geno's testimony. He exaggerated the gravity of the crimes and alluded to Matt as a shifty, behind the scenes manipulator bent on corrupting the system and using his medical degree as a shield to hide behind as he broke the law with impunity.

Matt could not imagine anything he had ever done that could have aroused such vindictiveness in Rupert Shimdugger. *Hell, I don't even know the man!*

When Shimdugger concluded, Judge Dana looked to Bernie. "Counselor, do you wish to make a statement or present witnesses?"

Rising to his feet, Bernie said, "Yes, thank you, Your Honor. I wish to say a few words, then Dr. Hightower will speak, and then there are a few members of the community who wish to speak on Dr. Hightower's behalf."

"Please, continue as you wish, Counselor." Judge Dana seemed genuinely concerned as she spoke pleasantly to Bernie.

"Contrary to Mr. Shimdugger's flamboyant and inaccurate rhetoric, Dr. Hightower is a good man. He has a record of achievements that include exemplary service to his nation and to this community. He is a good husband, a good father to his children and a good leader in this community.

"Dr. Hightower is also a man who made a mistake. He allowed himself to be pushed into a corner. He wasn't even aware of the road he was traveling on until it was too late. Far from being the manipulator described by Mr. Shimdugger, Dr. Hightower was himself expertly manipulated by Geno Geraldi who used his association with Dr. Hightower to make money. Then, when he got caught up in his own nefarious schemes, he embellished his association with Dr. Hightower, lied about the circumstances of that association, and sold his lies to the State in exchange for a reduced sentence.

"Geno Geraldi, Your Honor, has cut a deal with the State. Geno has only to testify against Dr. Hightower, and he is guaranteed not to receive a sentence of over five years for his own crimes. The true criminal, the man who arranged all these illegal transactions, made the pay-offs, supplied the influence, etc., etc., this known criminal with ties to the underworld gets a five year sentence while the State attempts to have this Court sentence Dr. Hightower to 20 years! This is a complete perversion of the criminal justice system. The founding fathers of this great country of ours must be rolling over in their graves!

"I can only hope that the Court looks at the actual record of Dr. Hightower's accomplishments; his past history of service to his country and this community; his complete lack of criminal history and indeed, complete lack of any criminal intent in this case, and compares this laudable record with the record of his accuser, Geno Geraldi. Geno is a known racketeer with a criminal history dating back to his early childhood as a hood on the tough streets of East Tampa. If the Court will compare the accuser with the accused, I believe the Court will agree with me that this is surely a time that justice should be tempered with mercy.

"And now, I'd like Dr. Hightower to say a few words."

Matt stood and was sworn in by the Clerk. "Your Honor, I stand before you, a humbled man. I have lost most of my worldly possessions. My prospering business is gone. My good name has been forever sullied. My license to practice medicine is revoked. I stand here in court, horrified at what I have brought about upon my family. These losses cannot be measured in dollars and cents.

"What was it all for, I ask myself? What did I do that was so terrible that this man," nodding to Shimdugger, "wants to send me to prison for the rest of my natural life? As God is my witness, I never asked Geno

Geraldi to intercede for me with anyone. Not the zoning board, not the planning board, not anyone. Not one time did I ever ask him.

"My crime was in not doing anything about Geno's stupendous drug usage after I had reason to suspect he had committed a crime in allowing others to share his drugs. That and just plain giving him too many drugs. I never knew he sold drugs. That never occurred to me. I believed he had acquired a huge tolerance to go along with his huge physique. I believed he was actually taking the medications prescribed and, at worst, sharing them with others. I was completely surprised when I was arrested and found out otherwise.

"In reality, I was set up. I was used by Geno to further his aim of reducing his own culpability and sentencing for his numerous crimes. He now has a deal for a five-year sentence, less than a quarter of the time the State is asking the Court to sentence me to. I honestly believe that would be a true miscarriage of justice.

"I never intentionally committed a crime. My crime was one of neglect. I neglected to stop what I should have investigated or reported. Surely that is not a crime of the magnitude to carry the penalties requested by Mr. Shimdugger.

"Your Honor, I ask that for my sake and the sake of my family, you be fair in your judgment.

"Thank you."

Matt sat down. He had hoped to come across as more humble, maybe even to cry, but it had not come out that way. Even so, Shimdugger looked worried.

Next Bernie called his character witnesses; six prominent community leaders in the Tampa area. One by one they told of Matt's exemplary life; his good deeds in the community; his efforts to improve the Bay area; and his many charitable contributions of both time and money.

Finally, Matt's family came up and told the judge what a good husband and father he had been. Each one cried as she told the Judge about her love for Matt and how good he was.

When they had finished, Bernie rested his defense.

Shimdugger asked for and was given one last rebuttal.

"Your Honor, Dr. Hightower stood here and told this Court he was a humbled man. But is he really? I never heard him admit to the crimes of which he has pled guilty. I never heard him say, 'I'm sorry' to the court. It appears to me that his so called humility was only a word used to elicit sympathy from this Court.

"Doctor Hightower presents a unique opportunity for the Court. Normally, when physicians become involved with drugs, their lives are in such a shamble and they have hurt so many people and owe so many people that the Court has to go light on them so that their victims stand a chance of repayment. That is not a problem here," Shimdugger explained. "Dr. Hightower's only victim is society as a whole. The only restitution due will be whatever punishment it requires to satisfy societal conscience. The Court can have it both ways. You can serve Dr. Hightower with a substantial sentence, thereby satisfying society's right of atonement for the crimes committed, and, at the same time, use Dr. Hightower as an example to the medical community. An example that will show they are not above the laws that affect the other members of society.

"Your Honor, the State requests that the Court exceed the maximum guidelines, based upon the magnitude of the crimes committed. There are 156 separate felonies committed by the Defendant. The State requests 44 years. That is only one-hundred days for each felony committed and pled to. That's a reasonable length of time for the crimes committed. Despite the guidelines, the State believes the punishment should at least represent a reasonable relationship to the crimes committed. One-hundred days per felony is reasonable.

"Thank you, Your Honor. The State rests its case."

Judge Dana's mind was on fire. Externally she appeared calm and almost aloof, but her thoughts belied the internal conflict she could not shed. *The press has already thrown me to the wolves, portraying me as too soft on criminals. Elections are only months away. On the other hand, this Doctor seems to have been caught up in something way over his head, and he obviously is not a hardnosed offender. Why the hell the State decided to use this as an in your face case I don't know, but I know what I have to do to survive election time and it's not pretty. Sorry Doc, but the dice have been cast and you lose. Ordinarily this case would scream for a downward departure, but today...*

"Will the Defendant please rise," Judge Dana said as Shimdugger sat down.

"Doctor Hightower. You have pled guilty to the charges brought against you by the State of Florida. Your counsel has argued that the Court go outside the guidelines and sentence you to a reduced term of imprisonment. The State, on the other hand, has requested the Court to exceed the guidelines, giving you over twice as much time as recommended by the statutory guidelines."

"The Court declines to accept either request for guideline departure. As to Count 1, Trafficking in Narcotics, the Court finds you guilty as charged and sentences you to 18 years in the state penitentiary. As to Count 2..."

Judge Dana went on for the next 54 counts, sentencing Matt to 18 years on each. Then she went on to the rest of the counts, all third degree felonies, and all sentenced to five years.

After the last one, Shimdugger spoke up. "All counts to run consecutively, Your Honor?"

"You know better, counselor. All counts to run concurrently, with five years probation to follow the Defendant's release from prison."

Matt was stunned. His family was openly weeping and his friends were looking at the Judge, in total shock.

Bernie spoke first. "Your Honor, we respectfully request that Dr. Hightower be allowed to remain free on bond for 30 days to wrap up his financial affairs prior to entering prison."

"What says the State, Mr. Shimdugger?"

"Your Honor, the State would oppose any such extension of time. Dr. Hightower has already had several months in which to take care of his affairs, financial or otherwise, prior to this sentencing hearing. Just because he is educated does not mean he is entitled to any more leniency than the next convicted felon. Additionally, he has sold all of his businesses, and with the sentence hanging over his head, he is an imminent risk for flight."

"Your Honor," Bernie began.

"I've heard enough, Counselor. Your motion is denied. Bailiff, take charge of the prisoner and cuff him. Court is adjourned."

As the cameras rolled, the bailiff put Matt's hands behind him and put the handcuffs on his wrists.

We had a deal. Thirty days to close out. Why?

Shimdugger! That's why. Shimdugger, that lying son of a bitch! From the beginning all he wanted to do was use me and to hell with me and my family; and the judge allowed it. Hell, she joined in with him.

Tears streaming down his face, Matt struggled to control his emotions and, gritting his teeth until his jaw ached, he forced himself to look at Marilyn and the girls.

If I look back at that scheming bitch of a judge or her pock-faced enforcer, I'll lose it! God, I have never hated anyone like this. Never.

Trying desperately to blink the tears from his eyes, Matt's face and gut screamed with anger as he was led out of the courtroom and into his new life.

As the tears streamed down Matt's face, he was unaware that deep inside of him the seeds of a fierce and lasting hatred had already sprouted and begun to grow.

CHAPTER THREE

The remainder of the hearing time was more of a blur to Matt than anything else. The Bailiff took him to the railing and shackled his legs, after which he had un-handcuffed Matt to allow him to remove his wallet, belt, tie, change and empty all the other things from his pockets. These belongings he permitted Matt to turn over to Marilyn. Matt was also permitted to hug Marilyn and each of the girls and to say his goodbyes.

After he had said his rapid, choked "I love yous," Matt was once again handcuffed and then led away, shuffling his feet and hanging his head in utter disgrace.

Sitting on the solid stainless steel bench in the holding cell, he watched for two hours as more men were thrown in with him following their sentencing hearings. All the others were repeat offenders and mostly mean looking. He was glad they all had cuffs on.

Matt had never felt like such an outsider in his entire life. The holding cell was bleak, damp and smelled of a mixture of disinfectant, human sweat and body odor. He sat there in his leg irons and cuffs, pondering his fate until the guards came and took them all to Orient Road. Once there, he was issued more jail clothes, assigned to a cell, and then left to his own thoughts.

During the week he remained in the Orient Road jail, Marilyn came to see him each morning and they talked through the Plexiglas, touching the glass together at the end of each meeting, pretending to actually feel the other. The girls came with her on the weekend and the little room on the other side of the Plexiglas looked as pretty to him as a vase full of beautiful flowers. The girls wore bright, spring-like dresses and were genuinely pleased to spend time with their dad. It was a bittersweet time for Matt.

Sam came once, bringing lots of paperwork for Matt to sign. As Matt's attorney, he was given a room with a table and chairs where he and Matt could meet in private. Matt signed over the forms for the sale of the clinics, Power of Attorney for Marilyn to be able to conduct all his business without him, and numerous other papers he never bothered to read. Sam agreed to guide Marilyn and help her manage the money. Four of the clinics had sold and the net result a little over $300,000 before taxes. The last and newest clinic had been sold and was set up on an eight-year mortgage to cover Matt's equity. This would provide Marilyn and the kids $40,000 a year to live on. Hopefully, the combined assets and income would provide Marilyn and the kids enough money to continue living in their home and take care of the girls' higher education costs as they came up.

Matt should be out in six years.

After eight days, he was awakened at 2: 00 AM and told to "Pack your shit and get ready to go."

* * * *

He and about 65 other inmates were taken to a large room several corridors down from his cellblock and given a change of clothing, which amounted to an orange jumpsuit for each of them. After the change they were lined up and issued a bag breakfast consisting of a peanut butter and jelly sandwich, a bologna sandwich, an apple and a small carton of milk.

As they finished their sandwiches they were told to make sure to use the restrooms if they had any urges because, for most of them it would be a long ride with no potty breaks.

About an hour later, they were lined up two abreast, by roll call. Each inmate in turn was cuffed and shackled, first together wrist to wrist and leg to leg and finally, with a chain connecting them together in groups of 12. They were then loaded into vans and seated in circles on a bench seat that ran the entire interior of each van. The interior of the van was covered with steel mesh and resembled a gigantic steel cage into which they were packed like sardines. Each movement of the van brought about different rattles and thumps; some from the van itself, but most from inmates and the metal they were involuntarily wearing.

It was extremely uncomfortable, horribly crowded and entirely unpleasant. The air was soon stagnant and stifling and it was impossible to sleep; and yet, after an hour, it was equally impossible to stay awake. As soon as a man fell asleep, he would fall forward, only to be snatched awake as his chains pulled on the two men directly attached to him. Soon the air became putrid by men letting out gas as their bowels swelled from the early morning meal.

* * * *

At four AM, Marilyn's over-taxed mind and body succumbed to her primal urge, falling into a restless sleep. Almost immediately she began to dream and soon she had a beautiful smile on her face as she relived her courtship with Matt.

They had made love for the first time and shared depths and sensations Marilyn had never thought possible when they heard some beachcombers coming toward them. Scrambling, they had just managed to get back into their swimsuits and begin shaking their towels when the group came in sight.

"Hi ya'll. Looks like you been having a late night swim," The unnamed girl called out to them.

"Nope, just sitting and watching the sunset." Matt called back, causing a torrent of guffaws and giggles to erupt from the crowd.

Marilyn was absolutely sure that every one in the group could see her bright red face in the moonlight and recognize the color was not all from the tan she was so proud of.

Putting his arm around her waist, Matt gently pulled her along and they were soon out of hearing range for the beachcombers.

"I guess we weren't quite as unobtrusive as we thought," Matt said. They'd both broken into gales of tension-relieving laughter.

As the laughter subsided, they took each other's hand and quietly walked back to her car.

"I need to see you again," Matt said. "Like tomorrow and the next day and forever, if that's OK with you."

"That almost sounds like a proposal," Marilyn answered back. "Seriously, we need to talk about something," she said, her voice expressing some nervousness.

"OK," Matt said with a quizzical look in his eyes.

"Matt, I'm scared. I just realized, we didn't use any protection and I'm not on the pill. What happens if I'm pregnant?"

"Why, that'll just give us a reason to get married sooner," he replied with a twinkle in his eye.

"Matt, I'm serious!" Marilyn said, frustration edging her voice.

"So am I." The twinkle was gone, replaced with a sincere and caring look that she knew was real.

"I was only half joking," he continued, "when I mentioned forever a while ago. If what I'm feeling now is anywhere near real, I don't ever want to lose it. I have never felt this way about anyone and I love it. If that means that I love you, than I welcome it with open arms. In other words, I love you. Period!"

Eight months later they married and a year after that came Jenny. Marilyn would never forget the look of pure ecstasy in Matt's eyes as he laid his head on Marilyn's left breast when the cleansed new baby, Jenny, was placed on her right breast to feed.

Watching Jenny suckle, at first Matt raised his loving eyes to Marilyn and then back to the baby. Finally, in a hoarse whisper, he said, "Will you look at the miracle you, God and I created? She is the most perfect and beautiful baby in the entire world. I love you so much."

Suddenly Shimdugger was staring straight at her with a leering grin on his pockmarked face and Matt was standing there in court, crying his eyes out. Marilyn began screaming at the prosecutor, crying and sobbing at the same time while flailing her arms at him in frustration.

"Mama, mama, what's wrong? Mama, wake up, please!" Jenny and her sisters were scared and trying to awaken Marilyn from what had blossomed into a full-blown nightmare.

Hearing their cries, Marilyn fought her way out of her dream-induced panic and quickly sat up, wrapping her arms around all of them and dragging them onto the bed with her, all of them crying together.

As she regained her composure, Marilyn knew a deep hatred had settled in her soul for a man she didn't even know. Shimdugger!

* * * *

By 6:30 AM, when they arrived at Lake Butler reception center, Matt was completely exhausted. As a doctor, he could not believe this inhumane treatment of men by the jailors. They were treated with less respect than would be given cattle.

Shimdugger! He and the bitch/Judge. They should be here, not me!

Pulling into a large garage at Lake Butler, the prisoners saw heavy steel doors that were electronically controlled and guards standing on either side of the entrance, armed with shotguns and rifles. When the doors rumbled shut, they were herded out of the van, their shackles and cuffs removed and then told to get out of the orange jump suits and turn them over to the county guards. As they turned in the jump suits they were handed their property bags; black garbage bags containing their personal belongings from the county jail. Matt's property bag contained one pair of tennis shoes, a pair of jeans, a T shirt, belt and fresh underwear. He also had a Timex Iron Man, bought for him to wear in prison. It was the last thing Marilyn had given him.

Unbeknown to Matt and the others from the van, they were being observed by three men from behind the windows of the doors to the building leading in from the garage. One man in particular, Sergeant Rufus Black, watched intently as he mentally separated the leaders from the sheep and the cons from the first timers. Black was a local farm boy whose daddy was a sharecropper in a small north Florida town which still had a full contingent of Clansmen who looked to abuse poor blacks as their chief source of entertainment on Saturday night.

Black had been headed down that same sharecropping road, until Viet Nam. In Nam he had distinguished himself on numerous occasions as a fighter and a man to be counted upon. He'd channeled the hatred his upbringing had given him upon the enemy. An untimely bullet that nearly severed his spinal cord ended his service career. Unnoticeable today, it had been all too prominent for the doctors to ignore; he had been retired with a 75% disability, several medals and a still burning hatred that no longer had an outlet.

He only lasted four months on the Highway Patrol before resigning in lieu of being fired for brutalizing two "suspected Mexican drug runners". Local orange pickers who had been good citizens for over twenty years, they just happened to be in the wrong place with the wrong man: Rufus Black.

His next stint lasted for 18 months, as a deputy county sheriff. That job had ended when he'd broken a suspect's back, causing Lake County to settle a law suit for half a million dollars. Black's luck changed when a friend told him about the Florida Department of Corrections. There, hatred, bigotry and racism made up the whole system, most of all, the inmates themselves. The department didn't care about brutality, at least not in certain prisons. Nobody really gave a damn what happened to inmates. Unless someone outside the system saw something happen, the guards would cover each other's backs. A man like Black was not just tolerated, but welcomed.

Black was no dummy, and he quickly learned when to kiss ass and when to kick it. In 14 months he had made sergeant, and had earned the reputation as the toughest sergeant in Butler. That was when he had been put in charge of incoming inductees to the penal system. He considered it his job to ensure that as these new prisoners left Butler for their permanent camps, they were softened up, and they were ready to comply with and accept orders from their new officers. Besides, as his three ex-wives had each testified to when divorcing him, Rufus didn't just like hurting people, he thrived on it. He enjoyed being the biggest, meanest son of a bitch you ever met, and he would tell you so every time he had the opportunity. Racial slurs were as much a part of Black's vocabulary as were any other words, and usually got him more attention. Watching his new recruits, he relished the thrill of anticipation as he selected his next victims.

Unaware of being scrutinized, Matt stood naked, watching as several others began to dress in their clothing from their property bags. The county guards were totally unresponsive, paying attention only to collecting the orange jumpers and stuffing them into more black garbage bags. Assuming that the others knew what they were doing, Matt followed suit, beginning to dress in his clothing from his property bag. He had just gotten into his under shorts when three large state officers walked inside the dark garage. The leader, a large black officer with sergeant's stripes on his collar, bellowed out in a deep, rasping voice, "Who in the hell told anybody here to put their fucking clothes on? I'll tell you motherfuckers what to do and when to do it. Meantime, unless you are told to do something, you are to do nothing! Understood?" His tone of voice left little doubt that he assumed everyone understood.

As everyone in the crowd nodded, the guard seemed to become infuriated. "I am a correctional officer, as are these gentlemen." He nodded to the other two guards. "When a correctional officer addresses you, you will address him. And when you address an officer, the *only* address you will use is 'sir'! Is that understood?" he screamed.

"Yes sir," they all answered.

"I did not fucking hear you!" he screamed again.

"Yes sir," they all screamed back.

"That's more like it," the sergeant screamed. "Now get your sorry asses in that room and line them up against the bench on the wall. Take off all your clothes and put them and your property on the floor in front of you. Do not, I repeat do not, sit your sorry bare asses on my bench. Is that clear?"

"Yes sir!" they all shouted.

As they lined up against the bench, a small 12-inch wide plank about 18 inches off the ground, Matt and most of the men stripped naked. A couple of men still retained their boxers.

"Are you deaf or just total fucking idiots?" the sergeant screamed. Matt noted the sergeant's name tag, Black.

"Get those God damn clothes off now!" Black screamed.

"All of you take your property bags and dump them on the floor, two spaces in front of you. Take all jewelry, watches, chains, navel rings, ear rings, titty rings and any other fucking thing that is removable from your otherwise naked body and drop it on the floor with the rest of your property. When you are finished, step back to the bench."

"When I call your name you will take one step forward. You will then shout out your full name, your date of birth and the county you were born in. When you have done that, one of these officers will step up to you and stand in front of you. You will raise your hands in the air, all the way up. You will then take your right hand and brush your left armpit thoroughly. You will then take your left hand and brush your right armpit. You will then take both hands and thoroughly brush out your hair. You will then put your left hand down at your side and open your mouth wide. You will run your tongue around the inside of your mouth and then lift it back against the roof of your mouth. Then you will take your right index finger and roll it completely around the outside of your teeth, inside your cheeks. You will then take your right hand and reach down and grab your dick and your nuts. You will raise them up as far as they will stretch. You will then turn around and bend over, drop your dick and grab the cheeks of your ass with both hands and pull your cheeks wide apart until your ass hole is pulled wide open. You will then squat like a duck and cough at the same time. You will then stand up, facing the wall, bend over and lift each foot with the bottom facing the officer, right foot first and then the left foot. Finally, you will turn back, face the officer and say, 'Sir,' and step back to the bench."

Pausing, Black looked around and then said, "Now, I hope all you fuckheads got that because I don't like to repeat myself."

Black called the first name and the process got underway. The first couple of men who were called obviously knew the procedure and that made it easier for the rest. It was embarrassing to say the least, but there was no room for any hesitation or false modesty.

Matt was dead tired by now. His mind was numb and he was incapable of accepting the current circumstances as real. It was much more like a hideous dream, a nightmare. As he bent over, squatting, coughing and spreading his cheeks, the ignominy of the entire thing was overwhelming. The very idea of standing there nude, lifting himself in front of these barbaric, foul mouthed men was enough to make him seriously wish he were dead.

At that moment, Matt wished he had a gun. He could practically feel the cool of blued steel against his forehead. The wave of nothingness that would follow his pulling the trigger would be a thousand times better than what he faced here.

His mind whirling, Matt tried to listen as Sergeant Black spoke again.

"It is time for you people to understand some things. You are no longer on the streets. You are convicted felons, inmates, sent here to do your time. We are here to see to it that you do that time. Now, you can do it easy, or you can do hard time. The choice is yours."

"Some of you always want to challenge the way we do things. Won't work! I always win. *Always!* We got special cells and special treatment for those of you who try me. It makes for real hard time."

Matt couldn't help himself. He did not even think. He was dead tired, mentally and physically exhausted. Unconsciously, he yawned.

"See now, that's what I'm talking about," Black said. "I'm being real nice and polite talking to you and some motherfucker just gonna disrespect me to my face. What's the matter dude? Am I boring you?"

Realizing that Black was talking to him, Matt gulped and said, "No, I was just..."

"No what?" screamed Black. "That's two times you done disrespected me, inmate. I got some special chores for you soon as we get inside. You gonna learn to respect me, boy."

"I'm sorry. It wasn't intentional, sir." Matt said. He was at least ten years older than the foul-mouthed sergeant and saw absolutely no reason to respect him, other than the circumstances, but he added the 'sir' anyway. Beyond everything that was happening, icy fingers of fear squeezed his mind and trickled down his back.

Two inmates dressed in white prison uniforms came in to the room carrying armloads of boxer shorts. Each new man was given a pair, and after everyone had theirs, Sergeant Black told them to put them on.

They were then told to sit down with their feet pulled under the bench and their backs straight. No slouching or putting feet flat in front of the bench was allowed. The position was extremely uncomfortable.

They were told to wait until their names were called and then to go to whomever was calling. No talking was allowed at any time. Nor could they go into their property bags that sat beside them on the bench.

After about 15 minutes, inmates began to droop from exhaustion and put their feet flat in front of themselves in order to stay on the bench. Matt himself was mentally exhausted, his mind far too numb from lack of sleep and all that had happened to keep a constant grasp on reality. Suddenly, a guard in combat boots came down Matt's row, stomping those heavy boots at the inmates' feet.

Matt snatched his feet back just as the guard's foot slammed down where they had been.

The man's boot barely clipped Matt's toes, but caused no pain. The officer was grinning as he went by, clearly enjoying himself as he forced everyone to pull their feet back in their uncomfortable positions.

Then Sergeant Black came out of the Plexiglas office where he had stepped for coffee and shouted, "You!" at Matt.

"Get your ass over here. Leave your property bag right where it is."

Matt rapidly walked over to Black. "Yes sir," he replied.

"Take this brush and sweep up all the tile grout in the hallway. I expect it to shine when you are through, inmate." Black grinned as he handed Matt a toothbrush.

Fuming, but maintaining enough sense not to argue or complain, Matt knelt and began sweeping with the toothbrush. He was still doing this, still in his boxer shorts, when his name was called about a half hour later.

He reported to the desk and was given two forms to fill out and sign. When he had finished he went back to the bench by his property and sat down, only to be summoned immediately by Black.

"Did I tell you to stop sweeping, inmate?"

"No sir," Matt replied.

"Then get you're lazy ass back to what you were doing, inmate."

"Yes sir," Matt answered.

Matt was unaware of how red his face had become with the effort it took to keep from confronting Sergeant Black. Sweat ran down his nose and his eyes squinted as he remembered what another inmate had told him. "If you ain't prejudiced now, you will be by the time you get out." Sergeant Black was well on the way toward helping to fulfill that prophecy.

The process continued as each new man went through each phase of initial reception at Butler. When they went to the property desk, Matt was informed he could only keep his belt, watch and shoes. The rest could be donated to charity or he could pay to have it sent home. If he elected to pay, it would keep his canteen account frozen for 30 days. Matt opted to donate.

Each new inmate received shots and scalp-like haircuts, then had to dry shave, answer numerous questions and fill out various forms. Additionally, they were photographed and all received new prison IDs.

At each step of the way, Sergeant Black confronted Matt. Recognizing Matt as a potential leader and non-conformist, Black was determined to send Matt away from Butler with a whole new outlook on life. Matt, meanwhile, had no idea of the reason behind Black's constant badgering and hateful language.

Before early afternoon, the room had filled with over 150 new inmates. Some were transfers from other institutions and had large amounts of property in laundry style bags, while others were new, like Matt and his group.

After the photo session, they were lined up in the hallway. Once again Sergeant Black came up to Matt. "I'm going to keep an eye on you, boy. You want any trouble, you just ask. I'm your worst nightmare. I'm the motherfucker your mama and your preacher told you to look out for. You hear me?"

What in God's name have I ever done to this racist bastard? Talk about nightmare, you son of a bitch! I'd like to show you a real nightmare. Just you and me, one on one.

But what he answered wisely was, "Yes sir."

"Good. I'll be looking for you."

They were then marched over to Building K. It was a two-story cellblock with three wings and a center control room. Each inmate was assigned a cell number and bunk. Two bunks per cell, one upper and one lower. Instructions were to make the bed with a six-inch collar and hospital corners. The bed was to remain made from 5:30 AM until after the master roster count at 8:00 PM. Inmates could only lie on top of the covers at any other time.

Walking into the dorm and seeing the cells lined up, two stories, automatic locks from the guard stationed behind the bullet proof glass, everything clanging and so impersonal, Matt could only describe his feelings as heavy. Heavy, as if the weight of all the steel bars around him were heaped upon his shoulders. Heavy with the loss of everything he held dear and laden with the sense of impending disaster. Overwhelmed by the total lack of humanity in what surrounded him. He felt as if his shoulders had never shared a greater burden than that which was thrust upon him as he entered this house of evil. He also felt as if he would never last to see the end of his sentence and ultimate release from this God-forsaken place. It was almost too much to bear as he shuffled his way to his cell.

As the door automatically slammed shut behind him, he felt as though the breath had been sucked from his lungs. Only an act of sheer will power allowed him to make up his bunk in time to follow the rest of the inmates out when the cells re-opened.

Matt was supposed to be at Butler for eight days and then be assigned to a permanent camp. Butler was the place for all inmates to be medically evaluated and then sent to a camp that was best suited for their particular needs. That was the theory, at least. In reality, his first visit to medical was a joke. He went in for a 'complete physical' and would have laughed out loud except that the conditions were real and utterly appalling. The 'doctors' were all Vietnamese medical personal and most did not speak English. None was a qualified MD. Matt was convinced that none of them could have passed any type of licensing requirement. The small amount of medical diagnosis and treatment Matt witnessed while at medical was outrageous. Exams were perfunctory at best. Most of the time it was nothing more than a 'doctor' filling in a blank on a State approved form or exing a mark in a box.

Medical evaluation was the least of Matt's problems, however, because every day, for three days, Sergeant Black sought him out. He deliberately singled out Matt and embarrassed him, having him sweep the sunlight off the sidewalk, or chase seagulls off the grounds. All the while, he screamed at Matt, shouting vile oaths that made Matt's blood boil and his hair stand up on the back of his neck. Twice he had to physically turn his attention from Black in order to hold on to the last vestiges of his ever-thinning temper. Sweat burned in his eyes, as much from squinting away the hatred that engulfed him, as from the sun or the work involved.

Black's constant fanning of the fires of his anger spread the sparks of his fast-growing hatred out to the Judge and prosecutor who sent him here to be taunted by this evil man. He began to relish his hate. Having no other outlet for emotion, he used his hatred to give him the energy and stamina to put up with whatever Black threw his way. He also became more and more of a loner, trusting no one to share confidences with.

None of the convicts would be able to call home or receive mail until they reached their permanent assignment, and he knew that all outgoing mail would be read before it left the camp by one or more of the camp officers. As a result, he had no one at all with whom to discuss his growing problem. Meanwhile, he continued to receive abuse from a jealous, bigoted Sergeant Black who was enjoying taking his frustrations out on a white doctor.

On the fourth day, in the morning on the way back from breakfast, Matt and the others heard gunshots. In the fog shrouded, early dawn light, he could barely make out two blankets thrown over the razor wire that surrounded the camp. Two fences were about ten feet apart, and blankets had been thrown over each. Two men were running over the sparse pasture-like sandy ground and, as the convicts watched, one went down. Almost simultaneously, the sound of a thud pierced the air. Matt knew it was the sound of a bullet hitting flesh. The man did not move again.

Abruptly, the other man fell, grabbing his right leg; they heard him grunt as he got back up and tried to run again. However, he was limping heavily and was no match for the sharp shooting guards in the towers. Matt and the others watched as three more shots found their mark and the second man fell about 20 feet from his companion. Two more shots were fired into his prone body, each one causing the body to jerk as the thud thud sound echoed back to Matt and the others. The fallen men moved no more.

Matt's mouth was dry and his pulse raced as he watched the two men die. If Black had given him an opening, he would have loved to have taken him out and then bolted from the prison himself. Matt's hands were sweaty as he clenched them, feeling more lost and further from sanity than at any time in his life. With senses heightened, it would not take much to drive him over the brink to insanity.

My God, my God. Is there anyone out there? Can anyone hear me? God, are you real? Can you hear me? Talk to me!

"All right, assholes." Black's voice came over the loudspeaker. "No more gawking. Party's over so back to your cells. Now!"

It was a very sober bunch that left the walkway and went into the cellblock. Matt never realized his own injury or felt any pain until after he unclenched his fists and saw blood dripping from where his nails had bitten into his palms.

* * * *

Throughout his few days there, Matt often had to pass by the area reserved for special prisoners. There were numerous offices on the ground floor, but the entire second floor of the long building was reserved for disciplinary confinement. Listening to the occasional noises from there, Matt knew he never wanted to be in DC. He also learned that Sergeant Black was one of the guards who inflicted punishment on confined inmates. When the inmates were punished, the ratio was usually six to one, guards over inmates. Matt wondered how good a fighter Sergeant Black really was. If he ever got the chance, he would find out.

He got the chance much sooner than he envisioned.

Just prior to Matt's expected departure from Lake Butler, Sergeant Black had Matt sweeping the sun off the sidewalk. Black instructed Matt to take his broom to the corner of the dental office, under the DC confinement unit. There was an alcove between the dental office and the stairs going to the upper level of the building. The whole area was about 15 feet wide and was pretty much concealed from the rest of the camp.

As Matt moved to the inside corner of the alcove, Sergeant Black told him to face the wall and put his hands against it.

Moving up behind him, Black took the broom from Matt's hand and stepped back. Suddenly Matt received two sharp blows to his kidneys, one on the left and one on the right. Over his shoulder, Matt saw Sergeant Black holding the broom handle in a classic jabbing stance, the same stance that Matt had learned when he was in the shore patrol in the Navy.

Following the kidney strikes, Sergeant Black jammed the broom handle straight into Matt's rectum. Even with the protection of the pants he was wearing, Matt could feel the clothing being forced into his body.

Sergeant Black pinned him against the wall and held him in place while he said, "Now, white boy doctor. Big man. You understand me. I don't care what you were on the street, you ain't nothing but a fucking con in here. And I hate cons! I eat them for breakfast, spit them out for lunch and shit the rest out at supper. You're my meat as long as you are in here and don't you ever forget it. You hear me, boy?"

In pain, embarrassed, scared, frustrated and madder than he had ever been in his life, Matt could only mumble, "Yes sir."

Mind still in shock and reeling from the episode Matt would never know what led him to his next move.

As Sergeant Black handed back the broom, Matt lost it. Before he could even think about what he was doing, Matt slammed his fist into Sergeant Black's face, rupturing his nose and causing blood to spurt freely. He pounded upon the sergeant, unmindful of where his punches landed, only caring to hit as hard as he could.

While Matt pounded away almost randomly, Black spun around. With his back to Matt, the sergeant pulled out a large black flashlight and a whistle. Sergeant Black blew three times on the whistle and then turned back to Matt, coming in sideways and low with the flashlight and catching Matt broadside in the face.

Matt's anger held him up through the first few strikes but the flashlight hit him hard and rapidly about his upper body. He soon collapsed under the steady blows. What he did not know in his near stupor was that four other guards had joined in with Sergeant Black to beat Matt, switching from beating to kicking as he got lower to the ground. Soon, the kicks rained in on his body, catching him in his kidneys, face, groin and rib area with such ferocity that Matt soon lost consciousness. His last thoughts as he left reality were:

God, I've done it now. They've killed me and I barely hurt the son of a bitch.

CHAPTER FOUR

When Matt was transferred, Marilyn and the girls had banded together, both out of fear and the frustration of the unknown. More and more, however, the girls were asking questions for which she had no answers. And which made their frustrations more acute. As the oldest, Jenny was the least argumentative, but she was also more thoughtful and it appeared she was retreating into a shell.

Carol and Eileen were best buds and seemed more fearful of being around others. Marilyn knew that all of them had been hurt by the unkind words of fellow students, even though their teachers were trying to help them in any way they could.

As the youngest, Rachael was the most disillusioned. All the girls were close to their daddy, but Rachael truly doted on him and her pain was the most obvious.

"Mommy, why can't daddy come home, at least for the weekend?" Rachael had entered the same plea several times before, never really accepting Marilyn's answer.

"Honey, your daddy would love to come home but he can't. It is not his fault. He loves you more than life itself, but he just can't."

"I'll talk to her, mom." Jenny said as she took her little sister by the arm and herded all three of the other girls off to the bedroom.

"Thanks, Jenny, I've got to call Sam and see if he needs me to do anything else about the transfer of the business mortgages. Let's all plan on going to Chuck-E-Cheese tonight. We need to lighten up and try to have a little fun."

"Sure, mom. That should help some."

Even though Jenny's answer was somewhat positive, Marilyn could see that she didn't smile as she whisked the girls into the other room. Matt had always handled the business and had been a good provider for her and the kids. Her job was to be a wife, mother and housekeeper, and she loved all three positions. Now she was everything. Even though Matt had done a good job setting up the business sales and making sure she and the kids had all the basics to keep things going in his absence, it was hard. It had been years since she ran the house on a budget, but now she and Abe had figured out just how much she could spend and keep things going without using any more of her principal than necessary. She no longer had a part-time maid and now did her own nails. Her one luxury that she allowed herself was her once a month hairstyle.

She was coping and she knew that as time went on, she would do better. Right now, though, it hurt.

"I don't want to, and you can't make me!"

Oh God, that's Carol. What now. This is the fourth time this week.

"Girls, girls, what's wrong?" Marilyn called out as she headed for the girls' bedroom at a fast walk.

"Jenny keeps telling me to sit here and let you have some time, but I'm scared and I need you. I need daddy!!" Carol broke out in tears, sobbing and grabbing her mother around the waist.

"There, there, it will be all right. We'll all go to see daddy as soon as he gets to his new camp, which shouldn't be too much longer." Marilyn rubbed Carol's back and tried not to join her in a good cry as the others gathered around.

"We have to be strong for daddy," Marilyn said, feeling anything but.

My God, my God. How do you tell a child to be strong when the center of her universe has been taken from her without warning? Why, why, why is this happening? What did any of us ever do to you, God? How did we hurt you so much to bring Shimdugger into our lives? I hate him, I hate him. He did this to four young girls and a good man. I hate him.

Forcing herself out of her reverie, Marilyn worked at calming the girls. No one wanted to go out for pizza so they stayed home and had macaroni and cheese and hot dogs. Even the TV didn't capture their interest; instead they all got books and read silently in the family room, together and quietly, almost as if in mourning.

* * * *

Dear God; I hurt! My arm is on fire! Oh God, It hurts so much when I move. Where am I?

Matt had remained unconscious for about eight hours. When he came to, he was lying on his back on a solid piece of concrete that was shaped like a bunk. There was no pillow, no mattress, no sheet or blanket: only concrete. He was covered, however; on his body was a moving mass of live cockroaches.

Shaking his head, he attempted to reach out to wipe the roaches off his face, but the intense pain he caused by his movements was too much to bear and he passed back into the dark but comfortable world of complete unconsciousness.

The next time he awoke, Matt shuddered with revulsion. Although his brain remained foggy, he forced himself to lie still and assess his situation as best he could. With hands cuffed behind his back, the first recognizable feeling was one of severe pain in his hand and arms; it only took him seconds to realize his left wrist was broken. His first move was to roll over on his side in an attempt to relieve the pain on his arms and hands.

"Yeaaaaaa! Dear God!"

It was his last move for over an hour, as the pain was so intense that he once again passed out.

When he came to for the third time, his arms were clear of body pressure and he very gingerly felt with his right hand to self diagnose the damage to the broken left wrist. In moments Matt realized that the handcuffs were biting into his wrist and causing even more swelling than should be normal from a broken wrist. Between the pain and the severity of swelling, it was impossible for him to get a finger between his wrist and the rim of the cuff. His flesh actually covered the cuff because of the swelling.

"Why, God. Why me. I'll develop gangrene, right? Oh it hurts so much!" Babbling, Matt talked to his invisible god as the intense pain made him virtually incoherent.

Had he access to a mirror, Matt would have seen something straight from a horror movie. His face, along with his entire head, was swollen to about twice its normal size. With cuts over both eyes, a broken nose, lacerated cheeks, and more cuts over his chin, forehead and lips, he appeared truly grotesque.

Additionally, at least two ribs were broken and his entire body was covered in so many bruises that a Dalmatian would have been poor competition in a spotted body contest. As he moved his legs, he realized that his testicles had been kicked so hard and so often that they were swollen to the size of baseballs.

Although his entire body hurt, Matt was primarily concerned with the severity of injury to his wrist and the risk that the handcuffs created. For three days, he drifted in and out of consciousness. Between bouts of intense pain, he attempted to cope with the biting handcuffs and increasing numbness in his hands. During this time, he received no food or medical assistance. On two occasions guards slipped water through the slot in the bottom of his door; otherwise, he would have died.

Unable to unbutton his prison pants, Matt lay in his own waste, and by the third day, he was sure he was going to die, actually welcomed the thought of death. At this point he was more scared of living than of dying.

As he fell asleep on the third night, he prayed for a just God to allow him to leave this world. He knew in his soul that whatever his sins may be, nothing he had ever done had condemned him to a hell worse than what he was going through now.

Awakening to excruciating pain, Matt screamed as the guard applied the 'jaws' to cut the cuffs from his wrists.

"Hold still, mother fucker. God, he stinks. You really are one filthy, stinking son of a bitch. I guess we are going to have to get him cleaned up before the 'doc' can see him. He wouldn't be able to touch him like this."

"You're right, Red, he really stinks. Last time I smelled one this bad, he had been dead for two days."

Babbling incessantly and pissing in his pants at the same time, Matt suffered through the pain and indignity.

One thought penetrated his confused mind. *If this shit happened in the county hospital to even the most indigent patient, he would be a multi-millionaire tomorrow.*

Groggy and drunk with the combination of pain and extreme malnutrition, Matt barely noticed as he was herded into the shower room.

"You want to take off his pants for him, Jimbo?"

"Hell no, I already touched more of him than I wanted to. He did it to himself, he can clean himself. Hell, he's still got one good hand."

Although Matt was barely able to stand, much less really help himself, the guards had him unbutton his filthy pants with his uninjured right wrist and let them fall to the floor. The shower was turned on full blast, cold water only, and Matt was thrust under the frigid stream.

There was no soap, so he rubbed the water on his body with as much gusto as he could muster, appreciating the cleansing effect while hating the pain that went with it.

Fecal waste had crusted on his buttocks and legs, and with only one hand to scrub with, it was remarkable that he accomplished as much as he did before the guards turned off the shower.

Allowing him to towel off for only a few moments, the guards then gave Matt a pair of boxer shorts, which he put on over his still wet body. Cradling his broken left arm with his right hand, Matt was then led back to his cell and given a bag lunch of a peanut butter and jelly sandwich, an apple and a half pint of milk.

With more sucking than chewing, he was able to eat the sandwich and drink the milk, but his mouth was far too sore to allow him to eat the apple.

I'll probably puke the whole mess up anyway, but at least it's food.

While he attempted to fashion a makeshift cast out of the milk carton, the paper bag and water from the cell commode, his cell door opened and a little Asian dressed in a white frock and stethoscope and carrying a black medical bag entered. Motioning him to move over on the concrete bunk, the 'Doctor' set his bag down and began to examine Matt.

Never actually saying a word, the 'doctor' *cluck clucked* his way through his examination and treatment of his patient, inmate Hightower. With local anesthetics he was able to stitch Matt's face, neck and arm before setting the broken wrist. No cast was used, only an Ace bandage wrapped tightly around the broken wrist. Finishing up, he stood and smiled, obviously very proud of his accomplishment. Still without uttering a single word, he gave Matt two aspirin and turned and walked over to the door whereupon the ever-watching guard opened the cell and allowed him to leave.

Matt later learned that no record, medical or otherwise, was ever made of the incident or the treatment. He also learned that the 'doctor' was actually a pharmacist, a refugee from Viet Nam, who was unable to pass the pharmaceutical tests in America and that only the low standards of the Florida Department of Corrections allowed him to practice as a pharmacist. This trend was prevalent among the vast majority of medical practitioners in the prison system of Florida.

As soon as the 'doctor' left, the guard came into Matt's cell and re-cuffed him, only this time it was with his hands in front to allow him to eat and function. The left cuff was loose, not cutting into the Ace bandage; for that, Matt was grateful.

Twice daily feedings ensued for three days and then were followed by the normal three times a day meals. The second week of confinement found Matt receiving better treatment, and on the ninth day, his handcuffs were removed. He was beginning to feel that life might not be quite a bad as he had begun to believe. That comforting thought was soon dispelled.

That night Sergeant Black returned to Matt's life, entering his cell with three other guards. All four carried large, black flashlights, the kind he had been beaten with before.

Matt's pulse raced and his face flushed as he tried desperately to hide first fear and then anger at the unwanted intrusion.

Sergeant Black had been through the routine too many times before to miss the signals Matt's body unconsciously sent. The sergeant nearly beamed as pleasure filled his demonic ego.

"Well, inmate, I just dropped in to see if you had learned your lesson. Still want to take this nigger on? Huh? Like I told you before, you may be a big shot doctor on the street, but in here you're my meat." Grinning broadly he took a step forward, slapped the flashlight in his hand and sucked in his breath. "Now turn around, inmate."

Feeling utterly intimidated, shamed and trying with all his manhood to blink back the stinging salty tears threatening to spill from his eyes,

Matt slowly did as he was told, turning his back to the Sergeant and facing his concrete bunk.

Dear God. I don't even have the balls to take on the son of a bitch. I'm so scared I'll be lucky if I don't piss my pants right in front of him.

"Now, inmate put your hands on that bunk and bend over!" Black yelled, causing Matt to involuntarily shudder with a combination of fear and revulsion.

Assuming the commanded position, Matt carefully ensured that most of his weight was supported by his good wrist. He almost lost it when he felt the butt of Sergeant Black's flashlight being forcefully rammed between his buttocks.

"What's the matter, white boy? You ain't never been fucked by no nigger before?" Well guess what? Lucky for you, this nigger don't want none of your sorry white ass. Not now, anyhow. Maybe tomorrow—we'll see then. Meanwhile, you sleep tight."

Sergeant Black burst out laughing. "Get it? Sleep tight? That's the way I wants you. I gets you the way I wants you, nice and tight."

Giving a final hard shove to his flashlight, Sergeant Black walked out of the cell, taking his officers with him.

Feeling alone, degraded and totally ashamed, Matt waited until he was certain that the Sergeant was really gone. He then pulled down his drawers, finding a large area of fecal stains in the bottom.

In a robotic state he washed his boxers as best he could in the toilet and hung them to dry on the end of the bunk. Climbing on the concrete he covered himself with the sheet, afraid to be seen naked by the guards.

Matt thought about the rumors he had heard of Sergeant Black's nightly episodes; beatings of inmates he disliked. Black made sure he brought enough guards to keep a four or five to one ratio, and usually dealt out severe damage.

Lying on the bunk Matt vowed that if he survived, he would find out how good Black was on a one to one basis. As the fear and shame of the moment abated, the hatred that had been building ever since the beginning of this ordeal threatened to overrun his logical mind. Only with great effort was he finally able to channel that hate into a force for survival. It would serve him well for the rest of his incarceration.

* * * *

Matt remained in the Lake Butler center for four weeks, total.

He was released from confinement one day and shipped out to a new camp the next. Awakened at 3:30 AM, he and several other inmates were told to "Pack your shit." and then herded to early chow and from there directly to the bus pickup area. After a two-hour wait they were loaded on to a Blue Bird bus that had seen many years of abuse. The seats were all hard plastic, no seat belts and no air conditioning. Windows were locked in place one-third open and covered with a heavy steel mesh. In front of the main seating was a steel cage for the inmates still in confinement and not allowed to settle in the general population. Ahead of them in the very front of the bus were the guards' seats, one for the driver and one for the shotgun rider. Both guards were armed with pistols and shotguns. Their cab was air conditioned and lined in the back with bullet proof Plexiglas with a pull-back curtain to shield them from the view of their captives.

Inmates had only one entrance in the back of the bus, a two-door opening with steps enabling them to reach the threshold. As they'd been previously shackled at the ankles, it would not have been possible for them to enter the bus without the steps. Each inmate approached the door, set his bag of belongings down, had his handcuffs removed, then picked up his belongings and entered the bus with strict orders to fill the front seats first. Overhead racks were shallow and had no constraints, causing many of the inmates to place their belongings on their laps.

Matt noticed that the old timers to the system had far more belongings than he and the new inductees. One obviously older, grizzled inmate had three large plastic garbage bags full of belongings. He later learned that as time passed, so did the rules of the prison system, and each change in the rules allowed less private ownership of possessions for the inmates. Usually when a new rule outlawed certain possessions, those in ownership of the now disallowed articles were grandfathered in to retain possession until their departure. With the passage of time, these outlawed items became premiere collectables on the prison black market.

Not having received his packages from home, Matt had only the clothes on his back and his toiletries, which easily fit the overhead rack. As he entered the bus, the first thing he noticed was the smell. A heavy odor of sweat, urine and fecal matter assaulted his nostrils with every breath. To his left, a funnel-shaped piece of tin, about eight inches around, stuck from the side of the bus and served as a urinal. It appeared to empty into a fifty gallon tank under the bus. A small steel pole attached from the floor to the ceiling to allow inmates to balance while using the urinal during transportation.

To his right was the *honey pot*, a standard igloo drinking cooler that served as a toilet for those who had to do more than urinate during the trip. There was neither toilet paper nor sink. Matt struggled not to gag as he got on the bus and took his seat next to a large black inmate with two super sized black plastic garbage bags of possessions.

My God! I can't believe the state allows this unsanitary and inhumane type of transportation to exist!

Two types of busses left Butler: local and long distance. Fortunately for Matt, he was on a local bus. Unfortunately, it was bound for Hamilton, a maximum-security facility that handles a large lifer population. Not being familiar with the prison system, Matt had no idea what a large population of lifers meant. Prisoners with life sentences had no place left to go. There was no reason for them to behave, except for what pain or discomfort the guards could do to them if they caught inmates doing something wrong. Even if they killed another inmate, the most severe punishment was generally a five-year sentence, a plea bargain type sentence, tacked onto the end of their life sentence. In time, Matt would meet many inmates with five or more of these short sentences tacked on to their permanent sentence. In a prison of 1800 inmates, with over a thousand of them serving life sentences, he would be one of less than 20 minimum-security inmates in the institution. He would learn that lifers had a totally different outlook on the sanctity of life. A large man himself, he was already feeling intimidated by the man beside him and Matt didn't offer any objection as one of his neighbor's property bags wound up in Matt's lap.

It was only a thirty minute run to Hamilton and as it turned out, all 55 inmates on the bus got off there.

Leaving the bus, it was easy for Matt to see the north Florida swamps in the distance. Hamilton Prison was located just outside the town of Jasper, about 20 miles from the Georgia-Florida border. It was not an inviting looking place, but after the Blue Bird ride, it sure was a relief to the olfactory senses.

As they unloaded prisoners from the bus, the guards took the shackles off and this time no handcuffs were used. The incoming inmates were lined up and then taken into a small room in the canteen area of the prison. Once inside, they were told to take a seat and then given a brief orientation speech by a sergeant who seemed far more human than Sergeant Black. During the speech, five classification officers, all in civilian clothes, came into the room and aligned themselves on a small stage overlooking the seated inmates. They were told that following the talk, they would be called up by a classification officer and given a job placement and told about how the system worked, etc.

"These people are your liaisons between you and the system. Your classification officer is not a standard corrections officer, but a qualified officer who will direct you to the right job and alert you to what you need to do to make you stay in the Florida State Penitentiary as painless as possible. They will insure that you are fairly represented, your rights are protected and you are fitted to the job that most suits your talents and abilities."

As the orientation officer finished his spiel, Matt began to realize that was only the theory. In truth, most of these officers quickly burned out and became as worthless to the inmates' welfare as were the regular prison guards.

As Matt watched the classification officers call up others, he soon realized that the worst appearing officer was a small, mousy looking woman who seemed to hate everyone. Her small, beady eyes were constantly cast downward, and on those rare occasions that she looked up, she radiated animosity. She obviously did not like doing what she did for a living and Matt wanted nothing to do with her. *Please God, don't let this be my officer.*

God apparently was not paying attention, because sure enough, Miss Mousy called him to her table.

"Sit down; I'm Mrs. Arnow, your new classification officer." She had completed the entire introduction without ever looking up into Matt's face.

"What did you do on the street, before you were arrested?"

"I am a medical doctor."

"What can you do?"

"I'm board certified in neurology."

"No. What I need is what you can do for the system?" Miss Mousy was persistent.

"I am a doctor." Matt said. Straightening up, shrugging his shoulders and spreading his hands, he said, "I do doctor things. I treat patients and diagnose their illnesses. I assume I can do something to assist the doctors in the system."

"I see you're going to make this difficult." Miss Mousy was becoming belligerent. Still looking down, she continued: "First, never assume anything while you are in prison. Second, what do you know about plumbing?"

"Plumbing?" Matt was so taken aback that he almost laughed. "Well, I know that you find plumbers in the yellow pages and they are twice as expensive on weekends and holidays." Matt's answer was at best only half joking.

Without even a wisp of a smile Miss Mousy looked directly at the papers in her hand and said to Matt: "We will evaluate this further and decide where you will do this institution the most good. You and I will meet every six months for a progress report. Unless there is some sort of emergency, that is all. You will be notified on the Friday callout where and when to report to work on Monday. If you do your job, and you follow all the rules, you may earn up to 20 days gain time a month. You may leave now, unless you have a question?"

Miss Mousy's tone implied that she expected no questions would be forthcoming, and Matt was happy to comply, as he had no reason to speak with anyone whom he considered an idiot. Immediately standing up, he quickly left and headed to his dorm.

Introducing himself to his dorm officer, Matt was shown to his bunk. After being assigned to a lower bunk in a double bed, the officer cautioned him, almost in a fatherly tone.

"You don't look like you're prejudiced, and you don't look like you belong here. Couple things you should know. The nigger that has your top bunk is one mean son of a bitch. Always look him in the eye when he talks to you, which won't be often. Try not to look afraid. Don't cross him or any other killer while you're here and you might just get through this alive. I'll do what I can to help, but know this. I ain't got but three years until I retire. I don't plan on cutting that time short by dying for you or any other inmate. Something serious goes down, we lock ourselves in that booth until help arrives. Keep that in mind, you'll live longer. Now, get yourself unpacked, make your bunk and then get out to the rec field."

Since the dorm was empty, Matt was able to get a good view of it as he made up his bunk with the provided bedroll. Unlike the single and double cell dorms at Butler, this was classified as an open bunk dorm with nothing separating the different bunks but space. The dorm itself was shaped like a 'T,' with two wings on either side of an officer station that constituted the head of the 'T.' Directly in front of the station was seating for a TV set that sat over the top of the bullet proof glass enclosure of the station. Going straight back from the station, one looked directly into the bathroom. Along the wall of each side of the bathroom were twelve toilets for sitting down. Made of porcelain, they were simple bowls with no seats and just slightly wider than normal rims.

In the center of the bathroom was an island with a row of sinks, with two urinals on each side. Eight showers framed the back wall and completed the room. There were no stalls, with all toilets and all showers open in full view of the officers. Privacy was a luxury not to be enjoyed by any member of the inmate population. From the officer's station, all activity in the dorm could be clearly monitored.

You can't even take a crap in private.

Matt made his bunk and stowed his few possessions in his locker. As instructed by the dorm officer, he then headed out to the rec yard to wait for chow and afternoon orientation.

For the next two days he went from place to place in orientation, but the actual orientation time involved was less than two hours: always brief segments at various locals delivered in monotone by an uncaring and uninteresting officer.

The first night, he met his bunkie, a huge black inmate who stood about six foot six and weighed over 250 pounds. He proceeded to instruct Matt as to bunk mate etiquette and informed him where he was to hang his laundry bag, which side of the bunk was his, how not to jostle the bunk and a number of home-made rules. It was an entirely unilateral discussion, with Matt nodding and his bunkie doing all the talking. No names were exchanged and when the discussion was over, his bunkie jumped up on the top rack, put his headphones on and closed his eyes. End of discussion. Matt heeded the earlier warnings of the officer and merely nodded and offered no argument to the diatribe from his bunkie. It turned out to be good advice.

Matt felt goose bumps run down his spine later that evening.

"Your bunkie returned home early one day to find his mother in bed with a man who wasn't his father. He took a 9 mil and shot the man in the stomach three times. He then went out to a tool shed, grabbed a machete, came back into the room and proceeded to whack off the man's arms and legs. Next, he took the machete and cut off the man's balls and dick and stuffed them in his mouth and calmly sat down and watched him bleed to death. He got ten years, but he's already tacked on ten more since he got here."

Bubba, one of Matt's new *roommates* was telling Matt about his bunkie's past.

Matt's bunkie had been given a ten year sentence for the brutal murder. Thinking about it, Matt felt as if he had been kicked in the stomach!

Ten years total! That's less time than I got. What the hell kind of justice is that?

On Thursday Matt's canteen account was turned on. He now had access to thirty of the most needed and useful dollars he had ever received. Deodorant, instant coffee, creamer and all the little necessary things he had not seen since coming to prison were now available to him. Each inmate was allowed thirty dollars a week canteen money, and Matt had instructed Marilyn to send two hundred dollars a month into his account.

His thoughts rambled: Marilyn and the kids. He remembered how excited he had been when he made his initial ten-minute call home that first night. Since all calls are monitored and recorded, he had made light of his plight and the reasons he had not called sooner. He was sure Marilyn noted his tone of voice, and he knew she would expect more complete answers to her questions at their first meeting, his third weekend at Hamilton.

* * * *

Friday morning arrived and the call outs were posted, with Matt's new job assignment right on top. Plumbing! It was only with time that he would learn that he would never be allowed to work in the medical department. It would be far too easy for a medically trained person to see through the façade called "treatment" that the Department proffered inmates. Men were routinely denied even the most basic of medical treatments and misdiagnosis of conditions by incompetent 'doctors' was standard, rather than rare. Needless permanent injury and death was incurred because of these shameful practices. Never in his wildest dreams would Matt have believed that such disgraceful medical treatment would be allowed anywhere in the United States. He had seen numerous humble street clinics in poverty areas that gave far better rudimentary treatment than this.

Reporting to his new job assignment on Friday, Matt met his new boss, a free man named Tommy.

"You got to work with Leroy here and learn how to handle letting out the tools from the plumbing cart to the plumbing inmates. All plumbing work is done from a cart that stays in the maintenance shed outside the compound fence except when we use it. The outside minimum custody inmates from the work camp bring it to the sally port where we pick it up. Once inside, you will be responsible for keeping track of who has each tool and make sure it is turned in at the end of the work shift. Any missing tools at the end of the day and you get loss of gain time and sentencing to time in solitary confinement, the box."

There were a total of 13 tools, including a box cutter. With the penalties involved surrounding missing tools, Matt put as much effort into insuring the return of the tools as he had given to prescribing the correct dosage of medicine to elderly patients.

While physically going over the tools for the first time, Matt was surprised to find that he was dripping in sweat as he thought wistfully of the things he could have done had he had just this one little tool back at Butler when Sergeant Black had confronted him. The razor projected and gleamed as he pushed the top ejection and retraction lever of the box cutter. He carefully hid his thoughts so as not to worry his new supervisor. But he was just beginning to realize the real depth of hatred accumulating in his soul since his incarceration. He welcomed his new job as providing something to think about other than his murderous thoughts.

Work days were short because of the necessary count procedures. Never could Matt have imagined that counting could be such an important part of daily existence. The first awakening count began at 4:30 in the morning. At this count, as with every 'formal count,' everyone was required to remain on their bunks until the 'clear count' signal was issued, usually after about 20 minutes. There was another such count following breakfast, and only when it was completed could all inmates report to their assigned job areas. There would be at least two 'freeze counts' during the morning where the job supervisor counted all the inmates in his charge and then all inmates would be released back to the dorms for a formal count and subsequent feeding in the chow hall.

After lunch, one more formal count and then back to the job site, followed by one or two more freeze counts during the afternoon work period and then a release back to the dorms for another formal count. Then evening chow and rec time, followed by another formal count at dusk and a final formal count at lights out, 10:00 PM. The rest of the night, the dormitory guard was to do a count every hour of the night, with frequent walk- through inspections in between. As Matt soon learned, not all the guards were observant or conscientious.

* * * *

"Mommy she's got my finger," two-year-old Jenny cried out as her new born sister, Carol held on tightly.

Both Matt and Marilyn laughed out loud as a nearly terrified Jenny struggled to get her finger away from her sister.

"Easy now," Matt said, still chuckling as he slowly separated finger from fist.

Jenny was sitting awkwardly on the hospital bed between her mom and dad the second day after the birth of her sister. Carol had just finished feeding and Matt had burped her and handed her back to Marilyn whereupon the tiny little fist had clamped down on her sister's unsuspecting finger as she tried to pet her.

"They're both as beautiful as their mom," Matt said as he lovingly brushed Marilyn's cheek with his lips.

"That's only possible because of how handsome their dad is," Marilyn shot back. "I don't think I'd win any beauty contest right now."

He looked down at her, remembering how she had sweat and suffered during the last hours of her pregnancy and could hardly believe how beautiful she looked now. His heart ached with all the love they shared, and the dreams he had for all of them.

"You are every bit as beautiful right now as you were the first time I looked at you on the beach, maybe even more. In fact..."

"God damn, what a fucking mess!"

Matt's loving dream was quickly cut off as on Wednesday, the third morning of Matt's new job, the dorm lights came on, curses flew and he awakened to blood spatters everywhere, the blood apparently coming from two bunks away.

The corpse, halfway off the bunk, was already stiff and contained at least 20 to 30 puncture wounds. One of the eyes had been gouged out and the nose had been severed.

Having seen numerous corpses in his career, Matt was surprised at how quickly the bile rose in his throat and he swallowed hard to keep from vomiting.

Dear God! This man was only eight feet away and I never heard a thing. It could just as easily have been me, and no one would have done squat!

He didn't have long to contemplate, however, because in seconds the whole world turned into a screaming nightmare. Guards appeared out of nowhere and inmates ran to their lockers and began dumping anything illegal in them, scattering the objects on the floor with no attempt to hide them. Shivs, porno books, food, watches, a complete mix of anything that did not belong in an inmate's locker appeared as if out of nowhere. One shiv landed on Matt's bunk, but even in his distraught state of mind, he quickly brushed it off.

No sooner had the shiv landed on the floor among the growing pile of contraband, than shrill whistles began blowing and guards were screaming for everyone to line up facing the bulkheads. "Against the wall and assume the position, shitheads! One false move and you're all going down! Now, up against the wall! Hustle, hustle motherfuckers! I said now!"

Herded like cattle, they were forced to bend over while being searched very roughly. Their undershirts and pants were torn off and while still bent over, they were ordered to spread their cheeks. In this position they were probed and prodded by the guards and their anuses pierced with the guards' fingers to see if anything was buried inside the rectum. Although the guards did have rubber gloves on, they did not change them as they proceeded from one inmate to the next. Other than the knives lying around on the floor, however, no more shivs were found.

Matt was shocked at how many knives were openly scattered about in a place where knives were outlawed and security was so tight. He vowed to himself that once things had settled down, he would have one too. It appeared to him that at least a third of the inmates had them and that meant his own chances of survival were lessened without an equalizer of some sort. Thinking back, he recalled his first conversation with his dorm officer and how he was told that his protection was limited by the amount of help available to assist the officer at any given time. He was just beginning to realize that any real protection of an immediate nature would not come from the prison guards, but from himself and whatever devices he managed to concoct.

For two hours they were threatened, cursed, yelled at and repeatedly searched. However, at the end of that time the guards were no further along the search for the murderer than when they started. No one had admitted to seeing, hearing or knowing anything about the stabbing.

They were allowed to dress and go to chow, but the rest of the day was spent sitting around as they were called in one by one for individual questioning.

By nightfall it was obvious that if anyone had seen anything, he was not talking.

That night, after lights out, Matt lay on his bunk in his own private hell. Sweating profusely and at times shaking as if he had a fever, he was struggling to cope with the fact that the dead man could just as easily been him.

No one would help. No one would care. I'm nothing but a disposable number!

As the trembling eased off and his sweat turned to cooling moisture, Matt's mind finally grabbed on to a nugget of purpose that turned his uncontrollable fear into controllable hatred.

If I can catch on fast enough, I might even live through this. I have to. There are too many people I owe to let these bastards win. The Judge, the prosecutor, Black, all of them have it coming and I intend to be the one who brings it to them. I don't deserve this shit but they brought it to me and by God they will pay for it! I'll either buy or build what I need to survive, but survive I will!

* * * *

Back on the job the next day, Matt figured out that he had easier access to knives, or shivs, than most inmates. Many of the tools he had accountability for were easy to convert into knives. Given the punishment for losing them, he knew that was not the answer. His first real inspiration came when he realized that the box cutter that he signed in and out all the time had a reservoir in the handle, with four extra blades that were not accounted for in the sign-in log. These blades were razor sharp, double ended and constructed of very heavy and completely non-flexible steel. On the top, flat side of each blade were two molded ridges and a hole to give solidity and grip to the blade as it was extended and retracted from the handle.

Using a criminal ingenuity he never knew he possessed, Matt devised a very passable plan for a shiv. First, he sawed off a piece of a broom handle about four inches long. He then split one end with a saw about one-and-a-half inches deep so that the blade would fit snugly in, especially when the point was forced into the handle. Cutting a notch in the wood and drilling a small hole through both sides of the handle allowed him to use the notches and hole in the flat part of the blade to maneuver the blade into its customized seat with a tight fit. Cinching a nut onto a bolt running through both handles and the blade itself, and heavily taping the handle with duct tape made it a manageable knife that would hold up in a fight. It would not stab deep, but it could slash very wickedly and effectively, drawing lots of blood, which quickly put an end to most fights.

That night Matt spent over two hours after lights out fitting his new shiv into its new home. First, he carefully ripped apart the end lining of his pillow cover, exposing the three tube-like cylinders inside. The actual rolls were similar to miniature rolls of pink insulation, tightly pressed into shape. At one time, he supposed, these had been soft, but now they were more like fireplace logs. He then slit open the middle tube and inserted the shiv about halfway into the center, keeping the now flakey stuffing from spilling out on the floor. The last task was sewing the cover up loosely and placing the loosely sewn end to the rear of the pillowcase.

Finished, Matt tested the pillow for touch and feel, and after punching it, squeezing it and manipulating it in every way he could, he was satisfied that no one would accidentally find his shiv. He estimated that it would take him 10 to 15 seconds to retrieve the knife if he needed it. He hoped that would be enough when the time came to use it.

The last thing he noticed as he lay back to try to sleep was that his T shirt was soaked with sweat and his hands were shaking. Not an auspicious beginning for a bad guy wannabee.

CHAPTER FIVE

Driving along Interstate 75, Marilyn couldn't help wondering why, with so many prisons in the State of Florida, her husband would be sent so far from Tampa. She had awakened at 4:00 AM in order to get ready. The hardest part had been leaving the kids, but until she saw the conditions at the visiting part of the prison, she wasn't about to bring the girls. By the time she left, they were all in tears, her included.

Marilyn considered herself a good mother and a good wife. She worked hard at both and damn anyone who came between her and her family. She was on her way to see her husband for the first time in months, the first time with Matt as a prisoner in the state penal system.

She remembered the first night they had made love. Coming in late was not something she ever heard about from her parents, so she had simply gone to bed and lay wide awake for about two hours. She remembered his kiss, his smile, his beautiful teeth. Blushingly, she also remembered his beautiful body. She finally fell asleep with his sweet, husky man scent still fresh on her mind and the tingling touch of his gentle hands fresh on her body.

The next morning she ate breakfast with her parents and calmly blurted out, "I've met the man I intend to marry, have children with and spend the rest of my life with."

"Really, dear? Isn't this quite sudden?" Emma, her mom said. "Is it the nice young doctor you told us about?"

Looking back over the years, Marilyn knew that she and Matt had had more than most couples ever dare dream. They both truly loved each other and, even better, they cared about each other and their children. Matt had provided well for her and the girls and even when everything fell apart, the first thing he had done was to make sure she and the girls were OK. She never doubted his love for her and she truly loved him. Now, she was on her way to see her man.

Marilyn knew something had gone wrong during Matt's indoctrination time at Butler. She didn't know what, but she knew. After two weeks of not hearing from him, she called Bernie's office and made an appointment to see him.

"I don't know how I know, but I know something is awfully wrong and I don't know where to turn," Marilyn said after the preliminaries were dispensed with. "I should have heard from Matt by now. What could have happened? Who do I contact? How can I help my husband?" These last words were spoken with such heartfelt tenderness and worry that Bernie felt truly sorry for her.

"You must understand the system before you can help your husband," Bernie started.

"The first thing to note is that if he were dead, you would know because they can't hide that. They would probably lie about the reason for his death, but they would disclose it immediately. The second thing is to realize that if he is in trouble he is a big boy and can probably fend for himself better alone than with outside help. Matt has one huge thing going for him in that he is a real doctor and can do things for other inmates that they can't do for themselves. This will help him immeasurably."

"But that will take time! I need to know if he needs help now!" Marilyn pleaded.

It was a bitter pill that she now had to swallow. Her body and soul constantly ached from missing her husband, especially at night when she lay awake until long hours of the night, often with one or more of the girls in the bed with her. Sometimes she spoke to him without thinking, before realizing that he wasn't anywhere around. Frequently she burst into tears as the enormity of loss cut into the depths of her soul, threatening to destroy her faith and even her sanity.

Even in the car going to see him for the first time in months, tears streamed down her face as she thought of her Matt.

Realizing that she was getting close to the prison and that she must look a mess, she pulled over into a rest area and went to the ladies room. After splashing water on her face she carefully applied fresh makeup and, adjusting her bra straps, she looked back at herself in the mirror.

I'm still a pretty fair looking gal, even if I do say so myself. I'm going to see the man I love and I'm going to get through this with him. I will raise our family as if he were there and I will make sure that the girls know how much he loves and cares for them. I will fill in for him until he returns to us. That is what I can do and what I will do.

She left the restroom a determined survivor. She could live with that. She was his woman.

* * * *

Matt fumed. He had seen Marilyn as she walked in and that was almost 45 minutes before. He had been subjected to a lengthy wait and then given a dressing down by an uneducated redneck half his age because Matt had neglected to call him 'sir.' For that infraction, he had been sent to the back of the line and had just now finished his strip search to be allowed into the visitation park. He had spread his cheeks, squatted and waddled like a duck, all at the whim of this juvenile acting officer.

Biting his lip, Matt resolved not to return the officer's comments lest he be forbidden to see Marilyn.

Finally cleared to go into the visitation park, Matt was given his conjugal instructions: One kiss and one hug upon arrival and one each at departure time. No other hugging and kissing in between; however, holding hands was permissible. If either of them was seen touching the other in the crotch or breast, the visit was over and no further visits would be allowed. He was to be polite to the officers at all times and when count was called, he was to report to his assigned area in the park ASAP.

The *visiting park* at Hamilton consisted of one inside room which contained a canteen for food and drinks and rest rooms divided, some for free people and some for inmates. There were also several tables and folding chairs to accommodate inmates and their guests. No smoking was allowed in the building. The rest of the park was outside and included two sheltered seating pavilions and several feet of grassy walking areas. The entire area was surrounded with fence and razor wire, double fencing on the outside parameters. They had all been warned not to get within five feet of the outside fence or they were subject to being shot and removed from the area. All of the fencing was electronically monitored and guards with shotguns and rifles watched from gun towers and roamed the perimeters in small pick up trucks.

Hell of a place to meet with my wife. Looks like something out of a bad war flick or something. My God, there she is.

As Matt watched, Marilyn came out of the visitors search area. She didn't see him at first and he had a second to observe her. She appeared to have lost about 20 lbs and was fit and more beautiful than he remembered. It was obvious she had been crying and she was now searching, almost frantically, for him. He was truly touched by the simple display of love and affection presented to him at this moment. They were only about ten feet apart when their eyes met and he swallowed his emotions as she choked down a sob while rushing into his arms.

It seemed as if only moments had passed as there bodies melded into one and he tasted her tears and smelled her fragrance. "Y'all goin' to have to get apart now or the major goin' to send her home. Ain't no carrying on allowed in the park. You hear me?"

Although not said loudly or in anger, the words had the desired effect of bringing them both back to reality. Marilyn was the first to speak. "All we did was hug." Sobbing, she continued, "Oh Matt, I missed you so. I can't tell you how much I love you; and the girls, they love you and miss you so…"

The rest of the day was spent with each of them rambling on and trying to catch up on what was happening in their lives. Matt was careful not to tell her too much because he knew that it would only hurt her to know how much he had suffered. But he did tell her enough so that if something happened she would have Sam do some kind of investigation to determine the real cause of his demise. However, his primary purpose in this visit was to soak up her very essence and catch up on the news of her and the girls.

All too soon, visiting hours were over and it was time for Marilyn to go.

"They tell me that I have to be here for a year before they will consider moving me to a camp near Tampa. I don't want to wait that long before I see the girls, so I guess we should schedule them to come up in a couple weeks. How about you coming up twice a month, once with the girls and once alone?"

"Why can't I come up each weekend?"

Looking deep into Marilyn's eyes, for the first time in this ordeal Matt realized how much this whole process had hurt the woman he loved. The weight loss, the dullness in her eyes, the tremor in her voice and the darting looks she unintentionally gave out whenever she sensed a guard approaching caused a deep stab of remorse to pierce his very soul.

My God, I didn't realize how much this has hurt her. And the girls? God damn the Judge and Shimdugger for what they have done!

Ignoring his deepening sense of pain for his family and struggling to keep all emotion off his face, Matt answered her.

"You and I both know that you and the girls have numerous things to do on the weekend. This is a very trying time in our lives and especially in the lives of the girls. I want them to have as normal a life as possible, but I want them to grow up with me also, as much as feasible. Once a month, at least until I get closer to home. OK?"

They parted, both in tears, the last ones to leave the park. As he watched her go, the bittersweet sorrow slowly turned to gut wrenching pain and then to searing hatred. Surrounded by thugs, rapists, murders and sexual predators, he knew that this place and this sentence were wrong. Marilyn and the kids needed him and he needed them.

An overwhelming sense of loneliness and despair settled in Matt's mind as he realized how many people were hurt by his imprisonment.

This is wrong. They don't deserve this! I don't deserve this!

This whole fucking mess is nothing more then the result of the blinding ambition of two people. A Judge and a prosecutor.

Looking up at the sky Matt invoked the assistance of a God he wasn't even sure existed and, as the hatred churned in his gut, Matt once again vowed that both of them would pay dearly for the pain they had cause him and his family.

* * * *

As the daily routine became more familiar, Matt quickly learned the ins and outs of survival in the Florida penal system. Although not unfriendly, he never attempted to make friends. As time went on, it became clear that in prison, true friends were rare indeed. However, as it became known that Matt was a real doctor, many inmates tried to show their friendly side to him in order to gain favors. Matt was quickly diagnosing everything from minor skin cancers to broken bones, most of which were never reported to prison officials. Since he never took payment for his services, he soon had numerous favors owed him, a blessing that would pay for itself many times over during his term. After less than two months, he was known by prisoners and guards alike as 'Doc.'"

Surgical procedures where supposed to carried out in a very sanitary and sterile environment: in prison, this was not always the case. Matt performed his first surgical procedure in his fifth month at Hamilton. It was after work hours and he was sitting in the bleachers with several other inmates watching a softball game when he was quickly and quietly surrounded by half a dozen inmates, one of whom was bleeding profusely. "Doc, you got to help my man here," said Largo, a gang leader of the local chapter of the Crips. "He done been stabbed by a rat. I'll take care of the rat, but you got to take care of my man. He can't go to the police cause they'll lock him up and then transfer him. Can't let that happen."

As he finished talking he handed Matt a needle, thread, a small amount of gauze, a roll of tape and a small container of bleach. He then looked Matt straight in the eye and waited for an answer.

Quickly assessing the situation, Matt weighed the pros and cons. If he got caught, it would be time in the box and loss of gain time. However, if he refused, he would be on the bad side of the Crips and that was not a good place to be. They stretched throughout the system and could help or hurt anyone they chose to.

Making up his mind, Matt pushed the wounded man, Chico's, shirt tail into his mouth to give him something to clench his teeth on as Matt cleaned the wound with bleach.

He found a jagged cut, about an inch deep and three inches long, located in the right side in what is commonly known as the love handle. Surrounded by several inmates who formed a barrier to the outside, visibility was thoroughly blocked. It was in this operating theater that Matt quickly and proficiently looped sixteen stitches, closing the wound as neatly as if it had been done in a hospital.

During the entire procedure, not a sound emanated from Chico's mouth as he chomped down on his bloody shirt tail.

With the bleeding stopped, Chico's friends quickly produced clean clothes and he was changed and walking away with a grin on his face within two minutes. He was strutting and acting for all the world as if nothing had happened, but Matt knew he was hurting.

"Doc, I owe you one. Let me know when you need a favor. OK?" Largo asked.

"Glad I could be of service. I can't think of anything right now. I'll let you know when I do."

"See you around, Doc."

"Later."

A few weeks later Matt called in his favor.

* * * *

Since Matt's arrival at Hamilton eight months previously, Marilyn had seen to it that he had a subscription to the Tampa Tribune delivered to him daily. As a prisoner, this was a welcome insight into life outside the fences. No other form of communication, other than limited television viewing, existed in the Florida system and only two other inmates received a paper of any kind and neither of them were from Matt's home area.

Matt had been particularly glad to receive a copy of a Sunday paper that ran a full page announcement of Judge Dana's campaign for re-election. Right in mid-page was her tough on crime pronouncement and Matt's case and result was prominently displayed as a confirmation of her toughness. In a related announcement on a separate page was an article with Shimdugger's promotion to Senior Assistant State Attorney. Matt now had proof of what he had believed all along. He had been used and both he and his family were sacrificial lambs to both the Shimdugger's and the judge's blind and uncaring ambitions.

I knew it! I never deserved what they did to me and even worse, neither did my family. Those sons of bitches will pay for what they have done! Christ, what a mess.

Matt continued to avidly scour all the news of the area until strangely, things began to change. For the last couple of months, Officer Jhonus had given Matt fits by holding his paper up for days at a time. By the time Matt saw it, it was old news. Often he had gone to the mailroom, stood in line and actually been able to see the paper in the back of the mailroom while being told by Jhonus that it had not yet arrived. Equally problematic, frequently parts of the paper were missing. He had Marilyn check with the publisher and found that the fault lay not with the paper but with the mail delivery at the prison.

Officer Jhonus was the mailroom officer, and was a mean mouthed woman; red headed and sharp nosed, she was skinny with several tattoos on her arms and neck. It was rumored that she had run with a motorcycle gang for years, and it was known that she was closely related to one of the camp supervisors. She seemed to take great delight in provoking inmates, especially ones with an education. Her favorite target of late had been Dr. Matthew Hightower. She was allowed to, and did read, all of his mail, both incoming and outgoing, and was keenly aware of all the people with whom Matt communicated. The only things she was not privy to were his legal correspondence. Those were required by law to be opened in front of him, still sealed and unread. She made it clear that she did not agree with the restrictions, often commenting upon a piece of legal mail.

Realizing that to acknowledge her comments might open a window into conversations about his legal affairs, Matt never responded, frustrating her even more.

She was also responsible for opening the mail containing the monthly money order to be posted in his canteen account. Normally those monies would be posted on the same day they were received, and the envelope would be marked as to the amount received and the date posted. Serious problems began when Matt's money began being posted days late and the envelopes mysteriously unaccounted for. Finally, he had Marilyn trace two money orders in a row. It was discovered that each had arrived on time and had been held in Jhonus's drawer for an undisclosed amount of time. It was not theft, as the money orders had not been cashed, but it was an illegal withholding of a prisoner's mail and Jhonus was called to task for it. Nothing ever came of the investigation, but Matt became a serious enemy of Jhonus and his mail and papers were always late.

One afternoon, having grown very weary of the constant friction between himself and Jhonus, Matt tried to talk to her and resolve the issue. After waiting in line for over an hour, he finally came face to face with her and politely requested an appointment to discuss their problem.

She instantly became red-faced, shouting at Matt that the only problem she had was him, and the worst problem he would ever have was her, especially after he had lied to the authorities about her. The shouting match went on in front of several inmates for a few minutes as Jhonus verbally ripped Matt apart with innuendos, half-truths and outright lies. She then called him around to the side entrance and, out of sight of the others, she slapped him full in the face, dragging her nails over the bottom of his chin.

Apparently realizing that she had left evidence of her assault, she slapped herself in the face, hard, yanked on her shirt, tearing off three buttons, and then began yelling for help.

While Matt watched in amazement, she yelled into her microphone that an officer needed help with a wild inmate who had attacked her, unprovoked.

It seemed like only seconds before several officers had surrounded Matt and began beating him down to the ground.

Still in a state of shock, he attempted to tell the officers what had really happened and that he was not resisting or fighting in any way.

Quickly realizing that no one was listening to him, Matt shut up and covered himself as best he could to avoid as much injury as possible.

"Asshole! Think you can beat up on a woman officer." A large white sergeant who Matt had thought of as decent led the pack of officers beating on Matt's body as he motioned to the others. "You ain't learned your lesson yet, dumbass! Haul him to L Dorm, boys; we'll show him what happens to big men who pick on little women."

Numb with disbelief, Matt was cuffed and shackled, then half drug, half walked to the confinement dorm where he was placed in a holding cell while the last six cells in the wing were cleared out.

Dear God, not again. God, I don't know if I can take another beating. Please God, help me, help me.

"Well, Doc. You went and done it this time. Didn't know you had it in you." The officer doing the talking was a large, physically challenging man, about 6'4" tall and fully 280 lbs, all muscle. "I think you screwed the pooch this time cause that's the Colonel's first cousin you took a swing at. He's up there giving instructions for your punishment, right now. It ain't going to be pretty. Meanwhile, come with me."

Officer Jawarski literally lifted Matt off his feet and carried him into the last cell on the block. Moments later, two additional guards came down, talked briefly, then cleared the remaining cells of inmates. Matt was the only inmate left on L block.

Still cuffed and shackled, Matt watched in horror as three guards dressed in goon-squad garb swarmed into the cellblock, pulling a fire hose. All three wore helmets with face shields, bulletproof vests, belly clubs, body shields, canisters of gas, jack boots and truly looked like shock troops from Hell. They followed this by pulling gas masks from over their shoulders and motioning the other guards to leave.

When all was clear they silently donned their masks and began spraying Matt with a combination of gasses, the most recognizable being tear gas and pepper gas.

Remembering his naval training, Matt dove to the floor, using his hands to cover his face as best he could. But soon the pepper spray penetrated his clothing and ate at his exposed flesh, feeling like droplets of hot grease from a frying pan that kept getting hotter and hotter.

After he'd made the mistake of opening his mouth and eyes to protest, the burning took on the feeling of real torture.

Knowing it would do more harm than good, but being unable to stop himself, Matt tried desperately to wipe the spray from his face and eyes with the back of his hands. He had only served to enhance his pain and now, he was quickly losing his grip on reality.

"All right, spray's gone. Let's give the Doc a little time to enjoy the sensation and then we'll give him a good bath and a sincere talking to. Chew on that, Doc, while you wallow in this gas for a while." The words were muffled as they came from the gas mask of the lead officer, but Matt could not mistake the animosity with which they were delivered.

It could have been minutes, maybe hours that he lay writhing in pain on the cell floor; Matt couldn't tell, only that it seemed like forever. Finally he heard them approaching and knew something was going to happen. Not caring what and prematurely breathing a sigh of relief, Matt believed that at this point anything would be an improvement.

BLAM, WOOSH, SLAM. The full force of the water hitting him first in the face and then in the stomach, sent him spinning into the steel wall from where he careened into the legs of the bunk. Sinuses already on fire from the gas, now screamed with additional pain from the forced infusion of the high-pressure water. Burning sinuses were his last thought as he lost consciousness when his body was slammed into the cell wall with enough force to shake the steel bars of his cell door.

Matt really never felt it when his back was wrenched almost in two as he bounced from the cell wall back into the steel bunk structure. His limp body continued to be thrown around by water pressure as the guards took turns spraying him, using the hose and his inert body as if playing a surreal game of pinball. When they finished, the unconscious Matt lay there; his shirt, shoes and socks had been torn from his body. Only his trousers remained.

Coming to, Matt was looking directly into the smiling face of the meanest man he thought he had ever seen. He was not a regular among the guards and Matt had no idea why he was here, only a gut feeling that whatever the reason, it wasn't good.

"Well, well, if it isn't the killer Doc. Heard about you and your exploits up at Butler, Doc. Thought you had learned your lesson, but apparently not. Seems like you're a hard learner. That's why they called me here, Doc. I teach hard learners. See, up at Butler they almost fucked up. Almost created a record. Would have, if you had croaked. I'm better than they are. When I'm through with you, you will have learned that you never win. The system always wins. You can't hit our women, Doc. Not now; not ever."

Looking the man straight in the eyes Matt said, "I never hit officer Jhonus. I never even raised my voice to her. I only asked her if we could meet and go over the problems with my mail. You've got to believe me. I've never hit a woman in my life."

"Doc, understand something. It don't matter what I believe. She says you hit her and for this get-together, that is what happened. Time to get started."

Without seeming to bat an eye and faster than Matt could keep up with him, the unnamed officer struck Matt in the breast so hard that he couldn't breathe. Almost lazily the officer stood up, striking Matt with the palm of his hand, crushing Matt's nose as if it were a paper cup. Pulling him up by the cuffs, the officer let go of him and before Matt's arms had a chance to drop, the officer jammed both of his thumbs rigidly up and into Matt's arm sockets, separating the connection between his shoulders and his arms as if slicing butter. They were left 100% disjointed.

Although in severe pain, Matt was now far enough into shock that he could observe what was going on above and beyond the feeling of the injuries themselves. He watched in awe as the officer raised his legs by the shackles and then dropped them, kicking first his left leg and then his right at the intersection of the knees and legs, once again separating the joints as if they were putty.

With Matt strewn out on the floor like a rag doll, he then reached down and jammed his fingers up and under his bare chest just below the bottom ribs. Seeming to exert no effort, the officer lifted Matt's body and sat it on the bunk, facing him.

"Now Doc, I'm about through. The only way you will ever see me again is if you are stupid enough to pull another stunt like this. If that happens, the results will be much worse. They're going to send a pharmacist to patch you up, build you a nose and pop your joints back and all that stuff. In about three or four weeks, when the bruises are gone, you'll be returned to the main compound. There is no record of any of this. Why, you won't even miss any gain time. See, as you already know, we protect our own here in the system. Do yourself a favor. Don't fuck up again. Understand?"

Unable to talk, Matt could only nod in agreement.

"Glad to see we understand each other, Doc. See you around."

As he walked out, Matt saw the other guards give him lots of leeway, as if he were something to be held in awe but never touched.

Over the next four weeks as he healed, Matt knew what he would do. It would take time, but another piece of scum, Jhonus, had been added to his hate list. There were now four. The playing field was sexually equal. Two men and two women. Plenty of time remained for him to figure out the best and most vicious method of vengeance he could wreak on them when he got out. Meanwhile, he had to stay alive. He had to survive.

God help me, but if it is the last thing I ever do, they will pay. They will pay!

* * * *

Knowing that he would need the names and addresses of the two officers on his list when he was close to getting out of confinement, Matt sent for Largo to call in his favor.

Although no visitors were allowed in confinement, the guards used inmates to clean the spaces, handle food trays, etc. The Crips always had someone on the confinement inmate work crew and it was simple for Matt to get word to Largo what was needed to satisfy the debt.

Largo had a network of men working back and forth from Butler to Hamilton, just as other Crips members had at other institutions. Since Butler was a central medical facility for all north Florida prisons, it was also a central point of communication for various gangs within the system. The day Matt left confinement, Largo walked up to him and gave him the information requested.

That night, sitting on his bunk with his Bible and several colored highlighters, Matt meticulously coded the license tag numbers, driver's license numbers, full names and addresses of Sergeant Black and Officer Jhonus.

I've got just over five years left. Even if they move and change addresses, with this information, I'll be able to track them down. These bastards will pay and so will the Judge and her pockmarked prosecutor friend!

Matt's hatred now had faces, addresses and a time-frame for revenge. The Florida system had exceeded itself in creating a bitter, vengeful man out of a former solid citizen. However, the system wasn't through, yet.

CHAPTER SIX

Matt remained at Hamilton for 14 more months without further damage to himself. True to his profession, he continued to help other inmates and guards alike, while, at the same time, building a solid base of favors owed when and if the time came to use them. The only thing that ever became of this effort was that on two occasions, when the visiting park was almost vacant, a guard who he had befriended and, over time, given a lot of help to, allowed him to use the inspection room for conjugal visits when Marilyn was there.

Sex was rushed and awkward, and the first time it almost didn't work for either of them. Afraid to completely undress, Marilyn had lowered her blouse and uncupped her breasts. With no bed available, they commandeered a sturdy aluminum-framed table, which she lay back on. Fearfully, she removed her panties, causing Matt to be instantly aroused and mortified at the same time. Calling it a *love making* session would have been a complete misnomer. Too scared to engage in foreplay, they grabbed each other with an intensity that took over on its own, and ejaculation came in less than a minute. Not daring to linger, they immediately dressed and, red-faced, left the room and walked back out to the park. Marilyn had been too embarrassed to look the officer in the face. Knowing the risk the officer had taken, Matt thanked him with his eyes. Other thanks would come later.

The second time was really no better, but even under the circumstances, it was something they both knew was special; and each time, afterward in the park, Marilyn had cried with gladness and relief at the joy she had been able to give to her man.

As Matt left Hamilton, on his way to Sumter Prison, he carried with him numerous messages for others. He would go first to a camp at Butler, Lake Butler West, known by inmates as The Wild, Wild West, and then to Orlando Regional, the reception center for Central Florida. By following through on delivery of the messages, Matt became known by other inmates in his new camps as reliable and one who could be trusted.

Matt had tried to get a camp closer to Tampa than Sumter, but even though he did not get the one he wanted, this was still only 50 minutes from Marilyn and the girls. It would make their visits more enjoyable, even if not more frequent. Most importantly, it would get him away from officer Jhonus. He had gone out of his way to keep as far away from her as possible upon his release from confinement. Even so, she had made a point of seeking him out at least once a month to leer at him, letting him know she was always superior to him and could have him thrown back in the box any time she wanted to. She never would have guessed that her behavior might be signing her own death warrant.

The last thoughts he had as the Blue Bird pulled away from Hamilton were of her.

Don't worry, bitch. I'll be back. Unless somebody kills me first, you will never tell a lie on anyone else, ever again. That's my promise to you, bitch! My solemn vow!

* * * *

By car, the distance from Hamilton to Sumter can be traveled in four to five hours. By Blue Bird, in the system, it took Matt 27 days to reach Sumter. During the process he had been shackled, searched, cuffed and treated like dirt more times than he would ever remember. However, he always had two things going for him. Every day he was getting further from Hamilton and, every day he was getting closer to Marilyn and the kids. It helped to keep things in perspective.

Finally arriving at Sumter, the indoctrination and orientation were basically the same as at Hamilton. However, it was a larger camp even though it still had more lifers than medium and minimum custody inmates. Matt was told that with his minimum custody, he would probably be assigned to the work camp shortly after his 90-day trial period was over. As usual for Matt, things never work out as easily as promised.

Sumter was a jitterbug camp, so named by older black inmates who wanted little to do with their younger counterparts. It was filled with young blacks called *jitterbugs*, whose primary ambition was to prove that they were "the man". To a point, all of their activities were very humorous, as all of them realized that they were subject to being trounced by better men at all times. However, they were dangerous because losing face was the one thing they would do almost anything to avoid.

Remembering his instructions from his first dorm officer, Matt never allowed himself to be cowered by the stare of one of these punks. It was a real test, as many of them were under 25, but carried life sentences for murder and trafficking and had little to fear from prison punishment. Matt was shocked to learn that men as young as 15 could be sentenced to life imprisonment for selling drugs, a trait very common to the men he now communed with on a regular basis.

Hamilton had its share of drug trafficking, but Sumter was far worse. It was rumored that the prison camp itself had more drug interaction than any place in the area, excepting only to the big Wildwood truck stop. Matt was in awe of the numerous drugs available and the various means of distribution. Each evening, as he walked back to his dorm from chow, he watched as pushers plied their trade. The wide sidewalks provided intersections reminiscent of the prostitution and drug areas of Tampa.

My God! If Hollywood portrayed this everyday scene in a movie, it would be seen as a total exaggeration. This is real! Not only pushers, but pimps as well!

In addition to drugs, Matt found prostitution readily available at Sumter. Homosexual sex was common in the prison system, as he had learned soon after entering it. But here he found prostitution from female guards. He had never suspected that could be a manageable and profitable enterprise in prison. True, the women did not last too long before getting caught, but punishment was so lenient, *i.e.,* resignation, that their ranks were filled rapidly. He soon learned that although prisoners were not allowed money in the system, it was readily available and freely spent for drugs and prostitution.

Methods of storing forbidden money were truly ingenious. Prison shoes were all made by PRIDE, and had no arches or inserts. Inserts were hard rubber sections that were issued at regular intervals with both new shoes and used. By combining two opposite inserts and gluing them together at all but the very end, inmates created storage places to hold and transport several bills per shoe. Coke cans would have the bottoms cut out and placed back in almost imperceptible fashion to store larger amounts of money and still keep it readily accessible. Bunk legs, pillows, mattresses and even buried jars became more permanent receptacles.

In short, what most men wanted to buy was for sale, and money was available to pay for it.

So much for the canteen cards limiting prisoner allowances.

Race was a much larger problem here than it had been at Hamilton. Florida's prison system is two thirds black and the rest divided between whites and Hispanics. Sumter was almost all black, but with a powerful, if small, Hispanic group. Matt was glad he had made his Latin contacts before getting here and proving them upon arrival with the delivery of his messages. Although not a member of any group, he possessed a talent they all needed from time to time and had already proven his trustworthiness. It undoubtedly saved his life.

* * * *

It is said that if you take the sweetest dog in the world, a Golden Retriever, for example, and cage it up, keeping it in a small pen; then you jab it with a sharp stick every time you pass by, in time it will become a vicious animal. Matt was becoming living proof of the theory, even though he did not realize it at the time.

On the one hand, he helped inmates and guards alike with medical problems from straightening broken limbs and stitching up wounds to giving free medical advice to camp officers about the problems they or their families were going through.

On the other hand, he was continually harassed by jitterbugs and officers alike. Jitterbugs were always trying to prove their manhood, especially over a white man whom they didn't perceive as a tough fighter. Some guards were just plain mean and enjoyed harassing inmates, especially those inmates who were educated and who they could never hold a candle to under any other circumstances.

One such guard was officer Stony, a mean hearted bull of a man who stood six foot four and weighed about 260 pounds, all raw, rock hard muscle. Stony worked out five times a week and considered himself a true man's man. He fished, played pool, and beat up women for fun, but his greatest pleasure other than beating up inmates was hunting. Every year, Stony planned his vacation time around the hunting season. He had a leased camp in the Withlacoochee Forest, which he proudly proclaimed produced more deer than any other camp regardless of the number of hunters involved. He always brought in pictures to show inmates and guards alike, and God help the inmate who didn't express proper appreciation for Stony's hunting prowess.

Matt first came into contact with Stony upon his arrival at Sumter. Assigned to inside grounds, as all inmates are upon arrival, he came under the direct supervision of Officer Stony. Recognizing a blowhard when he met one, Matt never was bowled over by Stony's bravado. Hunting was second nature to Matt, and Stony's stories always added so much hype that it would have taken a superhero to accomplish his feats. Stony had been divorced by three women before he hit thirty and had restraining orders issued against him, preventing him from visiting them and four other women as well. Knowing this, Matt figured Stony to be a pretty sadistic animal and he always attempted to give Stony a wide berth.

Sometimes, however, trouble has a way of looking for you whether you want it or not. During his second week on inside grounds, Matt was assigned to weeding and pruning the area just south of the chapel and alongside a sidewalk. His assignment consisted of a squared area of about 45 feet across, which he was to take care of with his partner, a young man named Jud.

That morning, Jud had checked out a hoe and Matt a rake, and both were now hot and sweaty from working about two hours. Usually, the men assigned to inside grounds knew their jobs were temporary and did as little as possible, but neither Jud nor Matt were ashamed to work, and so they were shocked when Stony appeared, cursing and ranting as though he had caught them napping.

"Son of a bitch! I thought niggers was lazy, but you two take the cake! Been here two goddamn hours and ain't done nothing! You boys want any gain time this month you'll have to do a lot better than this."

What the hell is this maniac talking about? We're the only two in this entire area who are actually working and he's raising hell with us. Stony, you are one sick son of a bitch.

Feeling himself tense up, Matt deliberately took a deep breath and let it out slowly as he waited for the tirade to continue.

Not so calmly, however, Jud shot back, "You don't go fucking around with my gain time, man. I ain't done nothing wrong. Hell, me an' the doc, we done more work than all them others you got out here. We been bustin' our asses 'stead of sittin' round."

Feral was the only word Matt could have used to describe the look on Stony's face after Jud's retort. "Gimme that hoe, boy. I'm gonna show you how to use this thing the right way."

Handing over the hoe, Jud stepped back, but not fast enough to avoid Stony's rapid advance.

"Let me show you how a real man handles a hoe, boy." Stony grunted as he flipped the hoe in his big hands, pointing the end of the handle at Jud's stomach.

Quicker than Matt had seen anyone ever move, other than the enforcer at Hamilton, Stony rammed the hoe handle into Jud's midsection three times; at least one of those times Matt was sure that Stony penetrated Jud's sternum.

Jud took two steps back and fell, unable to breathe and gasping for air that would not come.

Stony advanced as if to finish him off. Matt was appalled and scared at the same time. His better sense told him to stay out of the situation, but all the medical training he had received overruled his logical mind. Besides, he hated the injustice of a 260-pound guard with all the authority of God taking advantage of a skinny kid like Jud.

Before Stony could begin kicking Jud, Matt flung himself down on his knees between the two, cradling Jud's head in his lap and feeling for his sternum to see if it was truly ruptured.

"Damn you, inmate! What the hell you doin'? Can't you see that an officer is correcting another inmate? You know what happens to inmates that interfere with an officer in the performance of his duty."

Damn! I think that crazy loon has really hurt him. We need some medical help out here. Shit, we need someone to call off this goon. I think he wants to kill me, now.

Matt's mind was a blur as he waited for the next blow to descend, not on Jud, but on himself. However, the blow never came. Two other officers emerged from the gym area and called out to see what the trouble was. Even most of the officers thought Stony was nuts and far too aggressive, so it was with a less than brotherly attitude that they offered their assistance.

Stony had had numerous incidence reports written, and most of them were unfavorable. It was rumored that if he got another really bad one, it would be investigated by someone from another institution, or worse, Tallahassee. Neither of these two guards were his hunting nor fishing buddies, so he decided it was in his own best interest to cool down.

Tossing the hoe to the ground, Stony answered, "One of my inmates done fell down. Don't think it likely he hurt himself, but me and the doc here are checking him out."

Before he could catch himself, Matt said, "Bullshit!" He started to rise when Jud grabbed him tightly.

"Let it go, man. You can't win this one. I'll be OK. Let it go, please."

What the hell is this? First he is almost killed and now he doesn't want to do anything about it."

Matt's mind was in a whirl as he watched the three officers talk while, at the same time, Jud kept whispering for him to do nothing and keep his mouth shut.

Slowly, he came to understand that Jud was probably right. Meanwhile, Jud was asking for his help to stand up. Not really believing it was the wise thing to do, Matt nonetheless aided Jud in getting on his feet.

Recall had sounded and the two of them had to return the tools to the tool room and get back to their dorms. As they walked off, Matt helping Jud only slightly, Stony looked right into Matt's eyes.

"See you around, inmate," Stony said to Matt in a voice that rang full of menace and hatred. His eyes matched his voice as Jud pulled Matt away from any more confrontation.

Closer to the tool shed, Jud said, "Thanks, Doc. I appreciate what you done back there. But you got to watch that motherfucker. He's meaner than a snake. You got to watch your back. Ain't no telling what that crazy bastard might do."

That night as he lay in his bunk thinking, Matt knew he was in trouble with Stony. He knew it, but he had no idea just what kind of action Stony would take. They say ignorance is bliss. It proved to be true for a while, but what was coming would overcome blissful ignorance in a far more savage way than he would ever have anticipated.

With no wanted, usable, prison skills, Matt was given a position as a houseman, an inmate that cleaned up after the other inmates. Since everything in prison worked on a sort of intern basis, new housemen were typically assigned to bathroom duties. He was given an area consisting of eight sinks, two urinals and four commodes. Every morning after the men had left the dorms, the housemen were to clean the dorm, keeping it shiny and nice for all of two hours. Once a week, usually Wednesday or Thursday, inspection was held and the results were used to post the order in which the dorms were released for chow. Poor results meant cold food, often without the same selection as the menu called for.

One of the primary benefits of being a houseman was that by being present in the dorm during the day, you were aware of inmate transfers and therefore, inmate bunk changes. That was important, especially at Sumter, because it allowed Matt to get a bunk among his fellow housemen, all of whom were non-aggressive. Every night, after the lights out count, the guards left the dorm and gathered at the sergeant's shack for coffee. The dorm areas were divided into pods consisting of four buildings; three dorms and one multi-use building with a laundry as one half and the sergeant's office or *shack* as the other. These structures surrounded a courtyard with the phone stations, shuffleboard courts, tables and clotheslines. Each of these areas was like a separate mini-prison.

When lights were turned out, the dorm guards left the dorms, locking over 150 men in each dorm with no supervision. On his first night at Sumter, when the guard left, Matt knew he would never survive this camp. As the steel door clanged shut and the guard left the dorm, rock hard blocks of state soap were violently thrown across the dorm, hitting inmates and lockers alike, indiscriminately. At least a half dozen of them hit the door behind the departing guard and Matt heard him chuckle, as if he was merely leaving his kids off at a local movie, not abandoning his duties to the safety of those inside.

Then men jumped up from their bunks and began doing whatever they wanted with no fear of official retaliation. Several inmates began having sex; in one case three inmates joined together, but mostly in pairs. Even with minimal lighting, the violence of some of those encounters was enough to make Matt sick at his stomach.

Then the fighting broke out. First shouting and threats, but then serious fighting evolved. One inmate was thrown into a garbage can about three feet from the foot of Matt's bunk, head first. Matt watched in dismay as three other inmates tried to compact their victim into the can and close the lid.

Dear God in heaven. What kind of nut house am I in? These people are all insane. Where the hell are the guards? With all this racket I know they can't not hear it.

He thought of Marilyn and the girls, and what someone would tell them about this place.

Not the truth. I know that. No prison system could actually allow such a total disregard for the safety of the inmates. This is America, for God's sake. Hell, they even sound like animals.

Matt survived his first night and soon learned that the vast majority of fights in the dorm were programmed from earlier incidents. It was actually rare for a new fight to break out in the dorm after dark. But it did happen, and just as at Hamilton, Matt slept with his guard up at all times. It would eventually take months away from this environment before he could get a truly good night's sleep.

* * * *

Matt's ninety-day period came and went, and he remained in the main unit with no indication that he was being considered for the work camp. Matt placed requests with his classification officer, but that was useless. The head classification officer was a skinny little twerp who dressed in outdated, cheap polyester pants that were way too tight. The absurd part was that he had nothing to show off in his tight pants, except his total ignorance of any real style. He had a sign on his desk that read, "I AM GOD." The first time he saw the sign, Matt realized there were two words missing at the end: 'Damn Fool.'

With a small attack of the intelligence that got him through med school, he refrained from alerting the officer of the missing verbiage.

Eighteen months went by, then twenty and Matt thought he would never get to work camp. Then, before he could get away, his payback arrived from Officer Stony.

* * * *

It was Friday night, the second Friday of the month: fried chicken night. This was the one night of the month when all the dorms emptied out and everyone ate in the chow hall.

If you were one of the few who did not like fried chicken, you went and got your portion and sold or gave it to someone else. To let it go and not get your tray was an insult to your friends, and rarely forgiven.

Tonight was the first time that Matt's dorm had placed last on the inspection, making them the last dorm to be released for chow. When they were finally released and got to the chow hall, the line was still very long, with at least fifty men ahead of them, all being held up while the others inside finished eating. As they waited in line, Matt talked with his small Indian friend known in the prison as 'Papa Smurf.'

Papa Smurf was the first to notice the smell. When they had first arrived in line, the odor was of fried chicken, unmistakable when it only happened once a month. Now the smell was of hamburger meat: distinctly different. As they moved closer to the chow hall, the grumbling got louder and louder, beginning to sound ominous.

"Papa, what the hell is going on?" a concerned Matt asked his friend.

"Dunno, Doc, but it don't sound too good. Better we listen for the man, heh?"

As they passed through the doors into the chow hall, Matt noticed several inmates standing on the wall as if waiting for something else.

The officer at the food window spoke as they entered. "Anybody wants to wait for chicken, get over on the wall. The rest of you can eat hamburgers; double rations tonight."

Matt and Papa Smurf looked at each other, shrugged their shoulders and stepped up to the food window, taking their trays of hamburgers and making a beeline for the glasses and condiments.

Once seated, they began to eat and when they talked, it was with food and hands in front of their mouths and eyes down at the trays; in that manner, the guards could not see their lips forming words. Talking was strictly forbidden in the chow hall, but right now, most of the inmates were ignoring that rule.

This doesn't feel right. Those guys on the wall are very unhappy. Me thinks that Papa and I need to eat and get the hell out of here before something really bad happens.

"Papa, lets hurry up and get out of here. I haven't heard this much grumbling since my last riot at Hamilton, and that was no fun."

Matt had survived two riots at Hamilton, both small; fewer than 150 inmates involved in either of them, but nasty none-the-less. Both were ignited over simple things: a broken TV for one and a closed weight pile for the other. Although small, both inmates and guards had been injured, some seriously. Matt had never known that riots were so common in the prison system. The press rarely knew about them and the Department went to great lengths to keep them hidden.

Before they had finished bolting their meal, the Captain entered the chow hall with several other guards. It was obvious this was not a friendly visit, as the Captain and the guards all had their long handled flashlights in hand.

Taking a spot by the exit doors, he waited until his extra guards had moved completely around the inside of the chow hall and then announced that there was no more chicken and everyone who had not eaten was to get off the walls and grab a tray. Hamburgers would have to do.

As the inmates left the wall and started pushing and shoving their way back into the line, the grumbling got louder, until it sounded like a roaring waterfall in Matt's ear. As he picked up his tray to leave, a metal tray sailed through the chow hall like a square Frisbee, striking the Captain squarely in the mouth and knocking him to the floor.

The guards scrambled toward the tray's origin and more trays began to fly. In seconds, inmates were beating guards over the heads with the metal trays, plastic glasses and anything else they could grab, including the guards' flashlights.

Ten or twelve of the inmates ran into the now unguarded kitchen and grabbed heavy kitchen utensils, knives and anything that could be used as a weapon, keeping some things for themselves, and throwing the rest to other inmates. They began flowing out of the chow hall, knocking down and beating every guard who stood in their way. The Captain was stabbed seven times and left for dead. Matt first tried to make his way over and help the downed officer, but instantly realized if he was seen helping the 'enemy,' he would probably be killed as well. Papa was pulling on his arm shouting. "Come on, Doc. We got to get back to the dorm before this whole place goes to shit!"

Beginning to panic, Matt and Papa scrambled to get to their own courtyard before everything began to shut down. The possibility of being trapped with this wild bunch of screaming inmates scared the hell out of both of them. They both knew that most of these rioters had life sentences and little to fear as they went about the gruesome task of settling debts.

Matt gasped for air as he ran, pulling Papa most of the way.

His efforts went unrewarded as, just before they reached the gate, it was slammed shut by the sergeant on duty, leaving them and several other non-participating inmates struggling to climb over the gate to the safety of the courtyard. Already, helicopters swarmed overhead and canisters of tear gas were being shot out at random.

With the sure knowledge that they would die if they continued hanging on to the gate, Matt grabbed Papa, dropped to the ground and began wriggling his way out of the crowd and toward the gym; opting to get out in the open and as far away from the others as possible.

"Look, Doc!"

As Papa tugged at Matt and pointed to an area just outside the parameter fence, four helicopters were setting down and national guard troops with rifles locked, loaded and at the ready were streaming out, stationing themselves at intervals to ensure no inmates crossed over the fences.

God in heaven, has the whole world gone mad? There must be 600 inmates, some of them really bad, all gone crazy. We've got to get somewhere safe.

Spotting the huge oak tree located in the open in the center of the compound, Matt panted, "Papa, let's get over to the tree and sit up against it. That way nobody can mistake us for rioters. We'll wait for help to arrive and then go with them."

It sounded like a plan, and for a while it seemed to work. From their sitting position at the trunk of the tree, they watched the rioters continue to search out guards and inmates they didn't like, beating and stabbing the ones they caught. In a few minutes, the frenzy seemed to be calming down, but then the front gate opened up and at least fifty guards, armed with shotguns and rifles, poured through.

Inmates scrambled in all directions away from the central part of the prison, throwing anything they could grab at the guards as they ran.

In the midst of all this confusion, Matt was stunned when he saw an inmate he had always considered a pretty good guy, take a hit from a guard's shotgun and go down.

He didn't hesitate. Telling Papa to stay put, he ran out and began to administer to the inmate. Suddenly, he was slammed in the head from behind.

Jesus! What was that? I think my head has been split open.

On his knees and now reeling from the blow, Matt tried to turn around to confront his attacker when the second blow caught him with full force behind his right ear; he fell down as if he had been shot. Barely conscious, he couldn't even see his attacker. He was lying face down and he could feel the blood running from his head and on to the ground.

"Whatsamatter, Doc? You don't think I'd forgotten our little set to, do you?"

Oh my God. It's Stony!

With the coppery taste of his own blood filling his mouth and sending his senses whirling, Matt attempted to say something, but before he could respond, he was spun face up and then, kicked in the ribs with such force that it rolled him over, onto his back. As he looked up at Stony, his heart froze and his blood ran cold. Stony had a shotgun.

Shit! This crazy bastard's going to kill me.

Blood and patches of scalp covered the butt of the shotgun where it had been used as a club to Matt's head. Now, however, it was pointed directly at Matt's face from only about three feet away, with Stony's finger on the trigger.

"Doc. You gonna learn that nobody stops ol' Stony from doing his thing. Nobody!"

The tension of Stony's trigger finger began to increase as he kept the barrel pointed steadily at Matt. A crooked smile revealing stained yellow teeth loomed over the gun looking far more evil and demonic than anything Matt had ever imagined.

I'm going to die. Right here in this prison yard, I'm going to die. No more Marilyn; no more medical practice; nothing.

Reaching down deep in his inner self, Matt steeled himself and refused to let Stony see the fear that ate at his gut. He took a deep breath and waited for the explosion, curiously wondering if he would actually hear it before the blast took off his head.

"What's up Doc? How about it, Stony? Looks like you got ol' Denny taken care of, huh?"

Not trusting himself or Stony enough to turn his head, Matt shifted his eyes to his right and saw Officer Jawarski standing about four feet from Stony. Jawarski had his own shotgun, and it was pointed about knee level directly at Stony. Although the words were not menacing, his stance was clear and his intentions were obvious: if Stony shot Matt, he would go down too.

Stony knew his moment was lost. Any hope of an anonymous killing was gone, at least for this time. Besides, Stony knew that Jawarski was a Pole who fought with the Polish underground and he had been awarded several medals for bravery under fire. Almost retirement age now, and with a body that was beginning to show signs of arthritis and other ailments, Jawarski's eyes still held steady and had no compromise in them.

"Hey Ben", Stony said to Officer Jawarski. "Saw some trouble over here and came to see if the Doc needed help." Turning back to Matt, but without ever moving the gun away, Stony continued, "Ain't that right, Doc?"

Knowing that all three of them really knew what was going on, but also realizing that this was the only way out that would allow Stony to save face, Matt reluctantly agreed.

"Yeah, I guess. I came over to help Denny and somehow, I got hit from behind. But I think a few stitches will take care of me. Denny here is another matter. He needs help, bad. He may die anyway, but he will surely die without it."

Now that his ass was covered, Stony had no further use for Matt and he really wanted to get back to the action. Lowering his shotgun, he looked at Jawarski. "Looks like you got this under control. Pass the word on to medical about Doc and Denny and I'll go help the others."

With no other words spoken, Stony turned and ran toward the heaviest part of the fighting.

Watching him retreat, Matt was filled with a sense of revulsion and anger, incensed that Stony would get away with his brutality. As the guard waded back into the fight, Matt's anger stoked his hatred. It was like putting gas on an already burning fire, his hatred flaring up to the point that he almost choked.

"Cool it, Doc. You got real lucky that I saw what was going on before he blew you away. That is one mean son of a bitch and you won't live to leave this place standing up if you don't watch your back. I owed you one for helping me understand things when the missus had her surgery. But you can't count on me cuz I ain't always going to be around: I'm retiring in a few months."

Matt's vision was blurry, as much from the fires of his anger and hatred as from the blows Stony rained on his head. With the smoky, coppery taste of his own blood still in his mouth, he spit through clenched jaws before speaking to Officer Jawarski.

"Some day that bastard is going to pay for this." As he spoke, Matt's angry voice was more of an ominous hiss than anything else. He couldn't help himself. One minute he had been so scared and sure he was going to die that he almost crapped his pants. Now the shame of that moment, as well as the anger at the man who caused it, was almost overwhelming. One thing he knew for certain; if he lived through this, Stony would pay with his life, or worse.

Dear God. If you are really there; if you really exist, help me. Help me live so that I can kill this sorry son of a bitch! I will be your instrument of terror and rid the world of this sorry piece of shit. I make a solemn vow that if you let me live through this, he will pay, and pay dearly.

Feeling more like a man after saying his 'prayer.' Matt thanked Officer Jawarski and asked for help with Denny.

Surprisingly, Jawarski declined, telling Matt that Denny was just like any other convict and he would get help when this thing was over.

"You want to stay with him, that's up to you, Doc. Me, I got to get to work and help shut this place down. You need to watch your back; I'm telling you this for your own good. All them gunshots you hear ain't just being fired into the air. Stony ain't the only SOB on this compound. You get back over there with Papa and keep your head down until you hear them call everyone back to the dorms. Meanwhile, any officers come your way, you sit still and follow orders. Today ain't no day for questions, just 'yes sirs.' Understand?"

"You got it." Matt offered his hand to Jawarski for a shake.

"You still don't get it, Doc. You're an inmate and I'm an officer. At a time like this, we don't shake hands in public. Sorry to hurt your feelings, but I need to go to work and you need to get your ass back over there and out of the open. Now get to it!"

"Yes sir!" Matt began to rise and watched as Jawarski took off. Feeling bewildered and a little betrayed on top of all the other feelings, he thought, *If this isn't the most screwed up place I've ever been in. First he saves my life and then he refuses to shake my hand. Not only that, but he won't even help me save Denny's life. He probably would have let Stony shoot me if I hadn't spent so much time with him while his wife went through cervical cancer surgery and chemotherapy.*

Matt waved to Papa and soon both of them were pulling the inert Denny over to the tree. Once there, they waited for about 45 minutes, watching as inmates were knocked to the ground and wagonloads of cuffs and shackles were used to keep them down. Doc did what he could, but Denny died about half way through without ever regaining consciousness. It was a hell of a day and they both were glad when recall sounded and they were allowed to get back in the dorm. They left Denny lying under the tree and were never questioned by anyone about anything regarding his death.

One hell of a note. Really one hell of a note.

* * * *

Following the riot, they were locked down for four days, with all meals being brought in by selected kitchen inmates. Other than the few inmates needed for essential services, all others were subject to the lockdown. During this time, guards routinely came and got inmates identified by other guards or other inmates as having taken part in the rioting. These inmates never returned, but were immediately shipped to other camps to be confined in disciplinary blocks until they were tried by the normal Kangaroo Courts of the prison system. They were officially known as Disciplinary Hearings, but the outcome was almost always against the inmate, no matter the evidence.

Only a few of the worst violators were kept to undergo their hearings at Sumter. These would all be found guilty and subjected to extra forms of punishment. Matt was well aware of what that meant.

Stronger, heavier solid steel doors were ordered for the chow hall with the hope of shutting down or confining such a riot if it ever began again. More fencing was planned to cut down the ability of inmates to get across the compound freely. Other than the episode with Stony, the most important impact of the riot to Matt was that his possible transfer to the outside work camp was delayed for almost a year.

When he was finally transferred, he had only one and a half years to go. What he did not expect, however, was that while at the work camp, he would come in contact with the last of his future targets. More than enough reason would be given to insure that if any room was left in his heart for additional hatred, it soon would be filled to capacity.

CHAPTER SEVEN

Landing at the work camp with high expectations, Matt was not disappointed. Until now, all of his prison term had been spent in maximum custody confinement. The work camp still had fences, walls and guards, but inmates came and went out into the free world to work in various jobs. Once he was transferred to the camp, it would be 90 days until Matt would be allowed outside the main compound parameters, but he still would be working in relatively unguarded areas.

The most positive and notable part of the work camp was the prisoner's attitudes. All of these men were medium or minimum custody, and all were going home within a couple years. Killings were almost non-existent, and no one had a shiv. Although Matt had never had to use his shiv, he had always known it was there. Now, he didn't need that reassurance and his relief was palpable. Fights were infrequent and when one did occur, it was basically pushing, shoving or fistfights. It was a marked departure from the day-to-day existence of the main camp.

Three weeks after he arrived at the work camp, Matt got a full night's sleep, the first he had since entering the prison system. Without the constant pressure of living among lifers with nothing to fear, and who continuously engaged in fighting, stabbing and sexual aggression, he was finally able to relax enough to sleep. *Aaah, precious, precious sleep.*

Once again he was interviewed by a classification officer, and once again he was told that there was no use in the camp for his medical talents. Matt had expected nothing else.

Assigned to the warehouse, he quickly learned that some jobs were better than others. All food deliveries to the prison came through the warehouse and he soon adapted the skills allowing him to enjoy access to the best that came through the system.

Warehousemen had their own microwave and they added numerous food articles to the bag lunches that everyone in the work camp received each morning. Several of the deliverymen gave extras to the inmates so there was ice cream, cokes, cookies and other things available throughout the week to enhance their lunches. It was quite an enjoyable change for Matt, and he relished it. However, unknown to him, the best was yet to come.

After three months in the warehouse, he was transferred to the forestry work crew. Matt's job was to go with a forestry truck driver each day as they cleaned up the forestry camps in the Withlacoochee Forest. Often his job entailed walking through the woods with a large axe, clearing the visitors walking and jogging paths. It was the closest thing to being free that he had experienced in years. On one outing, he saw three doe standing in the woods watching him as he walked almost silently down the path. Feeling chill bumps run up his arms and down his spine, he almost cried as he watched them bound away, white tails flashing as they disappeared from his sight.

Oh my God! How much I have missed the woods. The sheer beauty of nature; it's awesome.

His boss was a good natured, friendly guy with no animosity toward prisoners, so as long as he did his job, Matt was allowed ample time to enjoy nature as he wished. For several weeks he marveled at the gators, beavers, snakes, squirrels, opossums, raccoons and all the animals of the forest.

This must be what is meant by being born again. If only Marilyn and the girls could be here to enjoy the peace and serenity of this place.

His luck improved even more when he was chosen to fill a vacancy in the Forestry food hall. The Division of Forestry people had nothing to do with the prison system other than to lease minimum custody inmates from the Department of Corrections for help with clean-up and preparation of food. Matt and the others cooked and ate real food. On his first morning there, he ate scrambled eggs, bacon, sausage, pancakes, toast and a wide variety of jellies and jams.

He ate like a madman. It had been over five years since he had bacon or link sausage; the same with the jams and jellies. When breakfast was over, he was taken to the kitchen where he was given the job of pot washer, the lowliest job in the kitchen. It would be his job until another inmate was brought in through attrition or whatever. Then he would be moved up the ladder. The pan of leftover sausage was brought to him to wash, and he was to throw away the 25 or so sausages left on it. Putting the pan to the side, Matt started popping the little sausages in his mouth as he washed the pans. Before he knew it, he had eaten all of them.

Within an hour, his stomach turned on him and he developed such a severe case of diarrhea that he swore he would never eat sausage again. Nauseous, clammy and sweating, he was so stuffed and queasy that he couldn't eat the charbroiled hamburgers they had for lunch, and only picked at the pork chops at supper. Even the salad bar with all the fixings did not appeal to him. Learning his lesson that first day, he vowed to be more controlled in his eating. His job assignment was the envy of the whole work camp and he was careful to do nothing that might jeopardize it.

Maybe it was the good food he was now able to enjoy, or maybe it was just that as a doctor he recognized a bad situation when it was presented, but Matt soon became concerned with the food that was served to the regular inmates, and especially the diabetics and special diet inmates. The food at the prison work camp was completely inferior to the food at the main unit, and diets were non-existent.

Diabetics were routinely forced to increase their insulin dosages after entering the work camp, even though the normal factors, stress, etc. were reduced with their transfer. Only food could make the difference and Matt was soon approached by several diabetics who sought his counsel.

Knowing that the meals being served were not healthy and did not provide minimal allowances of protein and other essentials, Matt decided to try and do something to help the inmates. If they wouldn't allow him to practice medicine, at least he could help with inmate welfare when it came to required allotments of food.

After first approaching the sergeant in charge of the work camp food services and getting nowhere, Matt wrote the kitchen officer a bad report, or grievance. This was a standard form that was usually ignored. Almost always, however, a copy was filed and it sometimes actually received attention. Two types of grievances existed: informal, which came first, and formal if the first one did not get the appropriate response. Informal grievances went directly to the officer grieved against, while formal grievances went either to the warden, or in some cases, Tallahassee itself.

After filing the informal grievance on the sergeant, Matt waited 15 days for his answer.

The response was a flagrant lie and a warning to keep his nose out of the camp kitchen business.

Knowing he probably should not get involved, but incensed at the food service and the unfair response he had received, Matt checked with a couple of the warehousemen that he knew from his past and began building a verifiable report on the amounts and types of food being delivered to the work camp. He then compared it with the menu supplied by Tallahassee, which was supposed to be followed throughout the system to provide the minimal food allowances for an average person. He soon had proof positive that less than half of the required meat allowances were being delivered to the camp, and even less was actually being served to the inmates.

Armed with his statistics, invoices, suggested menus and actual servings, Matt wrote another grievance, this time a formal grievance to Tallahassee. Matt heard nothing for several days, and then he received an answer that his grievance had been taken into account and turned over for further action and whatever corrections were needed would be made.

He was smiling as he left the gate for the forestry camp the next morning. The smile was erased when he returned that evening.

"Inmate Hightower."

Matt stepped through the metal detector and into the sally port to allow himself to be frisked, a ritual performed each time an inmate came back to camp. However, before he could be patted down, the Lieutenant stepped out from the main office with two guards and shouted, "Hightower! Over here and assume the position—now!"

What the hell is going on now? Dear Jesus, I haven't done anything wrong. Don't tell me that the Major was in on the food disappearance too?

The cold sweat of fear dripped down his back as he stepped forward and placed his hands on the wall of the building. With everyone watching, Matt's guts began churning as he waited for the next move, and he almost jumped out of his skin when the Lieutenant kicked his legs apart for the guard to attach the shackles to his shins.

He couldn't help but think of the other times he had been cuffed and shackled, and all the beatings he had taken following the lockdowns. Cold and clammy, his face and forehead broken out in beads of sweat, he couldn't control the involuntary wince as his hands were pulled behind and cuffed tightly.

God, I almost shit my pants. Come on, get a hold of yourself. Everyone is watching. Be a man, Hightower!

Feeling a kind of drunken sway taking over his body, Matt was pushed from behind as he followed the Lieutenant down the hall to the Major's office. Coal black eyes glared out of a rotund face whose solid black sheen stood in marked contrast to her starched white shirt collar. Standing about five feet two, the Major rose from her chair behind her desk.

"Hello, inmate Hightower. I am Major Kelly. Thank you, Lieutenant, you may go now. Take the others with you."

"Yes ma'am, Major. All right boys, lets get out of here. If you need me, Major, we'll be right down the hall."

"Thanks, but that shouldn't be necessary. You're going to be a good boy, right inmate Hightower?"

Garnering what few wits he still possessed, Matt answered, "Yes ma'am, Major. I thought I had been all along."

It was only after the door was shut and the others were safely down the hall that the Major spoke again.

"Inmate Hightower, you know that you have caused me and this institution a lot of problems. You also know that if any inmate has a problem in this camp, he can come to me and straighten it out. But not you; oh no, you got to go straight to Tallahassee. You only got a few months to go and already you think you are a free man and can decide how to run this camp.

"Let me tell you something you still ain't learned yet. You are a fucking inmate!"

Shit, she's mad as hell. If she wasn't black, her face would be crimson.

Feeling the hair rise up on the back of his neck, Matt waited for the Major to continue.

"Inmate Hightower; your gate pass is hereby revoked."

Saying that, the major actually took shears and cut his pass into several pieces, then continued. "You will be confined to this camp except when you must go to the main unit for medical or other mandatory purposes. Since you will no longer have a gate pass, every time you board the bus to go over there, every inmate on the bus will be subjected to security conditions and will be strip searched going and coming. They will all know who is responsible."

My God, she wants to alienate me from the rest of the camp.

"Since you apparently have a problem with the kitchen, you will spend the rest of your sentence there, seven days a week. You will find that this kitchen is somewhat different than the one you have been working in recently. You and your locker will be searched routinely, several times a week. If any contraband is discovered, even one extra pair of socks, you will be sanctioned severely, including loss of gain time and return to the main unit. An overdue library book will get you 30 days in DC, 60 days loss of gain time and return to the main unit. You clear on this so far?"

Clearing his throat, his head still swimming from the Major's pronouncement, Matt nodded: "Yes ma'am, Major."

Good Lord. If she has my locker checked right now, I'm on my way to confinement. I've got coffee packs from the Forestry camp, sugar, creamer, probably a dozen or more contraband items. Shit! Shit! Shit!

As if reading his thoughts, the Major continued. "As we speak, your dorm officer is going through your locker. Might be that you don't even make it to the kitchen after all. But, assuming you are currently squeaky clean, there's more news yet. As you already know, all mail coming and going is skimmed and randomly read. Not yours, not any longer. Every word you read or write will be examined to see if you attempt to communicate your condition as anything but normal for prison. I can promise you, it won't leave this institution, but when it is caught, it will be straight to DC confinement with several charges for which you will be incarcerated long past your Tentative Release Date before any appeal can ever be heard. And, I assume you are already aware that the survival rate in DC is not as healthy as it is over here?"

"Yes"

"Yes what, inmate? Insubordination will not serve you well at this time!"

"Yes Major, ma'am." Matt was so rattled by her venomous hiss as she delivered that last statement that he stammered all over his response.

"I'm telling you right now," she continued in a lower but equally evil tone. "One little fuck up on your part, only one, and you are my meat."

Replacing the evil growl with a forced smile and a more normal tone of voice, she continued, "You're going to walk out of here in a couple minutes."

Just then her phone rang. Picking up the phone she listened for a moment and said, "Put him on."

"Nothing, nothing at all? You're sure? OK then, but you know what I'm after, anything at all. I want him searched regularly."

Hanging up the phone she looked up at Matt. "It appears that this is your lucky day, Hightower. That was Officer Norton. He just completed a search of your locker and found it clean. So, to finish what I was saying, you will walk out of here shortly. If even one word of this conversation gets back to me, you will wish God had called you home years ago. I will make your life so miserable that suicide will be a definite option. I worked far too hard and sucked too many white dicks to get this far to let some high falootin inmate mar my record. You ain't the first white inmate who tried to hurt this black officer, and you sure as hell ain't going to be the first to succeed. One word, that's all I need. You know I got lots of snitches on this compound, so don't think I won't hear about it soon after it passes through your lips."

Punching her intercom button, she commanded, "Sergeant, come in here please. This inmate is ready to be escorted back to his dorm, and I want you to be the one to do it."

"Yes, Major, I'm on my way," came from the intercom.

That's got to be Sergeant Lacy. I've heard lots of rumors about her and the Major. At least I'm getting out of the office and will still be in the work camp.

Sergeant Lacy entered without knocking and stood, looking at the Major.

"Leave his shackles and cuffs on and parade him around the grounds in front of each dorm on the way to his own dorm. Make sure everyone possible sees him. I want him marked as trouble."

"Yes, Major. Come with me, inmate Hightower."

Taking him by the arm, Sergeant Lacy escorted Matt down the hall and out the door through the sally port, making sure that every one saw him shackled and cuffed and being led by the sergeant.

Although somewhat humiliated, Matt struggled to hide his relief at the leniency of this meeting. He didn't really give a damn what the other inmates thought, he only wanted to finish his time with no extensions and no more beatings.

Entering his dorm, Sergeant Lacy ordered his dorm officer to remove the cuffs and shackles. As she departed, she said, "You got the Major real pissed off, Hightower. Better think long and hard about every thing you do from here on out. Miss one step and you will regret it for the rest of your life. I'll be watching you. Bye bye now."

"Boy, have you fucked up now," said officer Newton.

* * * *

Looking into the dorm office, Matt saw what Officer Newton was pointing to. Coffee packets, creamer, most of the things he knew that were in his locker and could be called contraband were now in the trash can.

"The extra boxers, tees and socks were tossed into the dirty laundry hopper; no names are on them, at least not yours."

"Thanks, Mr. Newton, I really appreciate what you did."

"You're lucky it was me on duty when the major called. Somebody else might have helped the bitch nail you. I don't know exactly what you did; don't need to know. But you got trouble on your hands, be sure of that. Look over your head."

Matt looked to where Norton was pointing and saw a direct order from the major, handwritten by someone, probably Newton, which said that inmate Hightower was to be searched at least three times a week and the results forwarded to the major when each locker search was conducted.

"You got to keep your locker squeaky clean, Doc. Keep it locked at all times. Somebody who needs a few points with the major might accidentally drop something in your house, get my drift? Also, you got any friends that know your combination, buy a new lock and turn in the old one, immediately. If you even think someone else knows it, get rid of it. Gonna be a pain in the ass, but don't even get up to go piss without locking it."

"Something else you need to know. Word is that she's going to have you cuffed and paraded every couple weeks or so to remind you who's in charge. You just say yes ma'am and no ma'am, and don't give her any reason to accuse you of insubordination. Do your job, no matter how dirty, and you might make it. How much time you got left, anyway?"

"I've got 14 months left, if nothing is added on."

"I'll help you all I can, Doc. Remember, you got a lot of friends here, but our help is limited. Major knows about Stony, hell, we all do. Nothing she'd like better than to get you back over to him. Don't you be giving her no reason to do that. Don't do nothing stupid and you might just make the next 14 and go home."

Thanking Newton, Matt went to his bunk and checked his locker. It was as neat as a pin, with a considerable amount of space available that hadn't been there that morning. Heeding Officer Newton's words, Matt went to the canteen and bought a new lock, immediately giving the new combination to the dorm officer as required.

Lying in his bunk that night, Matt thought about the day's events. He still got a crawly sensation down his spine when he thought how close he had come to being sent back to the main compound. He also knew that if he was sent back, Stony would do anything in his power to salve his wounded pride.

He had wanted to talk about it all with Marilyn when he called her, but he knew that all phone calls were monitored and anything negative would get back to the Major. As the full impact of how much power the Major had and how she planned to use it to hurt him sank in, Matt became madder and madder. *This is wrong. I need to watch myself or the Major might really get to me. Got to cover my ass.*

With such thoughts, Matt fell into a restless and dreamless sleep.

* * * *

The next morning, Matt was summoned to his new job as a kitchen worker. Sergeant Abraham Lincoln Brown was in charge of the kitchen, and it was directly to him that Matt reported.

"Glad to have you back here, inmate Hightower. This ain't as fancy as where you been working, but it ain't bad. You pretty well get all you want to eat and you only work until your specific job is done. Gonna start you out as a swill man. Get with inmate Wilson and he will tell you all about it."

With that, Matt was shown out to the swill room and introduced to Racetrack Wilson, a thin, tall, black inmate with a mouth that looked like it never smiled. No attempt was made to alter that impression as he told Matt about how easy the job would be.

"We only work three times a day, hour or less each time. Rest of the time is yours. Find something to do, cause they won't let you in the library or nothing like that. I done finished for now, so you can go and I'll meet you back here after noon chow."

Since he couldn't go back to the dorm, Matt decided to walk the track, a clay walkway that covered about three-fourths of the total perimeter of the fence and was used as a running and walking track, as well as a place to smoke dope and talk privately by some.

He had only been on the track for a few minutes, wondering how he had gotten such a good assignment (except for the smell, it was a piece of cake), when his name was called over the loud speaker, with instructions to report to the kitchen.

Back in the kitchen, a very flustered Sergeant told him that his job placement had been counteracted, and his job was to be the only pot scrubber for the three hundred men in the camp. It was a seven day a week job, beginning at 4:00 AM every morning and ending about 8:00 PM. He would have as much time off as was available, depending on how much time he spent cleaning between meals. Also, he would have a replacement on the days he had to report to medical or when he had a visitor. He was warned, however, that if he took time for a visit, there better be a visitor. It would be a disciplinary action if he didn't; namely, the infraction of lying to staff.

Matt later learned that the reason the Major allowed the visitation privilege was because she was afraid that if she denied his visiting privileges, Matt's wife might get worried and report it.

He spent the next 14 months in the pot room, working a minimum of eight hours every weekday and more on the weekends. He was continuously harassed by the Major and her crony, Sergeant Lacy, but he never responded with anything other than politeness and respect. Several times he was set up and, had he not been vigilant, he would have been written up and sent to confinement. A favorite trick was for the kitchen officer to fail to place the required bleach allotment out for his use in the sink. It was a health requirement that three sinks were used: one for washing, one for disinfecting/rinsing, and the last one for final rinsing. If he had ever failed to pursue the officer and request the chlorine bleach, he would have broken a major rule. He never failed.

The Major also saw to it that his job was made tougher than it needed to be. Chicken was served twice a week, once baked and once baked with barbecue sauce added. The cooking process would leave Matt forty or more heavy aluminum sheets with baked on chicken to clean. Often, the cleaning pads would disappear and he would have only steel wool to scrub with, resulting in torn and bleeding fingers and a very sore back from hours of scrubbing. Each time he put his bleeding fingers into the stinging bleach water, his pain became fuel that brought the burning in his gut to a higher level. It was a long 14 months and he had plenty of opportunity to watch and secretly plot how he would carry out his revenge.

One of his friends, who worked on outside grounds, brought him the license numbers of both Officer Stony and the Major and he coded them into his Bible, just as before. He watched as the Major took long lunch breaks with Sgt. Lacy, often returning two hours later with fried chicken in a take out bag. He wondered what they were doing during lunch if they had to eat when they got back. Rumor had it that they were lesbians, but he wasn't sure. Besides, he never cared one way or the other about sexual preferences, until one acted like rutting animals as they often did on the main unit.

At least twice a month he would be shackled and cuffed and hauled up to the Major's office. She would smile and tell him that he was surprising her with his exemplary behavior.

He never reacted, even when the Sergeant, who was always there, told him that he must like his new job since there was no more writing going on. She and the Major got a real chuckle out of that one.

Matt stood there, choking back the puke he wanted to spew over both of them.

Every time he left the work camp, he had to be shackled and chained, and all the inmates with him were subjected to higher scrutiny. It interfered with their dealings back and forth with the main unit, and therefore he became about as welcomed as the plague, and was avoided whenever possible. He just soaked it all in, awaiting the day when he could pay back those responsible, in full measure.

Twelve days before he was scheduled to get out, the Major went on her annual two-week vacation. Not surprisingly, Sergeant Lacy's vacation also came about at the same time. What was surprising was that the Major never called Matt to her office to berate him before she left. In her stead, a lieutenant named Evelyn Dumas was appointed acting Major and Camp Superintendent. Rumors were that she too was a lesbian, but she was not necessarily a man hater. Most of the time, when Matt observed her, she seemed very pleasant and a little shy. Word had it that she was awaiting promotion to be a real Major and take over her own camp, but he had no idea where.

* * * *

It was a very surprised Matt who was called into her office Friday, the day before he was scheduled to get out of prison. Neither handcuffed nor shackled, he was led to the door of the Lieutenant's office and then called in by her.

"Inmate Hightower; Doctor, I'm Lieutenant Evelyn Dumas. Please close the door behind you and sit down, here, in front of my desk."

Although she didn't offer to shake hands, the Lieutenant gave Matt the most sincere and pleasant introduction he had experienced since coming to prison.

Nodding, he smiled in appreciation as he took the indicated chair.

Frowning for just a moment, the Lieutenant reached into the top drawer and pulled out an envelope, showing him the front of it in the process. It was addressed to the lieutenant and marked Personal and Confidential. The stationary was Major Kelly's official correspondence letterhead and return address.

Opening the envelope, Lieutenant Dumas spoke in a quiet voice. "Doctor Hightower, I need your word that everything we say here is completely confidential. Do I have it?"

"Yes Ma'am," Matt stammered, truly astonished by the use of his former title.

"You don't know me, doctor, but I am friends with one of your former office managers who speaks highly and fondly of you and thinks that you got a very harsh and undeserved sentence. When I took this assignment, I received this letter from the Major. I will read it to you."

"Lieutenant, Acting Major, Dumas. I understand you are looking for a promotion to actual major and a camp of your own, the juvenile facility in Bushnell. As you may know, I have friends who may be able to assist you in receiving that promotion. Rest assured that I will contact them upon my return from vacation and see what I can do.

"Meanwhile, I have a favor to ask of you. There is an inmate in my camp, Matthew Hightower, who is scheduled to depart prison the Saturday before I return. I would appreciate it if he did not go home at that time. I'm sure that given the 'proper' shakedown, some contraband will appear and he can be sent to confinement and then spend a few days at the main unit before returning to my custody."

"I thank you in advance for helping me with a difficult problem, and you can rest assured that I will do everything in my power to expedite your promotion. Sincerely, Major Kelly."

"Doctor Hightower, I don't know what you did to create such animosity from this woman toward you. Regardless of the cause, I want no part of the Major's retaliation. Luckily, just yesterday I received notice of my promotion and I have nothing to fear from the Major. As a matter of fact, I intend to hang on to this letter just in case I ever need it. She appears to be quite willing to be one nasty person."

"Barring something totally unforeseen, you will leave here tomorrow as scheduled. I wish you the best in your re-entry into society and hope that you realize that not all of us are cut from the same mold."

Having said what she wanted to say, she offered him her hand.

Taking her hand in his, Matt could only mutter a sincere "Thank You", while holding back the tears that threatened to stream from his eyes.

Leaving her office, the gratitude he felt was soon replaced by the enormity of what Major Kelly had attempted. Unjust confinement, loss of gain time and a return to Stony for further punishment or death while she and Sergeant Lacy enjoyed their vacations.

Grateful for the Lieutenant's intervention, he nonetheless felt that familiar searing burn his stomach with such intensity that he had to run to the bathroom as diarrhea spewed from his bowels.

Weak with the loss of energy from his bout on the toilet, Matt sat on his bunk, going through his property in preparation for leaving.

I will leave this God forsaken place, and when I do, there are six people who have no idea of what punishment really is. I **am** *the executioner of justice. I* **will** *have my day!*

CHAPTER EIGHT

All morning Matt waited for his name to be called. He had talked to Marilyn the night before and he had seen her arrive in the parking lot and go to the sally port to await his release. It was a Saturday morning and the Major wasn't there, but, especially since his talk with the Lieutenant, he was nervous anyway.

Finally he saw his classification officer enter the office and a few minutes later he was called to see him. He had already been to the lectures and received all the information regarding his probation, etc. He was now allowed to put on the clothes Marilyn brought, sign his release papers, collect his hundred dollars and walk out the gate—free!

Things began to blur in his sight; everything appeared surreal. He stumbled through the encounter in classification and then was allowed to pass through the gate, dressed in civilian clothes. Suddenly Marilyn was in his arms and they both were hugging and crying. Then, before he knew it, the girls were there; everyone was laughing and crying at the same time, all hugging each other and talking with no one making any sense. He didn't know if he could say anything that could express his feelings. He felt numb, shocked, excited, tense, unbelieving, and alive, all at once in a cacophony of emotions. After six years, he was a free man.

As his emotions began to calm down, he looked over his shoulder back at the sally port and saw one of the young black, female officers watching. She had tears in her eyes and she gave him the thumbs up sign and hollered, "That's from all of us who were rooting for you, Doc. Good luck and don't come back!"

He waved back, still too emotionally choked up to try to answer. As they turned toward the car, they decided that Marilyn would drive home so he could talk to them all and look at life without bars or screens for the first time in six years. It was a very happy Matt Hightower who rode home that day.

* * * *

Looking around at his new office, Matt felt a sense of satisfaction. Not the same as when he owned his own business and fleet of medical clinics, but satisfaction in the sense of freedom and the ability to make things happen without the asininity imposed while in the prison system. His office was impressive; a large desk was framed by a picture window overlooking the fountain in the center of a beautiful new complex. A leather couch and two wingback leather chairs were placed strategically to face the desk without blocking his view of the two machines centered in the front of the room.

The office was owned by Medi-Machine, a subsidiary of a large conglomerate. Medi-Mash as they all called it, manufactured and sold machines that allowed doctors to perform operations so delicate that humans could not attempt with their hands alone. The company also sold a special blaster that was used to remove skin blemishes without laser or cutting, and which could be used in a doctor's office. Both machines required extensive training to operate, and that is where Matt came in.

With medical training and MD certificates, even though he was no longer licensed to practice, Matt was knowledgeable enough to learn the product, and respected enough to be allowed into doctors' offices and even hospital surgeries to demonstrate the use of the machines. Medi-Mash paid him $125,000 per year, plus bonuses and a van to market their products. Although all inquiries within a 150 mile radius of Tampa were his for the taking, Matt had the authority to pick and choose those he wished to follow up on and determine those he believed to be wasted time. Having no immediate supervisor, his primary duty besides sales were the mandatory reports that needed filing. Fortunately, he had two administrative assistants to assist with the paperwork. He was as close to being his own boss as he could be without owning his own business.

The satisfaction he felt at his new job was tempered by the knowledge of what he had lost, and how much of an unreasonable price had been extracted from his very soul. He now was able to witness the effects his downfall had had on Marilyn and the girls. Not only did they all cling to him unexpectedly and without seeming provocation, but Marilyn and Rachel were still having nightmares on occasion. One night in particular, he had gotten up at two AM when he heard a noise from Rachel's room and as he entered it, he watched as she swung her arms and appeared to defend herself from an invisible foe, sobbing and gasping all the time. Matt had picked her up and held her close, soothing her with his touch and voice, all the while hating Shimdugger and the judge. Each stroke of his hand on his daughter's head stoked the fires of hatred in his own mind.

Equally as bad, two nights later, Marilyn had awakened him with her whimpering and thrashing in the bed. Matt would never forget the fear on her face as she grimaced, squeezing her eyes closed and at the same time, baring her teeth in absolute fear. Before he could reach out to her, the fearful look turned into one of hatred as she swung a blow at the imaginary invader of her dreams. As she hissed at her enemy, Matt recognized the name from between her clenched teeth: Shimdugger!

Grabbing his wife in an embrace and holding her as she woke up sobbing, Matt's own rage almost became more than he could handle. *There is no punishment to strong for those who caused this to happen. No matter what I may have done, the pain caused here and now is inexcusable. They have to pay. They have to pay!* Holding on to each other, he and Marilyn drifted off into a restless sleep with Matt's mind repeating over and over, "they have to pay."

Every morning on his way to the office he had to pass by his former flagship clinic near the University of South Florida Medical Center. Every morning he was reminded of what had been taken from him. Every morning he was witness to the success of his planning and prior efforts, and, every morning his gut churned with the hate that all but consumed him whenever he thought about his losses. Sometimes the hate was so strong that he would pull off the side of the road to compose himself prior to coming into the office for fear that his administrative assistants would see through the mask of blissful success he presented to the world.

Often, Matt would awaken at night, covered in sweat, startled to find that he was lying on soft sheets instead of on the cold, hard concrete bunk of Lake Butler prison. In his dreams he confused and mixed all the episodes where he was hurt and degraded. Sometimes Sergeant Black had a shotgun at his head, sometimes Stony had a flashlight, beating him all over his body and poking him in the rectum. Always, though, Judge Dana would oversee the action with a cold smile tightly sitting on her lips. Once the State Attorney, Shimdugger, stood against the cell wall, laughing and taunting him with cries of "What's up, Doc?"

Dear God, will this nightmare never end?

It was a silent prayer, pervasive and frequent and one to which he already knew the answer. Psychological help was not the answer. No, this was time for him to acknowledge the truth of the old axiom, "Physician heal thyself."

As if in confirmation of what had to take place, Matt was reading the Sunday business section when he came across the article headed, "Rupert Shimdugger promoted." It went on to say that Shimdugger was now a senior partner at his law firm and praised him for his conviction record at the State attorney's office and his ability to bring in new client's to the firm. *God damn his soul to hell! We suffer for years and this scumbag gets richer and richer! This has to stop! How much more can I take?*

True satisfaction and the silencing of the voices Matt now accepted, could only come when those responsible for his plight had been punished. The thin smile on his lips presented an almost evil twist when he acknowledged that the time had come to begin his mission. Once complete, he would allow himself to enjoy life. Meanwhile, he would start by wreaking revenge. He would make sure that those who had destroyed his life could never destroy those of anyone else. Ever.

* * * *

No more dreams. No more waiting. It is time.

On his way driving to Orlando where he had a demonstration scheduled for the skin blemish removing machine, Matt mused over his plans. He purposely had given himself several free hours in Orlando to do some research. He needed to be sure where his future victims lived.

Arriving at the Orlando Chat Room, a coffee house filled with computers where anyone could hook up to the Internet anonymously, he paid for one hour, in cash. Once on line, using the license numbers obtained at Sumter, he was able to retrieve the last two addresses he needed, as well as verify that Black and Jhonus were still at their former addresses. This time, he needed no biblical codes to hide them from the guards, just a small notebook and a pen.

Now he was ready to commit the crimes for which he had already served more than enough time.

* * * *

Sergeant Rufus Black was a single man who lived in a mobile home out in the country, less than one and a half miles from Butler prison. He had no immediate neighbors. Although unmarried, he had a live-in girlfriend, a pretty black girl who waited on tables at a nearby restaurant from 11:00 AM until 8:00 PM on weeknights; the only time of any concern to Matt.

Black was off by 4:00 PM every afternoon and each time Matt had scouted him out, he headed straight for home. Matt was counting on both of them adhering to their schedules today, the day of reckoning for Black.

After arranging his schedule to reflect three days of observation at USF medical college, Matt went by the operating theater each morning, donned scrubs and mask and went to the observation area above surgery. Each day, he chatted with a few colleagues and then slipped out after less than an hour and drove to Lake Butler. Yesterday, he had gone to Ocala first, stopping at Bill Jackson's Sporting Goods and paying cash for three baseball bats. Today, one bat was in his car and the other two were hidden in his garage at home.

The first two days of scouting were done in Matt's personal car, a Buick that he deliberately left dusty so as not to attract attention. Had he seen anyone who seemed even remotely suspicious or curious about him or the car, Matt would have delayed his plans. Nothing had occurred to alarm him, and so, today was the first day of payback time.

* * * *

Heading north on I-75, Matt felt a tremendous surge of excitement and exhilaration, tinged with just enough fear to keep him cautious. After almost ten years, he was finally striking back.

As the miles rolled by, both fear and exhilaration dwindled, only to be replaced with a calm sense of purpose. He knew what he was about and he intended to succeed.

He deliberately blocked out any thoughts of family, allowing nothing to interfere with his mission.

Now, Sergeant Black, we'll see just how good you really are.

Hitting Gainesville just before 2:00 in the afternoon, Matt pulled into the main parking lot for the University of Florida. Cruising through the lot, he searched until he spotted an older Dodge sedan that fitted the description of easy to break into cars that he had learned about from the best pros in prison. Once he had the car picked out, he parked his own car two blocks away in an automated parking lot.

Wearing a sport shirt and ball cap, Matt slung the baseball bat over his shoulder as he got out of his car and walked to the University lot. He attracted no unusual attention as he approached the older Dodge.

Taking one last glance around, Matt reached into his pocket and pulled out latex gloves, slipping them on with practiced ease. Then, after pulling out the screwdriver and flat metal ruler, he quickly entered the car. In seconds he had it hot-wired and was on his way out of the parking lot, completely unnoticed.

Turning the air conditioning up, he glanced at the gas gauge and was pleased to note that it was almost full.

Good, that means no extra stops. I didn't even work up a sweat and this is my first intentional felony. Shit, I learned a lot more in prison than I thought I did. I'm thinking and acting like a real pro!

Without letting himself feel too elated with his minor success, he went over the plans in his head as he drove the remaining distance to Lake Butler. He inventoried his tools: the bat; he was wearing the gloves; the ruler, not necessary any longer; the screwdriver and one piece of a leg of his wife's pantyhose. He had deliberated over the pantyhose versus a ski mask, and decided that for his use, the pantyhose would be sufficient and less traceable.

Arriving at Rufus Black's trailer at 3:30 PM, Matt pulled straight up in the driveway and parked near the front steps. It was a simple, older model doublewide mobile home. Nothing fancy or homey had been added and the front steps probably were the same steps that were delivered when the trailer arrived on the premises. Matt felt no remorse for what was about to occur. Taking a deep breath, he opened the car door and got out.

The only thing unusual about his actions was that he was wearing latex gloves, not readily noticeable at a distance. He held his breath and walked up the steps, knocking on the door immediately after reaching the top step. Silently thanking God that no one was home, he let out his breath and jumped back into the car.

I didn't think it would be any different today than the last two days, but I just had to know.

If anyone but God had been watching, Matt would have seemed like a very cool customer. Inside, he was tight as a piano string. Pulse racing, he backed the car up far enough to turn left in front of the trailer and drive to the far side of what was actually the rear of the mobile home. Parking the car he surveyed his placement, reassuring himself that the car couldn't be seen from the front of the trailer nor the side that Black would come in from.

Moving swiftly but carefully, Matt went to the rear entrance of the trailer. Both days that he had watched Rufus Black come home, the guard had entered through the front door. Matt was counting on the Sergeant being a man of habit and doing the same thing today. Using his screwdriver, he took less than 45 seconds to open the rear door of the trailer. It left a few scars on the metal doorframe, but it would be far too late to help Sergeant Black by the time the damage was discovered.

It was only when he entered the cool interior of the mobile home that Matt realized the extent to which he had been sweating. He was soaked. Thirsty, and with a pulse racing in high gear, he quickly surveyed the main room into which the front door opened.

Ignoring his thirst, he chose a small chair instead of the comfortable sofa and took his seat, facing the door and able to see the approach. If Rufus arrived with company, Matt could bolt for the back door and make his escape unseen. If not, he would do what he had come to do.

Regardless of the outcome, I'm not going back to prison. Not now, not ever.

He waited for a little over twenty minutes, deliberately reminding himself of the reasons he had so much hatred welling up inside him; his only outward sign of nerves was the occasional fiddling with his hands on the bat. It was placed in front of him, with the head of the bat on the floor and the handle on the chair at his lap. In his lap was the single leg of his wife's ruined pantyhose. Strangely, his mind held no doubt whether this was the right thing to do. Burning bands of hate had ripped through his very soul several hours out of every day, giving him all the justification he needed. The small amount of fear that accompanied him now was no match for ten years of searing hatred. He knew that he was exercising his well-earned need for revenge.

Suddenly he caught movement out of the corner of his left eye and soon discerned that Sergeant Rufus Black was alone and approaching the steps.

Silently, Matt slipped the pantyhose over his head and stepped to the side of the door. He saw Black stepping up, totally unconcerned as he held himself perfectly erect. Wearing his straw trooper hat at home, Black looked like the wannabe marine drill instructor that he really was.

Matt smiled. This was the last time in Black's life that he would ever look that cocky or confident.

Sergeant Rufus Black inserted his key and swung the front door open to step into his home. His face only began to register shock when the baseball bat, with the full strength of Matthew Hightower's six-foot frame behind it, caught him fully in the mouth.

The tremendous impact crushed his lips into his mouth. His jaw completely disappeared as the bat continued forward, taking out all of his teeth in the process. Before Black could hit the floor, his teeth had scattered around him like a spilled box of Chiclets, while his face appeared to have a gaping cavern where a mouth used to be.

As soon as the body hit, Matt dropped the bat and pulled the unconscious Black into the center of the living room floor. Then he went back, closed the door and picked up the bat and returned to the inert body.

Matt was almost in a sort of super trance, more alive than at any time in his life. It was almost as if he occupied another person's body, watching as he did what he had dreamed of for so long. Feeling the same raw power that his caveman ancestors must have felt when they beat their enemies with clubs, Matt looked down at his victim.

Well, well, Sergeant Rufus. I think that will take care of your ability to run that nasty mouth at any more inmates. Now let's see what I can do about the rest of you.

He removed the pantyhose from his face, stuffing it in his pocket and leaned over the body. First he made sure that Black was breathing with no obstructions in his air passages.

OK, I haven't killed you. Good.

Methodically Matt straightened out Black's limp arms and legs, taking books off the shelf and propping up the elbows and knees.

Standing over the prone figure, Matt brought the bat down with crushing force, on each collarbone, one at a time. Then, grunting with each exertion, he swung the bat with all the strength he could muster, completely crushing each elbow and each knee.

I don't think I have any machines for sale that can repair these for you Mr. Rufus. Sorry about that.

Finishing with the elbows and knees, he made two more adjustments, taking two more books from the shelf and placing each under Black's hands.

I think this will keep that nasty ole flashlight from finding its way into someone else's asshole at your hands.

Taking a deep breath and swinging like an experienced coal miner with a pick, Matt brought the bat down on each hand repeatedly, until a bloody, mashed pulp dangled at the end of each wrist.

Now let's see how many helpless inmates you can cuff and beat up, Sergeant Black.

Once more he checked to insure that Black was breathing unobstructed and would live. He was alive and breathing well, and that was all Matt wanted. Black would come to long before his girlfriend came home but be able to do nothing but hurt until she arrived.

Hurt, you son of a bitch! Hurt! Hurt! Hurt!

Taking a deep breath, Matt carefully checked himself to make sure he acquired no blood or signs of a scuffle. Satisfied, he then counted his tools, bat and pantyhose. Once sure he had everything, he let himself out the back door and got into the old Dodge, hot wired it and drove off. He never even met another vehicle until he got back on the interstate. He felt good: real good.

Careful dude, don't get too satisfied. You've still got to get your car back.

Driving carefully and always doing the speed limit, Matt returned to Gainesville and drove to a spot a block away from the parking lot and about the same distance from his car. The area was almost deserted now and no one noticed as he threw the bat and pantyhose into a nearby dumpster. He then took off the latex gloves and put them in his pocket, finally throwing them into another dumpster nearer to his own car. The ruler and screwdriver were safely hidden in his pockets as he walked from the Dodge to his car.

Feeling very satisfied, and enjoying a newfound surge of excitement, Matt drove off and headed for home. He wasn't even shaking as he got back on the interstate. *I really did it. I pulled it off. Only five more to go.*

CHAPTER NINE

Three months passed before Matt started working on his next victim, Officer Jhonus, the woman who lied and had him locked up and beaten. Enough time had now passed that nothing should arise to connect the two incidences in the eyes of the police. The temporary taste of vengeance he had experienced with the assault on Black had worn off, but the searing fires in his gut had, if anything, increased. Now that he knew he could actually do something to sate his lust for vengeance, each day that passed with no action only seemed to enhance the all-consuming passion within him. Even Marilyn, who rarely questioned him about anything, had remarked that he seemed pre-occupied.

It is time. I can't even look at a garden hose and not recall being nearly drowned and beaten by the water pressure from the fire hose. My eyes still burn with mace and tear gas and my mind does crazy things. I've got to put out the fire. The woman has got to go.

On his first trip to the Jasper area where Jhonus lived, it became apparent that this attack would not be as easy to carry out as the last one. Officer Jhonus and her family lived in a cheap, concrete block home in a rural development that never really expanded after the first few houses were built. There were about 20 houses in the area, all connected by a thinly sprayed asphalt road, long since riddled with potholes and choked with weeds. None of the houses had lawns, and barely clad children with dirty hands and faces populated most of the yards, floating freely from house to house.

Matt gleaned most of his information from afar, too concerned with being noticed as an outsider in this remote subdivision to actually go into the community. After driving by the development twice, he returned to the main intersection of roads that he believed Jhonus would have to travel back and forth to work. It was about 3:45 PM, and he didn't think he would have too long to wait. He stopped and bought a Coke at a Junior store, and sure enough, in about five minutes, Officer Jhonus drove by.

Feeling a tightening in his gut and with a few drops of sweat beading on his forehead, Matt slowly returned to his car and kept Jhonus just barely in sight. Puzzled when she turned off on a smaller county road, he followed her and soon realized that this was a short cut he hadn't picked up on by looking at the map.

They passed no other traffic on the way and the county road cut back in to the state road about a mile from Jhonus's subdivision.

She gets off earlier than most people in this community do because of where she works. I'll bet she never passes anyone on the way home after cutting off on this county road.

Driving back to Tampa, and glad that he had a job that allowed him almost complete freedom to move about unreported, Matt began formulating a plan in his mind. First, he had to be sure about Jhonus's routine. The next day he drove to Gainesville, parked about two blocks away from Rent-A-Wreck where, with a phony driver's license and lots of cash, he rented a cheap but serviceable car. He now had two false licenses, both purchased from an individual referred to him by one of his contacts in prison. They were absolutely genuine in all respects except for name, address and social security numbers and depicted him with longer hair and a scruff of a beard; enough to alter his looks without raising questions.

Since the car's only purpose was allow him to legally, albeit anonymously, drive by Jhonus's place one more time, he wasn't overly concerned about it being traced to him. This time, he went straight to the county road and drove the distance, marking it as 11 miles long and with two fairly sharp curves. One curve was in the open, but the second one was wrapped around a field of planted pines, probably eight years old and thick enough to hide him from view. There were only two rusty old fence wires strung between old pine lighter posts at about 16 feet apart. A cheap pair of wire cutters would take care of that, and no one would notice it, at least not for the few minutes that would count.

Finished with his scouting project, Matt returned to the main crossroads and waited less than five minutes to watch Jhonus come by. He followed her only far enough to watch her take the deserted county road once more, and then he turned off and headed back to Gainesville. Returning the rental was simple, and after picking up his deposit, he walked to his own car and was quickly on his way back to Tampa, satisfied, with a completed plan formulated in his mind.

The woman is mine, now. After tomorrow, I don't think she will be thinking at all about fucking up inmates' lives anymore.

Matt was actually tapping his hands to the music as he drove, the fire in his gut temporarily sated with the knowledge that tomorrow would mark two down on his list.

* * * *

Shortly after getting out of prison, Matt had installed custom workbenches and cabinets in his garage, telling Marilyn that they would be necessary in his new profession. That had been true enough, and he had legitimately used the garage for that purpose as well as normal garage use. However, unknown to anyone but himself, he had purchased a large, deep gun safe and installed it in such a way that it was completely hidden; it could not be accessed except through a Formica cover with a trick opening. It was in this safe that he kept equipment purchased for his exploits. In addition to spare baseball bats, he had several guns and ammunition, all purchased at gun shows with no ID required. He had bullets and shells and two extremely sharp stilettos with razor edges on both sides of the locking blades. He had a handmade ignition lock pick, fashioned after one an inmate friend had made for him in Sumter. A pair of binoculars sat in the corner, a cash purchase from Sports Authority in Brandon. Two thin, steel rulers completed his hidden collection.

He went to this safe that night, picking out a 22 long handled target pistol, a full clip of soft, hollow point long rifle bullets, the pick, the binoculars and one of the stilettos. Locking the safe, he placed these items in a small paper bag in his trunk. Adding a full shield motorcycle riding helmet that he purchased at a K-Mart in Orlando, he then completed his trunk collection with a small bottle of ether and a handkerchief. In his line of work, ether was easy to come by. He had purchased the hanky in a pack of three cheap ones at Eckerd's in St. Pete. His trunk already held surgical gloves, routine in his work.

After grabbing a small pair of wire cutters off the bench, he needed only a light jacket, which he would get in the morning. He had the perfect one, once again purchased with cash, a cheap but presentable one, this time from Wal-Mart in Ocala. He was ready.

That night, he made love to Marilyn in a very sweet, satisfying fashion. They were both so fulfilled that when finished, they never even parted, but instead fell asleep still joined and wrapped in each other's arms. It was deep in the middle of the night before they separated, and then only to turn on their sides and fall back asleep, cupped together like a pair of spoons.

The next morning, Matt felt more alive than he could ever remember. Before leaving for the office, he kissed Marilyn and she had responded so fiercely, passionately and lovingly that he almost didn't leave. He told her he would try not to be too late, but that she better not hold dinner up for him because his last presentation was a late one in Ocala.

Driving toward his office and picturing her in his mind, Matt had second thoughts about what he was going to do today. For the first time since getting out of prison, he wondered, "What if?" What if he were caught? Could he survive once again without Marilyn? She had become more to him than he had realized. He had always loved her, but not with the same deep feeling that now wanted to engulf him and make him want to play it safe.

God, I've got to stop this shit. I'll drive myself crazy. Think. Just think.

Steeling himself, he deliberately turned his thoughts to his past pain and present need for revenge and welcomed the burning hatred finding its way back into his guts. Gradually, Marilyn receded from his conscious mind and thoughts of what had happened to him because of Jhonus replaced her. Wiping his damp brow, he once again felt the motivation move in, encapsulating his soul.

The bitch has got to pay, and today is the payday.

The words began to play like a litany in his mind, and as he rode toward Gainesville, he tapped in tune to the little ditty his vengeful mind had created.

The bitch has got to pay and today is the payday. The bitch has got to pay and today is the payday. The bitch...

* * * *

Reaching Gainesville, Matt pulled off at the third exit, the one that would take him straight to the main campus of the University of Florida. The parking lots were full of vehicles for the choosing, and this time he needed something different.

Driving around slowly, he found and discarded several choices, until he spotted what he was looking for—an older Honda, 1100 CC motorcycle. It appeared to be in excellent running condition, but was not new enough, nor fancy enough, to draw attention. Better yet, it was one of the types a former inmate had instructed him how to hotwire and unlock the front wheel.

There was almost no pedestrian traffic in the parking lot, so he knew classes were still in session. Matt drove a block away to another pay parking lot and parked his car. Quickly he gathered his gear, putting on the jacket sans helmet and then placed everything else in his pockets. Locking the car, he put the helmet under his arm and walked off, carrying it easily and naturally, as if he had done it thousands of times before.

Luckily, the lot was still deserted. As he approached the bike, Matt placed the helmet on his head and pulled the visor down. His face was now totally invisible to the rest of the world.

Straddling the bike, he kicked up the stand and leaned over the key lock, pick in hand, as casually as if he were inserting the key into his own bike.

In seconds, the bike was running smoothly and the front wheel was free.

Flipping the headlight on, he eased out of the parking lot drawing no attention to his leaving.

How wonderful, the things one learns in prison!

The bike continued to run smoothly, and soon Matt was heading north on I 75. However, the owner of the bike had not been as generous as the owner of the old Dodge, and as he looked at the gas gauge he saw it was almost empty.

Pulling off at the first small town the other side of Gainesville, into a Stucky's Texaco, Matt left the full-face visor in place. He quickly filled up the tank and paid at the outside window, also buying a pecan roll to take with him for energy. No one looked twice at him and he felt very confident as he pulled back onto the interstate.

* * * *

As he had surmised, the fence was rusty and aged and fell apart with the touch of the wire cutters. Two quick clips and he had all the room he needed to move the bike back, off the road and out of sight.

Careful not to move too deeply into the woods, Matt moved the bike back about three trees deep, just far enough to hide it, but not so far as to get it off the grassy carpet and into the softer sand. He wasn't concerned about going too deep anyway, since he was on the far side of the woods that she would see as she came out of the curve.

Taking his binoculars, Matt walked the fifty or so feet to the front side of the woods, staying back far enough to be unnoticed by any passersby, including Jhonus.

Waiting propped against one of the pines, it was a long thirty minutes before he saw her car.

Taking one moment to focus the binoculars on the car, he quickly ascertained that she was alone. There were no other cars on the road, nor had he seen any during his wait.

Moving rapidly, Matt rolled the bike forward to the edge of the trees and pulled out the pistol, checking it for bullets and making sure the chamber was loaded and the safety off.

Watching as she came around the curve at about 25 miles per hour, he took careful aim with the 22 and shot two rounds into the left front tire, causing it to make a simple popping sound, deflating almost instantly.

Jhonus had already begun to accelerate coming out of the curve when the deflated tire began to send severe vibrations throughout the car, causing her to brake and pull over. As distracted as she was handling her vehicle, she never noticed Matt as he left the woods and drove up behind her.

Other than the two of them, the road was still deserted as Matt pulled over just in front of her car while she simultaneously got out to see what was wrong. Still wearing his helmet with the visor pulled down, he set the kickstand on the edge of the road and pointed at the left front tire of her car.

"Son of a bitch," she railed as she saw what he was pointing at. "Those are brand new fucking tires and I just paid good money for them."

She never noticed as Matt poured ether onto the handkerchief and stepped closer to her.

"I'm not fucking eating the cost of this! That fucking Jimmy is getting these back…" Her mouth was open and it was only seconds before she was completely out cold as Matt held the soaked handkerchief against her face.

See, that mouth got you in trouble this time. So busy running that foul mouth and blaming others that you never saw what was really wrong. Got you now. In a few moments, you'll have a hard time ever running that filthy mouth again.

Momentarily setting her down against his legs, Matt put the ether back in his pocket and brought out his gloves, pulling them on quickly and easily. In seconds he had picked her up and moved her around to the passenger side of the car, opening the back door and throwing her partly on the seat. Beads of sweat lined his forehead and upper lip and his hands felt clammy inside the gloves; but his purpose never wavered.

In her drug-induced stupor, her mouth gaped open, making it that much easier to do what he had in mind.

All right, woman. Last chance to wag that nasty tongue of yours. What? Not even going to try? So be it. Say goodbye.

Expertly, Matt reached into Jhonus's mouth and grabbed her tongue with his left hand, pulling it forward while he took the stiletto and severed it at the root. Although there was a lot of blood, he knew it would clot soon and the injury would not be fatal. He was now totally into his job, all doubts and worries gone, replaced by a calm efficiency that belied his inner heat and excitement. The rage-filled memories he had held for so long were imploding inside him, giving him fuel for the burning in his gut, while at the same time, giving him a near sexual relief.

No one will ever suffer from the whiplash of that filthy, foul, lying tongue again.

Grunting with a combination of exertion and satisfaction, he reached down and grabbed her right hand, and, with his surgeon's skill, sliced away her index finger and adjacent finger. Placing both fingers on the floor of the car alongside the severed tongue, he repeated the process on the left hand, leaving both hands minus two fingers.

Gonna be a little more difficult writing lies and false reports on helpless inmates now, don't you think?

Almost giddy with excitement and a sense of wonder at his accomplishments, he nonetheless took care to check for any oncoming traffic. There was none.

Too bad, Bitch. Now for the grand finale. You've been kicking people while they were down for far too long. Let's see if we can do something about that.

Unbuckling her prison guard belt and unzipping her male-style fly, Matt flipped her over on her stomach and pulled down her pants from behind.

Damn, even you're underwear is nasty!

Sex wasn't even remotely on his mind as he took the stiletto and inserted it into her knee joints and sliced the tendons and muscles, totally debilitating her lower legs.

Be a little more difficult to kick now. So sorry…Hah!

After double-checking to ensure that none of the wounds were severe enough to cause death, he picked up the severed parts and threw them as far back into the woods as he could. He almost put her fully into the car, but then decided to let her ass hang out. She would wake up soon anyway, so it would be up to her to cover up, if she even cared to at that point.

Next, he removed his gloves and wiped the knife off in the grass; but that did not satisfy him. Reaching into his pocket he pulled out the ether soaked hanky, wiped the knife completely. Careful not to touch the car, he took one last look at the still sleeping Jhonus and nodded with satisfaction at his latest handiwork. After looking over his own clothing to make sure that he had no tell tale signs of the encounter, he cranked the bike and headed back to Gainesville.

About a mile from the interstate, Matt pulled over at the foot of a bridge overlooking a deep, muddy river. He took out the knife and wiped it down one final time, carefully handling it with the hanky and making sure there were no fingerprints anywhere on it. He then wrapped the knife with the hanky and threw it into the deepest part of the river. He really didn't think it would be found, but even if it was, it couldn't be traced to him.

Reaching into his pocket, he pulled out the gun, and with the same precision, he used a rag from the bike saddlebag and wiped it down.

Checking to make sure he was still unobserved, he tied the gloves to the gun and threw the gun toward the same spot in the river. He did not throw away the ether, as the numbered can was the one thing that might possibly be traced back to him. He would chance taking it with him back to his car. Once there, it was a normal accessory to his profession.

Heading the bike toward the interstate and Gainesville, Matt began to come off the natural high he had been on for the last hour. However, rather than the depression drug addicts go through when coming down off a high, he was feeling contented and more than a little sated.

Easy, boy. You've still got to get this bike back and make it home. But damn it man, I feel good! That liar will never do to anyone else what she did to me. Amazing how an act of pure violence can cleanse the soul.

With the wind whipping around his helmet and clothes, Matt hummed a catchy little ditty all the way to Gainesville. Taking a cue from the Wizard of Oz, he re-arranged the words in his mind to chant,

Hi ho, *the wicked bitch is dead...*

He had never felt so empowered. His was a righteous mission to help others; he was the avenging angel, the left hand of God.

Four more to go.

The wicked bitch is dead...

* * * *

Once in Gainesville, Matt pulled into a vacant self-parking lot about four blocks from where his Buick was waiting. After backing into a remote spot, he wiped the bike clean of all fingerprints and debris and walked away, paying the cost of four hours parking as he left the lot. His helmet remained on until he was safely around the corner and sure that no one had paid any attention to him, whereupon he swept it from his head and casually carried it under his arm until he came to his car.

It took no more than ten seconds to hide the ether in his pseudo-doctor bag in the trunk and place the helmet next to it. It was only when he threw the jacket into the back seat that he realized he was soaked in sweat.

I'll bet I lost five pounds today. Too bad I can't sell my routine as a weight loss program. Matt's Marquis De Sade Weight Reduction Center. Lose your unwanted pounds and your unwanted enemies at the same time.

In spite of the childish nature of the pun, Matt had to smile. He really felt good.

Only thing I regret is that I'll never get to hear her try to talk. Bet her lisp will make Daffy Duck sound like Julie Andrews. Oh well, you can't have it all.

As the interstate glided beneath him, Matt settled back into the soft luxury of the large Buick seats and turned the air up to high. His shirt and pants would dry on the way back to Tampa where he would arrive home in a triumphant mood as if he had made all three sales today. A wistful smile played on his lips as he thought of how he would celebrate his accomplishment by making love to his wife tonight. *We'll start in the hot tub...*

CHAPTER TEN

He decided to wait four months before tackling Stony. During the interim, he continued to exhibit superior skills as a businessman and a salesman. His quotas were exceeded and bonuses were soaring, even as he took off time to be with Marilyn and the kids. Marilyn was the most important thing in his life, and his relationship with the girls was only second to that. Although he had never considered himself a true family man, Matt was beginning to show all the signs of a man madly in love with life, family and his job, in that order. To the casual observer it would appear that the man who survived Hell had now created his own little piece of heaven on earth. But then, the casual observer never got to see the gut wrenching night sweats that soaked the bed at least once a week as his fires of hatred still burned intensely.

Matt began to fear that there was something really wrong with him. Any just God would surely allow him to overcome this raging inferno in his gut, especially now, with the help of his loving family, the community of friends and a new, but highly successful career. Unfortunately, hatred turned to fire burns deep, and can only be sated with action. Finally, he set out to continue his quest to satisfy the wrongs done. Stony had tried to kill him. Stony had hurt him. Stony had caused pain and death to many others, usually those who could not help themselves. Stony had to be stopped, *and I'm the man to do it. I took an oath and Stony is part of that vow.*

By now, Matt was ready for a new car, especially since his company would now pay half of the cost of his personal car as part of the bonus he received for his exemplary performance. He had put it off, however. A Lincoln Continental, being his first choice, would stand out like a sore thumb in Sumter County, especially near the trailer trash areas where many of the State's finest lived.

Fall was in the air and that meant hunting and guns. Perfect combinations for what Matt had in mind. Stony was an avid hunter, so much so that he bragged on his bird dogs and had leased prime hunting camps from the state for so long that he had first choice of sites every year. They had even let him get away with using a chain saw a few years back to clear his site just the way he wanted it. He would be getting antsy for hunting season to open. He would be getting ready. He would be practicing. He would be careless.

He will be my meat.

* * * *

Every time Matt thought about Stony, his pulse got quicker and his senses heightened. It was if he could smell the guard, just as when he'd been in the hunt for a deer when he was a kid. He had used real urine, picked up behind doe deer that Matt had watched urinate while scouting the woods days before. With Stony, it wasn't the scent of urine Matt remembered; it was the stench of bad breath and unwashed, putrid armpits that still flooded his senses. Those memories produced a fire that no amount of antacids could calm.

When it burned so fiercely and often, like now, Marilyn would become concerned. No matter how hard he tried, Matt couldn't hide the groans and sweats in the middle of the night. He placated her by blaming it on reruns of prison times, knowing that she did not want details of those experiences.

She chose to believe him and was satisfied. Had she known what he had in mind to eliminate the fires, she would have thought him mad.

They were all Christians, and lately, even Matt had begun to attend Sunday church with Marilyn and the girls. At night, he prayed to God that his family would be well and safe, and he thanked God for the many blessings he now enjoyed. But he never talked to God about his oath, the ones who had felt the wrath of his oath, nor the ones who were to follow. That was between Matt and them; God, he thought, had no say in the matter.

Matt was ready. The time was right. The fires were hot. He began to scout and plan his absences.

* * * *

True to form, Stony, a divorced man, lived alone in a doublewide trailer on a five-acre plot in the woods.

All these guards must be inbred. Apparently it goes with the mindset and ability, as well as the limited ambition.

Tracking down rural addresses can be challenging, but Matt had been surprised to find that Stony's place was deep in his own patch of woods and completely concealed from the highway. As a result, he had spent two days of watching a presumed driveway to make sure no one was home and no other homeowners used the same trail as Stony. It turned out that the lane was not a lane or driveway after all, but what looked like a former logging trail or something that had later been converted into a connecting link of dirt road that passed by three parcels of land as it meandered between two paved county roads. Stony's was the only residence sitting off the dirt road and was in clear sight of the intersection of his private driveway and the lane.

Although the place was surrounded with trees, there were about one and a half acres of cleared land upon which his trailer and a dilapidated barn sat, along with a dog pen and a large garden area, which now looked like a deserted cornfield.

Probably uses that field as a baited area to attract doves. Not really legal, but then, neither is Stony.

About 200 yards from Stony's entrance off the dirt road was a cleared out patch of ground where there apparently had once been a residence or barn, long since rotted or burned down. It provided an easy place for Matt to pull off the road, completely out of view of anyone going to Stony's place from the main road. A short walk and he was at the edge of the woods where he could observe without being seen.

Stony was a day worker and got off around 4:00 PM. Like most of the others, routine was a normal part of his life. Always coming home from the same direction, he drove into his driveway by 4:20 every day. He never used his front door, preferring instead to park next to the dilapidated barn-like structure and enter through the back door of the trailer. It never took him more than ten minutes to emerge with a cold beer in one hand and a shotgun in the other. Target practice would commence with two bird dogs in attendance, albeit watching from their pen.

Apparently Stony either had some limited mechanical expertise, or he had a friend who had some. Matt would have seriously doubted the actuality of either proposition, but there it was: a homemade trap-shooting device that really worked. Stony had merely to hit the foot pedal with his boot and the thing threw discs far into the air, just waiting for Stony to shoot them down. This he did with apparently practiced ease.

As he watched from the trees, a plan began to develop in Matt's mind.

* * * *

On his way home the second night, Matt stopped at a Scotty's in Temple Terrace and picked up a tube of fast drying liquid nails. It was like the super glue of super glues, and would fill a large hole and dry in minutes. It was all he needed, other than his normal break-in tools. He was ready.

* * * *

This time, Matt drove past the Sumter exit and up to the second exit in Ocala. There were two hospitals in the city, a north and south one, both sporting lots of parking spaces with plenty of other spaces in the two blocks between them. The number of cars and trucks available in the confined area was staggering, but it only took him a few minutes to find the perfect old Dodge parked in a remote, out of the way, spot surrounded with oleander bushes on two sides in the south hospital parking lot.

Matt then drove to the north hospital lot. After putting on his jacket, collected his tools and liquid nails and headed to the Dodge. This time was easier than before, as the owner of the car had neglected to lock it up. He slipped on his gloves and merely grabbed the handle and pushed the button and the door opened with ease. With a half tank of gas showing on the gauge, he knew he had no need for extra stops or exposure; it was only about forty miles each way, and he was covered. When he leaned over to hot wire the car, he had an even more pleasant surprise: a set of keys was lying in the floorboard.

I don't really think it's appropriate to think, 'thank God' at this point, but wow, this is great!

He really hadn't slept well for the last three nights. Visions of Stony holding a shotgun in Matt's face while wearing that evil grin kept creeping into his mind. Last night Marilyn had wanted to make love and, unable to get an erection, he had feigned flu-like symptoms and begged off.

That was a first. Even in the prison bathroom in the visitation park, Big Dude responded with class. Marilyn and I both where scared shitless, but I was still hard as a rock. Don't know what happened last night, but I don't like it.

Pulling out of the parking lot, he allowed his mind to wander, thinking about the differences now as opposed to the first time he had risked it all to obey his sworn oath. The fires of hate that had ruled his mind and body for so long still churned in his guts, but only occasionally. The 24-hour hate spells had been replaced by memories that needed flogging to burn as deep and as hot. Now, as the time approached, he had to shut out the questions and concentrate on picturing what had been done to him. Without those pictures, he was afraid he would lose the incentive to continue.

What the hell is happening to me? I cannot and I will not allow those bastards to get away after what they did to me and what they are surely doing to others right now while I have this stupid conversation with myself. Damn them! Damn them all straight to hell! They earned my hate. They earned a shortened route to Hell. But most of all, I earned the right to send them there!

Having quashed his doubts and stilled his unwanted humanity, Matt continued toward Sumter County and Stony. It wasn't even 1:00 PM, so he pulled straight into Stony's driveway.

Alighting from the car, he headed up to the front door. He had his trusty screwdriver in his pocket, but he left it there until he had knocked several times on the door to ensure no one was home.

Satisfied, he inserted the screwdriver into the doorjamb and with a loud pop, the door swung part way open.

Startled, Matt looked into the crack and saw a little brass chain that prevented the door from opening.

Shit! How many idiots use their front door so little that they leave the door chain on while they're out? I guess this classless dolt brings everyone in through his back door.

Shrugging his shoulders, Matt pushed the cheap trailer door almost closed and then yanked it hard, snapping the little chain as if it were thread.

Disgusted that someone who considered himself a law enforcement officer would have such a rinky-dink *security system*, Matt walked through the door feeling better about himself and what he was doing than he had in a long while. His mental reservations were rapidly receding into the nether regions of his brain and with their departure came the return of the sharp, dedicated professional avenger he had become.

After securing the front door, he looked around and saw a trailer devoid of any woman's touch. The furniture was cheap and manly, large wooden arms and big, dark faux leather pillows and backs. One well-worn easy chair appeared to be the obvious choice of the master of the estate. An extra-large TV appeared to be the only relatively new living room piece. Next to the remote control was a pile of girlie books and a vibrator.

I guess if you're too damn mean to keep a woman, a vibrator would have to be your best friend.

Moving into the dining room he saw a gun rack with two guns hanging on the wall. That was it. No pictures or anything else to soften the room, just two guns. The top rack held a rifle, a Marlin 306 with a scope. Cheap, but effective. The lower rack held a 12 gauge shotgun: a Browning gold trigger. This was a much more expensive weapon and probably represented the reason for the skeet shooting and the bird dogs, as well as the baited field. It was this gun that Matt lifted from its resting place.

A gas operated semi-automatic, the shotgun was fully loaded, even to a shell in the chamber. The only thing keeping the gun from going off with a touch to the trigger was the safety. Matt ejected all three shells and looked into the barrel.

Well oiled, the gun had been cleaned expertly and had no residue anywhere. All the mechanisms worked freely and it was obvious that this was the one piece of equipment that Stony had real pride in keeping perfect.

Gun in hand, Matt surveyed the rest of the room. On the dining room table he saw gun-cleaning tools, oil and patches. All were neatly arranged, and the barrel rods were screwed together the appropriate length and with the right patch holder to accommodate the shotgun.

Below the table were two stacks of ammunition: the smaller of the two was a pile of bullets, 306 caliber. The larger stack consisted of at least 70 or 80 boxes of shotgun shells, some target and some two and a half-inch standard load.

Matt looked at the shells he had ejected from the gun and found them to be target load, shells with less powder and less kick than standard load. Looking even further back in the stack, he saw a box of express shells, a much stronger magnum load for heavy shooting. They had quite a bit more kick to go with the larger powder load.

After pulling several paper towels off the roll hanging over the sink, he wadded up two of them and, using the cleaning rod, he forced them down the barrel. Breaking open the breach by pulling open the lock and exposing the automatic mechanisms, he locked the breach in open and forced the towels out of the barrel and through the opening. He repeated the same procedure twice, using clean towels each time.

There, that should get rid of all the gun oil in the barrel.

Squinting down the barrel, he held it facing into the light and satisfied himself that the barrel was indeed dry and free of gun oil. Borrowing a kitchen knife from the counter top, he clipped off the end of the tube of liquid nails. A caulk like substance, it was guaranteed to dry in 45 minutes or less. Matt figured he had two hours, so that was fine. He crammed the end of the tube well up into the barrel and squeezed it until over half of the tube was in the gun barrel. Removing the tube, he looked into the barrel and was pleased that the substance was over an inch into the barrel from the loading breach and clearly invisible unless you opened the gun and stared up into it. From the other end, it was over 15 inches deep in the barrel. Again, nearly invisible unless you were looking for it.

Stony cleans the gun, oils it and loads it, all the night before, so that he can use every minute of daylight when he gets home. By the time he realizes something is wrong, he'll already be fucked.

Reaching back to the rear of the pile, Matt took the box of express magnums and opened them. There were four shells missing, probably from a former hunt.

Matt reached in and removed the one remaining top row shell, and two more rows of shells. He put the three shells he had removed from the gun into the box, and then covered them with all but the last three shells, which he then inserted into the gun, one in the chamber and two in reserve. It was impossible to look at the gun and tell that the low power shells had been switched for the magnums.

It probably won't make any difference anyway, but why take chances? After all, nobody deserves the best more than Officer Stony.

Wiping the barrel down with one of Stony's cleaning rags, Matt made sure that all smudges were removed and the gun looked as well maintained as before he'd taken it down.

Satisfied, he placed the gun back in the rack and cleaned up his mess, wiping the table top down and replacing the magnum box back were it belonged. Finally, he put the knife back where it came from and stuffed the dirty paper towels down in the garbage can under other trash.

Leaving no noticeable trace of himself, he shut the front door and got back into the Dodge. In less than a minute he had driven back to the old abandoned area where he parked his car and walked back to the edge of the woods to await Stony's return. He had thought about taking a beer from Stony's fridge, poetic justice and all that, but he decided against it. He was taking no chances, at least none more than he deemed necessary. He sat down on the thick pine straw with his back to a tree and lifted his binoculars. When he had adjusted the lenses to where he could see the space between the bird dog's eyes, he set the binoculars down and began his wait.

Over two hours later, Stony finally came home.

Watching the guard pull into his driveway, Matt ignored the stiffness of the long sitting wait and sat up straighter, placing the binoculars to his face while resting his elbows on his knees. As he watched, Story jumped out of his car and headed to the back door, pulling off his shirt as he went. Matt held his breath as he watched Stony go into the trailer, and almost turned red in the face before he realized what he was doing.

Get a grip you idiot. Passing out from holding your breath will not get anything done any faster.

Forcing himself to relax, he had only a few minutes to wait before Stony emerged with the shotgun in one hand, a beer in the other and two boxes of shells under his left arm. Just as Matt had seen him do before, Stony walked over to the part of the fence where his trap contraption was located and set everything down while he adjusted and loaded the skeet machine.

Apparently satisfied with his efforts, he took a long pull on his beer and stepped back a few feet. Placing the beer on the fence post, he picked up the shotgun and deliberately placed his right foot to the right and brought the shotgun into a waist high position. As soon as he stepped down on the lever, the machine threw two clay discs straight up in an arching pattern and Stony, in a very practiced and smooth move, swung the shotgun up, sighted and then pulled the trigger.

Even from this distance, the noise almost deafened Matt as the entire gun barrel exploded about two inches from the stock. The blast turned the barrel into fine metal shrapnel, spraying everything within a few feet with its deadly armament.

Matt watched in awe as Stony's face and stomach instantly turned into a bloody mess of pulp and bone. Matt had once heard a bobcat scream in pain when it was caught in a bear trap with its intestines being ripped out and its foot nearly severed. That was the only familiar thing he could recount to describe the sounds now erupting from what was left of Stony's mouth.

Watching with grim fascination, Matt focused on Stony's face, absolutely sure that Stony's bad boy days were over. His face could never be repaired. His eyes were gone and only blackened holes remained where they had once looked out at inmates with hate and abuse. His mouth would never tell lies or order inmates to satisfy his perverted humor. This was one sadist who would never again hurt anyone. He would live, but he would never again have a life.

Standing up to leave, Matt felt how rubbery his own legs were and wondered if it was just from sitting so long, or if the savagery of what he had done had affected him. He hoped not: he was only halfway finished.

* * * *

On the way back to Ocala, Matt passed over the Lake Panasoffkee Bridge. There was no traffic behind him and it only took a second to throw the half tube of liquid nails over the railing. He also finally acknowledged to himself that it wasn't just the heat that had caused him to sweat during his last two missions: even though the temperature was now chilly, he was still soaked.

I know that what I am doing is justified. I know that even though my main motivation is revenge, I am truly helping to prevent cruelty to others who cannot help themselves. What I don't know, and am afraid to ask is, am I condemning my very soul to Hell? Or, if there really is no Hell, am I ruining my chances of regaining my life and building on my ever deepening relationship with my wife and the girls? What am I becoming? What have I become?

After about ten minutes of soul searching, Matt realized he was almost dry and his burning belly had settled instead into another peaceful part of his body. The fire was out and he was satisfied. Satisfaction breeds satisfaction and soon the doubtful misgivings were put to rest and he was keeping time to the music. No longer doubtful, his mind turned to the justice of his actions, and soon, he was sure that he was in the right. More than that, he convinced himself he was a leader of a heroic moment in time. He'd claimed a small place in history where one man made a difference because he was willing to take the chance to do what he had vowed to do. He would not fail. He would keep his promise, if not for himself, for the others he could help.

His minimal psychiatric training from medical school would have alerted him to the fact that he was merely justifying his own self doubts by making something otherwise unconscionable into a palatable situation; but he was not interested in psychiatry—only in getting through the next three victims. So he drove back to Ocala in very high, albeit falsely high, spirits.

The car swap in Ocala was a piece of cake, with Matt parking less than a few spaces away from his own car and dropping the keys on the floorboard and walking only about thirty feet. As he pulled off his gloves he thought how easily he had become a successful criminal. Well, he had been to the best schools of all: the State Penal System.

Dropping his gloves in a nearby dumpster, he got in his car and drove off. The music was country western, something he only listened to while on the road, and he was not in the mood for the sad whiny song that was playing. Flipping the stations he came to an upbeat boy band song that reminded him a little of the Beatles and he began to keep time with the music. As his mood lightened, he thought of Marilyn.

I never knew how much I really loved you. I do know now. More than I have ever loved anyone else. More than I could ever love anyone else. In some strange way, this is for us. I hope you would understand, but I will make sure that you never have to.

As he drove homeward, tapping to the tune of the music, he knew that his body would not fail him tonight. He was already rising to the occasion.

CHAPTER ELEVEN

OK, Major Kelly. Time to pay up for all your sins. Most people get to wait for God to demand retribution. You don't. You blew it; you hurt me, hurt my friends, and tried to get others to do your dirty work. Now, it's time! There is a time for all things and this is your time and I am the Grim Reaper.

Unconsciously, Matt was paraphrasing from the Bible.

A time to live,
A time to die,
A time to play,
And a time to pay.
Paybacks are hell, Major. Your hell, my creation. I'm on my way.

Maybe it was because he really hadn't figured out what he would do to the Major, or maybe it was an effort to keep his hate fired up enough to carry out this part of his mission; he didn't consciously know. His mind worked furiously at times, and then lapsing into poetic mantras at others.

Realizing that he had to keep moving faster in order to complete the last half of his sworn duty, Matt worked diligently to remind himself of how much she had hurt him and how much he hated her. Although the pangs of hate and fires of vengeance still burned in his stomach, they had been dampened and were far less intense than when he had taken his oath of vengeance. To enhance his memories of the months of servitude caused by the Major, the prisoners who suffered because of her greed and how she had tried to have him sent back to the main unit for a lengthier sentence or even worse, death by Stony, he took over washing the dishes and pots and pans by hand as Marilyn and the girls watched dumbfounded.

Acknowledging to himself that Marilyn and the girls were more responsible for his departure from the dedication to his oath than was the dwindling internal furnace, he began to do mental exercises when he was away from them. Unable to bring himself to reduce the loving feelings that had built up so strongly between he and his family, he developed a game of mental gymnastics that involved deliberately shutting them out of his mind when he walked out the door each morning. For the rest of the day, anytime he thought of them, he would perform mental exorcisms until he lost their images, and then replace them with the hatefully smiling face of Major Kelly.

In his car at a red light or stop sign, he would conjure up the short, curly hair; the flat nose and oversized lips that barely parted to reveal a thin tight smile over bright white teeth. Almost wincing, he stared into her eyes: coal black pupils surrounded by snow white blankets that looked at him as if he were a piece of trash waiting to be thrown in the garbage.

When he focused strongly and visualized her as if she were real, the sweat popped out on his forehead and bile rose in his throat. Pulse quickening and stomach burning with the familiar fire, he knew he could follow through with his mission. It was this image and these feelings that filled his mind as he left Tampa Thursday afternoon on his way to Bushnell, a small town a few miles from Sumter Prison, and the home of Major Beulah Kelly, his next victim.

After picking up a street map from a local Texaco, Matt proceeded to track down the Major's home. What he found was a small, stucco home in an older subdivision of Bushnell. Any special name or designation for the area had long since disappeared, but it was a well kept, neat little community with most homes sporting carports instead of garages. The Major's house was no exception. A small home, maybe 1,700 or 1,800 square feet, it sported a well-manicured front yard, faux brick about half way up the front wall and one large oak tree right in the middle of the lawn. Neatly trimmed azalea bushes surrounded the tree and lined the driveway, the carport, the house and the roadway, and also acted as a dividing line between her and her neighbor.

Not really what I expected; but then, they can't all be trailer aficionados. Apparently her off duty personality is far nicer than when she's in uniform and in charge. Let's see what I can come up with: something truly inspirational for this very special person.

As Matt he drove past Major Kelly's corner lot, he saw that the house diagonally across from her had a "For Sale" sign in the front yard. Looking closely, he noticed that the yard had not been mowed in several weeks and the house appeared to have been vacant for quite some time. The carport was partially enclosed with a brick wall on the outside facing the road that ran alongside the house. The bricks were spaced so that squares of light showed through, and, although the open spaces had been almost completely filled in by honeysuckle vines, it afforded a pretty good spot from which Matt could watch the Major's house undetected.

He backed up the driveway and into the carport to not expose his license tag, then looked around. He was sure that no one had noticed him. If anyone questioned him, he would merely express interest in the home as an investment. That would explain why a man in a brand new Lincoln would be in this neighborhood. The next time he came, it would be in a Rent-a -Wreck vehicle, not the Continental.

Shaking his head to stay awake, three hours later Matt spotted the Major pulling into her driveway at 5:15 PM. He had begun to get nervous as several other cars had passed his parking space on their way home from work.

Damn, I don't remember her leaving this late. She was always out of the camp before four. Shit, this may really complicate matters.

Relief flooded him when she got out of her car and moved to the back door and removed two bags of groceries, leaving the car door open to return for more.

Well, well, it looks as if Thursday is shopping day for the Major. Apparently, she likes to shop in her uniform. Probably gives her a sense of superiority.

When she went back into her house with her second load of groceries, he pulled out of his hiding place and drove off, sure that she had never suspected that she was being watched. He still had no plan, but he was mulling over all that he witnessed and storing it for future use. On the good side, he had seen no one until after 4:45 PM. That gave him a lot of time to go about whatever his business was, unobserved. The downside, of course, was that it would do him no good to have all that time if she were not there. He had never missed watching his victims pay, and he wouldn't start now.

He was still thinking along those lines as he drove all the way back to Tampa.

* * * *

Friday morning, Matt parked his car in one of the extreme remote parking lots close to the Tampa airport. It was an automated lot that dispensed tickets upon arrival and charged fees for two hours, and a daily rate for anything over that. Five dollars a day placed in the slot provided a ticket to get you out without having to see a cashier.

From Tampa, he flew to Orlando, caught the van to Rent-a-Wreck and rented a Ford Taurus for a week. Once again he paid cash and used his phony ID card to secure the rental. Recognizing that this would be his most difficult mission, he had blocked out a week full of false meetings and surgical observations to give himself time to come up with and activate a plan. He still had no idea of what was really an appropriate sentence, nor what he would do.

By the time he reached Bushnell, it was already after three Friday afternoon. As he pulled into the carport, he noticed that the neighborhood was once again very quiet. The shock was that he was only there for 15 minutes before he saw the Major's car pull up.

Damn, what kind of schedule does this woman keep?

Matt watched as she entered her home and appeared to lock the door behind her. An hour later, he pulled out of the driveway, no more sure of what to do than when he had arrived. Even though he was keyed up, being on the *mission* as he now routinely thought of it, he was acutely frustrated.

Swapping the rental for his own car at the remote parking lot in Tampa, he knew it would be a long weekend.

Monday was equally frustrating, and by Tuesday he knew something had to change. Even Marilyn could sense the change in him, but she wisely refrained from saying anything. Once again, sex was a problem.

*Got to get a friend to prescribe some Viagra for these times when I can't perform. Marilyn is puzzled and I never **ever**, want her to blame herself! God, I love her. When this is over, all over, I'll have to do something special for her. Then something else special for her and the girls.*

It took him two hours Tuesday morning to clear his mind and get in the right mindset to continue with his mission. He decided it was time to do something, so he left early, intending to break into the Major's home to see what it could tell him.

Parking the rental in the now routine spot, he carefully looked around in preparation for his entry into the Major's home. In his pocket was a thin metal ruler, credit cards and a screwdriver. His hunch was that the lock would be an old one and either the ruler or the credit cards would work. If not, the trusty screwdriver would. His only worry about the screwdriver was that the Major always entered through the front door and would surely notice if it were scarred.

Oh well, nothing is ever perfect.

At exactly 11:30, he opened his car door and started to get out. Less than two seconds later, he froze. The Major's car was pulling into her driveway and she was not alone. As he sank back into the seat of the Taurus, Matt unconsciously wiped the sweat from his brow. His interest deepened as he saw her passenger.

I'll be damned. It's Sergeant Lacy! So this is what they were doing on their long Tuesday lunches.

Totally enraptured, he watched as they left the car and entered the house, very friendly and oblivious to the rest of the world. They obviously had no fear of getting caught.

Maybe it's silly, and maybe I am getting ahead of myself, but methinks I'm beginning to get a feel for this operation. Now, let's see what happens.

With a calmness that he did not have to work at, he sat in his car for one and a half hours as the two women did their thing, whatever that was. He remembered all the talk about the two women and how many times they had gone for lunch for two or more hours, returning with lunches to be eaten at the camp.

Finally the front door opened and both women returned to the car, driving off in an apparently very good mood.

Perfect, let's see what can be seen, not just imagined.

He cranked up the Taurus and slowly pulled out of the driveway he had hidden in and into the Major's driveway. Quickly he slipped on his gloves. Acting for all the world as if he had every right to be here, he stepped out of the car and walked up to the front door.

There was a small overhead roof cover which protected people as they opened the door, but he could see no security devices, nor had he seen the Major activate or deactivate one as he'd watched her enter and leave.

Quickly he opened the screen door and exposed the old, solid wooden door with a thirty-year-old lock. One swipe with the ruler and he was in the house; no scars or other noticeable signs of entry present.

Plush, neither masculine nor feminine but sexually neutral, with a certain flair for leather and oversized pillows, the Major's living room was spotlessly clean. Across the room, the small dining room, equally spotless, was filled with a table, chairs and china cabinet. All real wood, but not overly expensive. Walking down the hall he observed no less than twenty pictures. The most intriguing thing about the photos was that they were all of one person, the Major, and most of them were of her in various uniforms.

She really lets this Major thing go to her head. Wow! Here's one in a Girl Scout uniform. I've known women with a thing for uniforms, but I was usually in them. Not this female. She's obviously in love with herself, and likes it when she can show off in a uniform.

Proceeding to the end of the hall he noticed it had two bedrooms with one bath connecting between them. Opening the second bedroom first, Matt noticed it looked picture perfect. It was a simple but nice bedroom suite with twin beds and comforters that matched the drapes.

As he opened the master bedroom, however, he realized the key to his dilemma was now in his grasp. At the center of the room was a round, king sized waterbed surrounded with mirrors, both on the walls and on the ceiling. With dressers in the closet and storage drawers hidden in the bed siding, the only other piece of furniture in the room was a nightstand with a single, long, deep drawer.

Almost reverently he pulled the drawer open, and then he burst out laughing.

Major Kelly! You deviant bitch. All the photos, all the mirrors. You don't love any other person. You love yourself. And Sergeant Lacy helps you do it.

Feeling as giddy as a kid in a candy store with a pocket full of money, Matt looked at the various items in the drawer. There was a plethora of sexual toys, the most notable of which was a super sized, latex dildo with a large penis head on either end. It had to measure 2 inches thick and 18 inches long. It lined the back of the drawer while numerous other toys lay in front of it, including a slender vibrator about 8 inches long; a vibrating latex penis of rather large proportions, a smaller dildo, again with heads on both ends for joint usage and two other smaller vibrators whose purpose Matt was not even going to guess. All sorts of creams and ointments were lined up on the left side, along with two tubes of KY jelly.

Nothing like making sure the old engine keeps well oiled.

Very carefully pushing the drawer back so as not to disturb anything, Matt double-checked the room. The only thing amiss was the bedspread, and that had been sloppily thrown over the bed with no intent to hide the fact that it had been used. He pulled the spread back and observed the wet, oily spots at various places and figured that the Major would use the unclean bed to put her back in the mood once again that night. As he pulled the cover back, he had a flash of inspiration. Remembering the old Mission Impossible TV series, he thought, *Your mission, if you accept it, Matt, is to change this lady's sexual habits. If you can't do that, then at least you are to insure that she no longer enjoys the habits she now has. Your time in this house will temporarily expire in ten seconds. Good luck, Matthew!*

Keeping the ruler in the door as he closed it, Matt was able to pull it out and lock the front door; once again, he left no sign of his entry. He had a spring in his step as he walked to his rental car and he wasn't even sweating as he pulled away from the Major's house.

Realizing that he would not need the rental car again, he headed straight for Orlando when he left Bushnell. He would not be back here for a week, and then it would be time for another old Dodge.

As he drove, his mind regurgitated all the chemistry he learned at med school, and he developed his plans. Now all he needed was some time, some reference material and a little more inspiration. The job would also take a little more time than he had thought, but that, too, was OK.

Major Beulah Kelly gets to play one more time, then pay forever.

A time to live,
A time to die,
A time to play,
And a time to pay!

He was a happy man, having found a way to complete his mission, and a reason to feel like it was worthwhile. Even Marilyn put aside her doubts about his behavior as he made love to her that night in a very satisfying, almost electric way. Starting slowly, they climbed to a rushing crescendo, with Matt almost smugly watching Marilyn as she came in a series of strong orgasms until he could hang on no longer and joined her in a final gasp of pleasure. As they fell asleep, wrapped in each others arms and encased in the warm glow of the aftermath of their love, Matt could hear the little ditty running softly in the far recesses of his mind; *A time to play, And a time to pay.*

* * * *

The University of Florida Medical School has a very comprehensive medical and chemical library, with access to computerized research that connects this university with almost any major facility in the world. Matt spent the next three days here, doing research and establishing a formula that would provide the results he wanted.

By the second day, he was sure that what he needed was an acid. It had to have properties that would not affect plastic or rubber, and that would not be diluted by oils and lotions so as to be impervious to the play jells in the Major's toy drawer. It would have to dry and be harmless to the touch, until wet with water or body fluids, and then become activated to cause severe damage to human tissue.

Wednesday afternoon, he decided upon the formula for the acid compound he would use. The components were simple enough, and by Thursday afternoon he had everything he needed in his office. After his admins left, he mixed a half-pint of the acid in a glass jar and ran two tests. The first test involved simply dipping a round, oversized Q-Tip in the acid and removing it. Placing it in front of a fan, he watched as the liquid dried in less than ten minutes. Next, he wiped the now dry Q-tip on the end of his right pinky. It only took about sixty seconds for the burn to start less than a minute later the skin was blistering and painful. Quickly dipping his very painful finger into his prepared solution, he extinguished the pain and rubbed Neosporin onto the sore before placing a small Band-Aid over the finger.

After carefully sealing the acid in the jar, he headed for home, stopping at Scotty's on the way. The small brush he needed was only $1.99. He placed both the brush and the acid on a shelf in his special safe in the garage when he got home. He was now ready for next Tuesday.

A time to live,
A time to die,
A time to play,

And a time to pay!

The weekend was a complete family weekend with Matt taking his wife and daughters to Bush Gardens on Saturday and then springing for pizza and a movie for the two youngest, while the older two went on their own dates. Marilyn and he went to Bern's Steak House and shared a bottle of Perrier Jouet Champagne followed by a fantastic cut of Chateaubriand and a bottle of Louis Martini Cabernet Sauvignon. It was a beautiful evening, and they were both a little lightheaded when they returned home.

In their room, Marilyn had planned to put on her sexiest nighty, but she never got that far. As they kissed, the entire world became a distant planet and the only real life was the two of them, fusing into one. Controlled but passionate, they undressed each other slowly, milking every erotic sensation as each piece of clothing fell from their bodies. Hunger filled both of them so completely that each touch was as though electricity flew from their fingertips.

As he traced her body with his mouth, kissing her breasts and nuzzling his way to her navel, she whimpered, shaking uncontrollably as the goose bumps jumped up the instant his tongue touched a new part of her body. Finally, neither of them could wait any longer and they fell back on the bed as she pulled him into her, wrapping her legs around him and accepting him with a fervor they had never experienced before. They rode the wild winds of their combined passion until each of them was about to explode, trying desperately to hang on as far into the sea of sensuality as possible, until finally bursting in a burst of sheer ecstasy that left them both panting and heaving; breaths coming out as quick sobs while they floated back to earth.

Afterward, as they lay contentedly in each other's arms, she with her face against his chest and he with his nose pressed into her soft hair, he drifted slowly off to sleep knowing he was right with the world. *A time to play, And a time to pay.*

Sunday morning they woke up, still wrapped in each other's arms. They made love, again before getting out of bed. This time was slow and loving, without the intensity of the night before. When they had finished and cleaned up, they lay back in bed and talked. They talked about the future, the girls, his job and its potential and, most of all, they talked about how much they had come to mean to each other.

Later they ate a quick breakfast and went to church, together as a family, and then out to lunch at Mel's Diner, the girls' favorite restaurant. After a variety of hot dogs and french fries, with beer for Matt and Marilyn, they returned home and spent the rest of the day in a lazy, family kind of way, popping popcorn and playing Monopoly, Parcheesi, and cards until they finally drifted off to their own devises.

The last thing Matt thought as he fell asleep Sunday night was:

I can't remember a better weekend in all my life.

* * * *

Tuesday morning, Matt loaded his tools, two large pieces of plastic coated cloth (3' x 3' unfolded, but only a minor pocketful when folded) and his jar of acid. After a quick stop at the office, he drove into Ocala. Instead of the hospital parking lots, he decided to head for the large 24 hour Publix on Silver Springs Boulevard. It was shortly after nine in the morning, but even now there were a large number of cars in the lot. He figured that at this hour, most of the cars on the outside parameter would belong to employees and he could borrow one if he could find the one he wanted and no one would notice before he returned it.

He spotted exactly what he was looking for and he parked three rows over, a mere 50 yards away. Satisfied that no one was paying any attention to him, he quickly donned his gloves and made sure his tools and acid were in his jacket pockets and the ruler in the lining. It was the same reversible jacket he had worn before, and it served him well again. In less than 30 seconds he was inside the older Plymouth and in a few more seconds, he was pulling out of the lot and headed back to Bushnell.

Without hesitation, he drove straight up the Major's driveway and got out of the Plymouth as if he was an invited guest.

Just as before, the ruler quickly opened the ancient lock and he was inside, headed to the master bedroom. This time, the bed was neatly made and the room appeared spotless.

The mighty major and her playmate haven't had a chance to muss things up, yet. Let's see if I can't give them some new covers for their toys.

As he pulled out the two sheets of plastic, his hands were steady and his mind was clear. He wasn't even sweating, but rather, he was as cool as the proverbial cucumber. It actually felt good to be there, good to be getting two-thirds through with his mission. Really good to be evening out the score with the major.

Placing the sheets of plastic one on top of the other, he covered the nightstand from end to end. Then he placed the jar of acid and the small paintbrush on one end, carefully opening the acid and dropping the lid alongside the jar. Opening the drawer fully, Matt took the first vibrator out and carefully painted it with the acid, setting it down on the plastic in the same position as it occupied in the drawer beneath it. Even before he had finished with the second sex toy, the first had dried; he began a rotation, putting one toy back and pulling the other out, always being careful to position each one in the same place each time. The last one he painted was the oversized double dildo in the back of the drawer, and it took almost as much acid as the others combined.

Shaking his head in amazement, he placed the oversized toy in the back of the drawer and studied the whole arrangement to ensure that it was exactly as it had appeared before. Satisfied that everything was in order, he shut the drawer, placed the cap on the jar and tightened it securely. Now, he had on a pair of gloves that had acid on them from handling the sex toys, so he folded up the plastic, placing the brush inside the folds and then taking off his gloves and replacing them with another, clean pair. He then wrapped the whole small bundle tightly and placed everything in a small plastic grocery bag and dropped it into his pocket. After double-checking his handiwork one last time, he walked out the door, locking it as before as he headed to the Plymouth.

This time he drove the Plymouth around for about ten minutes, and then back to the carport from where he would wait and observe.

Less than ten minutes after he parked in his hidden spot, the Major drove up. Sergeant Lacy was with her and they both acted as though they couldn't wait to get inside, hurrying up the sidewalk and crowding together as they stepped inside.

Must have had a little foreplay on the way over.

They remained inside for about 20 minutes before he saw the front door fly open and a crouched over Sergeant Lacy emerged holding up a staggering Major Kelly. As they made their way to the car, he could see that the Major's pants were not belted, and the front of her crotch and upper thighs were covered in blood. She writhed in agony and whimpered like a little puppy.

Sergeant Lacy was a little better off, but blood spots were beginning to show as she shoved the Major into the back seat and jumped behind the wheel to drive to the hospital.

The door to the house was still wide open as she peeled rubber out of the driveway and Matt wondered which toy or toys had been responsible for the job. He had not expected them to hit the dildo that quickly, but obviously they both were on the receiving end of a dose of acid, so they must have skipped the vibrators all together.

Well, well, Sergeant Lacy. Should have been a little more choosy with the company you keep.

Even though he was curious, he was not stupid. He was in the clear and he intended to remain that way. He never even looked back at the open door as he drove off on his way to Ocala. The only stop he made was at the open dump site on the way out of Bushnell where he tossed the set of gloves, the acid, the plastic sheets and the brush deep back into the area soon to be covered. He waved to the crane operator on his way out, sure that his distance was great enough to prevent any recognition.

When you get to the hospital, they will know right away that it is acid that is eating you up, and they will dilute it soon enough to save you. Depends on how fast you get there as to whether or not you will shit in a bag for the rest of your life. One thing for sure, everyone will know what you were doing. Bet you won't feel like harassing inmates again, not now, not ever!

He was so engrossed in his vengeful thoughts that he almost missed it. After he stopped at the traffic light across from Publix, he was in the inside left turn lane, ready to pull into the parking lot when he noticed three police cars with lights flashing just off to his left, in the lot where he had borrowed the Plymouth. An elderly woman was waiving her arms, obviously distraught and crying.

Holy cow! This must be her car. Damn, damn, damn.

He could do nothing but sweat and wait for the light to change, hoping she didn't look his way. When the light changed, there was no one behind him so he sat out the left turn signal and waited for the through traffic to pass him so he could blend in and move away quietly. His hands were soaked inside the gloves, and his eyes were stinging from the salt dripping off of his sweaty brow. The longer he had to wait, the more his bowels screamed for relief. His guts were like jelly and he was about to pee his pants.

Dear God. Not now. It can't end this way. I won't let it. I'm not going back. Not now, not ever!

Getting a grip on his emotions, he sat and looked straight ahead as he waited to go forward. Then, just as he thought he had made it, out of the corner of his eye he saw the old woman pointing at him and jumping up and down. He couldn't hear her, but he could see she was shouting and suddenly the police were jumping into their cars.

Knowing that stealth was no longer an option, he blasted through the light and roared down Silver Springs Boulevard as fast as the old Plymouth would go, running two stop lights and then cutting into a side road across the street, on the same side of Silver Springs Boulevard as Publix, but several blocks away. He had a full minute's head start and he was sure that no one knew which side road he had turned into. His mind racing furiously, he had only two or three minutes, at best, before the old Plymouth was spotted.

Two blocks off the main road he spun the wheel hard left and headed back toward Publix. His heart was beating so hard he thought it might jump right out of his chest, but his thoughts remained focused.

All right, I've got a few seconds to hide this car and get to walking. Come on, Matt, you can do it. Look, look, something is here, just find it!

The neighborhood was an older one that had once been a bright, middle class area but had long since run down and was no longer well kept. He was going slowly, looking hard for somewhere to hide the car when he spotted two For Sale signs on front lawns, just ahead on his right. The first house, seriously overgrown and with no fencing, offered no concealment possibilities. The second one, however, had a privacy fence around the back yard and right now it was the only game in town.

Without hesitation, Matt swung the Plymouth into the driveway. Veering to the left, he crashed through the fence alongside the garage, intending to hide the car behind the house. He figured that the fence down on a deserted house would not attract too much attention, at least not real soon.

What he did not figure into the equation was the pool, which only became visible when he crashed through the fence. Once again, he let his instincts take over and he instantly bailed out of the car, rolling with the flow of movement as he hit the ground and stopping just short of the tiled pool walkway. The Plymouth did not stop. With a tremendous splash, it plunged into the pool, its momentum carrying it into the other side where it cracked the wall as it stopped and gradually sunk. Although it seemed like a lifetime, the entire crash, bailout and sinking had taken less than 15 seconds. Even the steam had already dissipated and the car was securely out of sight.

Rolling to his feet, Matt immediately stripped off his jacket and used it to wipe off the ruler and the screwdriver so that no fingerprints were left. He then took off the gloves and rolled the entire bundle tightly, tossing jacket and all into the next lot alongside the fence. It was overgrown and hidden, and by the time anyone came up with any connection to the auto, he would either be in jail or long gone. He was opting for long gone.

Rolling up the sleeves of his plaid shirt, he felt the cool air on his now sweat-soaked body.

Ignoring the minor discomfort, he looked both ways as he came to the front of the house and saw no traffic, most importantly, no cop cars. He could clearly hear the sirens, though, as he fast walked across the street and turned down a trash pick up alley and came out one block over.

Just as he got to the new block and turned right, headed back to Publix, he heard the siren of a police car as it flew down the street he had just left. It did not stop, so he assumed they were still looking for the Plymouth, not a man on foot.

The longest distance he ever walked in his entire life came about when he reached the Publix parking lot. Although this time he was approaching from the down side of the store, he could still see the commotion going on to his left, out toward the main drag. The old lady was still there and so were two police cars. They were apparently monitoring the chase and were holding her to identify a suspect when one was caught.

He wanted to run. His stomach was in knots and his bowels were almost beyond control. He did not want to look at the crime scene. Even if they never connected him to the Major, the grand theft auto charge would come on top of his probation. At least twenty years hard time.

All right, Doc. Get a grip on yourself. You ain't caught yet and you ain't going to give yourself away. Now get on into that store!

Not looking at police cars with lights flashing in a parking lot would be unnatural, so he deliberately stared at the action out front as he made his way into the store.

Inside several people were standing at the large picture windows, watching everything. Except for a couple of curt nods, no one paid him any attention as he picked up a small shopping basket and headed to the back of the store.

He sat on the stool in the men's room for ten minutes; even though he had blown his entire system in the first two seconds after his butt hit the rim. The rest of the time was devoted to regaining his composure, and he did a remarkable job of it.

Emerging from the stall, he washed his face and hands, and, using his fingertips, he combed his hair and became just another shopper.

Leaving the restroom he spotted the little hand basket he had left on the shelf before he went in. As he collected the basket, he noticed that the deli had stacks of Cuban sandwiches piled high. Realizing that it was lunchtime, he picked up a Cuban and had them add mustard and mayo. Everything else was already on it.

He added a six-pack of Michelob Light to his basket and checked out at the front counter.

No one gave him a second glance as he carried his bag of groceries from the store to his car, and he drove off knowing that no one had paid attention to his car or tag. Obviously, why would a man in a brand new Continental steal an old Plymouth?

Just outside Ocala, two miles past State Highway 200, Matt pulled into the rest stop and parked away from the main entrance, back behind the building and near a dog walk trail in the woods. There he ate his sandwich and drank two of the beers while allowing himself the joy of feeling relief. He knew how close he had come. He could still smell the rank fear that had permeated every pore if his body when he saw the woman point at him. He knew that the small satisfaction he felt at completing his mission with the Major would never overcome the absolute terror that consumed his body when he thought he might be sent back to prison.

Now, however, was the time to heal, to enjoy his freedom and his family. He would need some time off before he continued his mission. He had earned it. Once again, he realized that he was a satisfied man.

CHAPTER TWELVE

It was two months before the fires of hatred began to burn bright again: another two months before Matt decided it was time to do something about it. Initially, he was having trouble reviving the reasons why he shared such a deep hatred with Shimdugger and Judge Dana. All the love he was experiencing with Marilyn and his family overshadowed the deep animosity he felt for these two people. His sworn mission had become a remote dream rather than a certain reality. On top of that, the close call he had in Ocala had taken much of the wind out of his sails.

He knew he had to make a final decision, and he knew it would have to be a fair one or he could not live in peace with himself, especially if the decision was to abandon his mission. First, he went to his storage files and retrieved the transcript of his sentencing hearing and the copies of his two depositions. The University of South Florida, a sprawling university, has numerous wide sidewalks, bike trails and lawns for the students and faculty to enjoy while attending school. It was to one of these lawns, a five-acre park area, that Matt brought his folding chair and his reading material. From under the large oak tree where he sat, he could look out and see the flagship clinic that had been stolen from him during the process of unjustly convicting him. It made an appropriate background for his readings. Two hours later, the decision was made and it was final. His mission must be completed.

Since Shimdugger was no longer with the State Attorney's office, Matt tracked him down through the Bar Journal, which listed him as a partner in private practice in Sarasota. Bar journals never list the member's private residences or phone numbers, so it would be up to Matt to track him down and decide where he would take him out, and what method he would use. Of all the methods he had used so far, the baseball bat had yielded the most personal gratification, and he favored it with Shimdugger.

Memorizing the information in the Bar Journal, Matt thought, *I'd bet a large piece of my retirement that your salary and partnership were aided by the publicity involved in my case. Now it's time to see if you still think it a worthwhile investment.*

On his first drive to Sarasota, Matt used his own car. He was not looking for Shimdugger, but merely wanted to scout out the office where the lawyer worked; then he would work out his game plan. This would be his toughest assignment of all, and he would not be rushed into anything of which he was not completely sure.

Once he located Shimdugger's office, he drove by, noting the settings near the courthouse, the one-way streets with short-timed parking meters and the numerous parking lots that filled every available nook and cranny in the vicinity.

Early the next morning, he drove to his office before any other employees were there, parked his car in his spot and caught a cab to the airport. He then caught a Delta flight to Atlanta where he transferred to a Conair flight to Dothan, Alabama. In Dothan, he went to the loop on the south side, which contains a series of new and used car lots that stretches for several miles. It did not take long for him to find what he was looking for. Using his phony driver's license and $2,100 cash, he bought an older, but seemingly reliable, Honda Accord.

As he drove back through Florida, he got off at the Lake City exit and went to the first combination gas station and convenience store where he purchased a screwdriver.

Armed with his new tool, he proceeded to the rear of a very crowded Cracker Barrel restaurant adjacent to an outlet mall. Cruising slowly, he passed two other Accords before he found one of the same approximate age and color as the one he was driving. It only took him a moment to stop and remove the tag.

Back on the interstate, he took the first rest stop exit and pulled to the rear where he put the stolen tag on his car.

Stolen cars are easy for the cops to keep an eye out for, once they have been reported. Stolen tags never turn up unless an accident occurs or it is used in a crime and spotted that way. Once again, a little helpful prison logic.

He was grinning as he left the rest area, almost feeling a little giddy.

Don't you just love it when a plan comes together?

He pulled into the automated remote parking lot for USF personnel a little after six that night. He had purchased two monthly spots with cash and he could transfer from one car to the other as he came and went. It was only five blocks to his office where he picked up his car to ride home in. Since professors and students worked all hours of the day and night, no one would question the cars being there several hours at a time. Matt Hightower was a tired, but happy man. He was on a mission and he would not be deterred.

* * * *

Matt was good at his work, and his primary source of business was the almost staggering number of referrals he received from his clients. It only took him a few minutes on the phone to tell if the referral was serious about buying, and it was only to those who almost bought over the phone that he now addressed his sales time. He might miss a few that way, but he did not have time to do otherwise and still continue his mission.

Damn, I'm already the number one salesman in the company. Wonder how much I could sell if I really dedicated myself to this business? Guess I'll find out after two more piles of shit hit the fan.

Since he answered to no one for his time, and since his sales were extraordinarily high, no one questioned his long absences from the office. Nor did he tell Marilyn about all of his bonuses. He had amassed a war chest of several thousand dollars cash which he kept in his office safe, and which he used to finance his mission. It seemed only fair: bonuses from healing machines to heal his wounded psyche and body. It was what it did to the other bodies, he enjoyed the most. It was time to concentrate on exactly that.

Sitting in the Honda, Matt watched as Shimdugger got into his new Mercedes and drove out of his firm's parking lot.

I wonder how much of that car my case paid for?

Even after all these years, he still felt the hair stand up on the back of his neck at the sight of his sworn enemy. His pulse was racing and in spite of himself, he felt a touch of fear grab him in his gut.

Dear God. How can any man possess such power over me? I hate him so much I can't even swallow my spit right now. And yet, he still scares the shit out of me. I could crap all over the front seat if I only relaxed for a second. No question, Shimdugger has got to pay!

Watching the car pull away, he committed the tag numbers to memory. He had no intention of following Shimdugger at this time; it was much too risky. Instead, he would track his address down through the USF computer system. Only then would he begin to track the man's movements.

He wanted no more incidents like Ocala.

The computer did its thing and he had an address.

As he cruised down the streets in the upscale subdivision where Shimdugger lived, Matt felt like the Continental would be less obvious than the Honda.

Shimdugger lived in a newly developed subdivision about halfway between Sarasota and Venice. Houses there must have started in the quarter-million-dollar range. The neighborhood was full of Volvos, Mercedes and BMWs, as well as a sprinkling of American Cadillacs and Lincolns. Only a few lesser cars were noticeable, and those were probably the kids' cars.

It was also obvious that many of these families had young children, and Shimdugger was no exception. It was on Matt's second pass through the neighborhood that he spotted the Mercedes station wagon pulling up in the driveway. Easing over to the opposite curb so as not to attract attention, he watched as an attractive woman with medium length blonde hair, a pretty face and a full figure, which she wore clothes to accentuate, got out of the car and herded three stepping-stone children up to the front door of the house. The youngest child appeared to be about four, and the oldest, no more than ten. All boys.

For a moment, he almost lost his resolve. Then, to his dismay the woman broke the idyllic scene by yelling at the oldest child, "If you don't get your fucking ass in that door, I'm gonna let your daddy bust it for you when he gets home!"

Obviously, our Mr. Shimdugger has met the woman who appeals to his sensibilities.

While pulling away from the curb and slowly making his way out of the neighborhood, Matt recognized just how hard this was going to be. At least he thought he did.

* * * *

Two weeks later, Matt was still unaware of how to complete his *mission*. Shimdugger kept no schedule that allowed a predictable interception. The only thing close was that on Fridays, he appeared to head home shortly after five. That put him getting home at the same time as most of his neighbors in a highly congested area full of children as well as adults. Not a good setting for a baseball bat beating.

Matt was determined that the bat was his weapon of choice, and he would do almost anything to see Shimdugger's face as he laid into him with it. But he still had no way of pulling it off and not getting caught.

Worried about spending too much time going through the neighborhood or following Shimdugger, Matt took two weeks off and thought the problem over.

It was as if the devil himself had heard his prayers and answered them. Matt had forgotten his birthday and Marilyn and the girls had surprised him. He was home at about 7:00 PM when the doorbell rang and no one wanted to answer it.

He got up from his easy chair and when he opened the door, a lady with a bunch of balloons sang a little ditty and handed him the balloons and a gift, with a card signed by Marilyn and the girls. At first stunned, he then became extremely happy, first for the birthday surprise, and then later for the phenomenal idea. His family, not aware of his vengeful dilemma, attributed all of his happiness to their surprise, and the evening was a huge success. It was also the first time in two weeks that he had sex with his wife.

Matt loved Marilyn almost more than life itself. But he had a mission, and when he was actively engaged in his mission, it was almost impossible for him to relax or to enjoy himself. All of his physical signs of enjoyment were external during these times, with no real joy able to penetrate the depths of his anger and vengeance. It was the only way he could keep his mission paramount.

He had gone to a friend to get a prescription for Viagra, and in the end, had alluded to some nocturnal delights other than Marilyn as the reason behind the request. Laughingly, his friend had agreed, joking about the real money Matt must be making now that he no longer had to carry medical malpractice insurance and how that would allow him to keep a mistress on the side. Matt left, feeling dirty and sullied, almost as if he had deliberately denigrated Marilyn.

Hell, I'm doing it for her. I don't want her to get caught up in this mess.

Then, *Bullshit. You sorry asshole! Don't blame her for your not being able to get a hard on. She loves you far more than you're worth and don't you forget it. The blame is on you and your mission and nothing else. Get it done. Get it over. Then you can get on with your life and stop blaming others for your wimpish misgivings.*

He had yet to use the Viagra, feeling as if it would somehow be an excuse from which he could never recover. During his mission, he needed the pain of doing without almost as much as he needed the fires of hate churning in his gut. All too frequently, both of those desires were at low ebb.

The night of his birthday, long after he and Marilyn made love and she fell asleep, it finally came to him. Not surprisingly, it came from a conversation he had back in Sumter, with an inmate who had once been a loan shark enforcer.

The following Monday he was on a plane for New York.

* * * *

When he pulled this off, law enforcement would cover every lead possible, so Matt took no chances with buying what he needed from anywhere local, not even as close as Orlando. No, this had to come from either New York or California, the states known for anonymity. New York was an easy up and back in one day with plenty of time for shopping, so, New York was the choice. At 10:30 in the morning, he was standing in a phone booth along the wall just inside the Delta terminal.

Looking up the address of the three largest costume sales stores in Manhattan, he took a cab to a hotel two blocks from the first one and walked to the store. Clown suits were apparently very popular, and he found exactly what he wanted in minutes.

After paying for his purchase, he went on to the second store in the same fashion as the first, and quickly found the facemask he wanted to accompany the suit. The third and last store had the largest selection of oversized shoes, and he was very selective of the shoes he wanted. They had to accommodate his normal sized shoes and be removable with ease. He didn't intend to be tangled up in a pair of shoes when the time came to escape.

After finding what he was looking for, he went into one of the numerous discount stores on 42nd Street and purchased a nylon carry-on bag large enough to hold his purchases. On his return flight, he looked just like any other businessman returning home from an overnight meeting. The only things he hadn't bought that he would need were the balloons and a small gas container to blow them up with. The cylinder might have caused concern and focused attention on him, so he waited for them.

The next day he found that Spencer's, in the University Square Mall, carried both the balloons and the gas cylinders. Still leery of buying anything local, he drove to Orlando and found a Spencer's in the mall on Orange Blossom Trail where he made his purchases. Everything he bought, he packed away in the gun safe in his garage, out of sight and ready for immediate usage. It was Wednesday; he did not expect to use them until Friday.

Thursday was a regular workday, with him actually making two sales, one of each machine. Banner days in sales were anything but uncommon for Matt, but two in one day without even making the appointments in advance was something unique.

It must be a sign. I'm going to make tonight a special evening for myself and Marilyn. Tomorrow will make this mission almost complete and she deserves anything I can give her, especially myself.

Having spent the last few weeks working himself up to the task at hand, he had neglected Marilyn more than he intended. He knew she deserved better, and he resolved to make this a night she would remember fondly.

It was an unmitigated disaster.

Stopping first to buy flowers and a special wine, he then stopped by the meat market in Whaley's, an upscale store in the better part of South Tampa. After purchasing two nice Porterhouse steaks, prime Black Angus of course, and some special dinner rolls, he headed home. He had already arranged for his oldest daughter to take all the girls out to supper and a movie, using his new car, and they were excited and eager to comply.

After the girls left, he placed two large baking potatoes in the oven and lit the charcoal grill; he opened the wine to let it breathe and poured them both a drink, her favorite, Crown Royal over ice with Maraschino cherry juice and ginger ale. Moving into the master bedroom, he slipped into his best silk robe and slippers and she followed suit, putting on his favorite silk top and shorts with a lacy thin mesh robe as an inviting cover. In the bathroom, he secretly popped a Viagra and followed it with a glass of water. He was taking no chances. When he opened the bathroom door, she was standing, slightly bent over the bed with a full profile of her attractive figure achingly visible against the bed stand light.

God, she's lost 20 pounds these last few months. She really is beautiful, and I really do love her.

When the potatoes had less than 15 minutes, he stirred the coals and placed the steaks on the grill. The steaks were thick, but they both liked them rare, so five minutes on each side would do the job. Marilyn melted into his arms and buried her head in his chest while he waited for the steaks to cook. So engrossed in the moment was he that he almost forgot the steaks. It was obvious that she felt the same, and for a fleeting moment, he almost abandoned the food for the bedroom.

Common sense overtook each of them, and they moved into the dining room and enjoyed a candlelight dinner in their nightclothes. They made it about half way through the steaks and then jointly stood up and came together, wine glasses in hand and held each other close. As they gazed into each others eyes, Marilyn took her hand and reached down to hold him. He was already hard as a rock and she smiled. She moved her hand and grabbed his, placing it on her left breast, and gently pushed her pelvis up against his straining member.

"A toast, Matt, my darling; to us, to tonight, and to tomorrow and all the days hereafter."

So saying, she lifted her glass to his and waited expectantly.

Following her cue, he replied:

"A toast back to you, my darling; for tonight, tomorrow..."

Tomorrow! My God, Tomorrow!

Right in the middle of his toast the thoughts of what he had planned for tomorrow hit him like a ton of bricks. His member shrank and became as limp as a wet dishrag and the look on his face was so stricken that Marilyn was afraid he had had a heart attack.

"Matt, Matt! Speak to me darling! Are you OK? Talk to me baby. What's wrong? Oh God, what's happening?"

Sweat had already popped up heavily on his brow and upper lip, and he felt sick to his stomach. He knew he had to supply some sort of explanation, but he couldn't stop the intense feeling of disaster that seared his guts like a hot iron poker, threatening to explode at both ends. He was clammy all over and he knew that he was pale and looked like shit.

Swallowing the acidic bile that threatened to spew out of his mouth, he told her, "I think I'm all right, but I'm going to be sick. Must have been something wrong with the meat."

Almost flying into their master bathroom, he barely made it before he began heaving. The revulsion and fear in his belly was so strong that he continued with the dry heaves long after his stomach had emptied its contents into the porcelain bowl. After finally holding back the heaves long enough to rinse his mouth out with mouthwash, it was a very shaken and sickly Matt that emerged from the bathroom and allowed his wife to guide him to bed.

He assured her that he would be OK, and she assured him that she was right here to help him any way she could. She finally fell asleep in his arms, and, as her breathing became steady, he lay there thinking. At first, he was scared that he had lost his nerve, then glad, if that meant it was over. Then, after a little while, the hatred that had abandoned him for so long returned a hundred-fold.

If anything that has to do with that son of a bitch can cause this much pain for me and my wife then it's my sworn duty and obligation to end it, once and for all. Tomorrow, you sorry bastard. Tomorrow. After tomorrow, you will never put me or anyone else through this much pain. Never.

It was 3:00 AM before he finally fell off into a fitful sleep, all the while dreaming of finishing his mission against Shimdugger with a final, ruthless action.

* * * *

Parking at Sarasota Memorial Hospital was spread out into at least six different lots, as well as numerous side areas that even included using the back street medians as parking spaces. One thing that he looked for though, was the area that was reserved for employees. It was 2:30, and shift changes were just beginning to take place as he waited and watched for just the right car and driver.

He thought back to leaving home that morning. He had reassured Marilyn that he was OK, and that if anything came up to the contrary, he would let her know. Unbeknown to her, he had also taken two Lomotil and a double capful of Pepto-Bismol; he could not afford another incidence like last night. He did not intend to shit all over himself or puke his guts out when he had to do his thing. He had gathered his bat, costume and accessories, and the steel ruler and put them in the trunk of the Continental. Fifteen minutes later, he transferred them into the trunk of the Honda and set out for Sarasota and his mission.

Finally, he spotted the Dodge that fit his needs, pulling up into the employee parking lot and stopping in an open area near the rear entrance to the Hospital. It wasn't the best parking location to steal from, but it would do. As he pulled out from his spot, he drove away and rode across the causeway into Ana Maria Island, a former fishing village turned major tourist area and home to some of the most exclusive residences in the Sarasota locale. With no interest in the area itself, he drove to kill time without attracting attention. He didn't come back to the parking lot until after 3:45, when the shift changes had ended and the lot was free of moving traffic, human and auto.

The Dodge was still parked and so he drove to a remote automated parking lot three blocks away and left his Honda in a covered area, one level up. After walking back to the hospital, he took less than 30 seconds to get in the Dodge and only a few more to start it and drive away. No one noticed as he drove off and headed for the Honda. When he had left the Honda, there was an open space next to it; however, in his short absence it had become occupied and he hesitated when he got there, making sure no one was on the floor to question his next actions.

Once he was sure he was alone on the upper level, he pulled the Dodge behind the Honda, in a catty corner, trunk to passenger door arrangement. Rapidly, he opened the trunk of the Honda and transferred the clown suit and all accessories, including the bat, to the passenger side of the Dodge and closed the trunk and door. As he walked around the Dodge, he let his gaze sweep the parking area to insure no one had seen the transfer. Satisfied that he was alone and unseen, he checked the gas in the Dodge.

Half a tank. Plenty enough to do what I need you to do, old-timer. Nothing fancy, just a few miles, a couple stops and then I'll take you back to your mistress.

Quickly slipping into the clown suit, he pulled the front zipper up to about the halfway point, just above the navel. Rolling the top half down, he shoved the remainder behind his back, with the arms lying to his sides. No one who looked into his car would be able to see the clown suit, only a casually dressed man who was on his way somewhere.

As he moved closer to his target, his body began to betray him once more, with sweat and clamminess taking over beneath his clothes. Briefly his mind began to flirt with the pictures of Marilyn as she looked last night, just before his repulsive reaction.

No, damnit. Get hold of yourself. There is nothing you can do to change last night. But you can stop it from ever happening again. Do your job. Complete your mission and go home. Make love to your wife. Be a man.

With the cool breeze of the moving vehicle blowing on his face and his mind back on track, his body began to dry up and the clamminess fell off to a minimum. He was ready to complete his mission and, as he pulled in to his parking space where he could observe Shimdugger's office parking lot, he began to carry out the last details of his plan.

The gas cylinder felt cool to the touch as he set it beside himself and unpacked the rest of his bag of goodies. He'd already wiped down everything twice, except the paper bag and the bat, which he now proceeded to do. He had his rubber gloves on and fingerprints were the last thing he wanted on any of the toys.

With the fingerprints no longer an issue, he took the gas cylinder and began blowing up the balloons, tying off each one with four foot pieces of string. After securing the stem of the balloons, he placed them in the bag, upside down, and placed the bat through the handles to weigh the whole thing down and keep the balloons from floating all over the car and attracting attention. When he finished all the balloons, he had nothing to do but wait, which he did for just over an hour, until he saw Shimdugger drive out of the lot.

All right, you son of a bitch. You're my meat now.

Hands breaking back into a sweat inside his rubber gloves, Matt pulled out five car lengths and two cars behind Shimdugger. Following him only long enough to ensure that he was headed for home, Matt pulled off at a small wayside park and waited for five minutes before driving the rest of the way into Shimdugger's neighborhood.

Kids were playing half a block away from Shimdugger's residence and Matt took careful note of any activity as he drove around the block twice before driving up to Shimdugger's garage door.

Breathing deeply, he zipped the clown suit all the way up, opened the car door and put on the shoes. Then, from the seat next to him, he produced the full face mask with attached ears, bulbous nose and widened-out eyes to see better, and slipped it over his head and adjusted it to his face. Before stepping out of the car he grabbed the balloons in his left hand and the bat in the right one and stood up outside the car in plain view of God and anyone else who might be watching.

The car was still running as he walked up to the front foyer and hammered the knocker, hard. His breath was coming in deep gulps and his heart felt as though it would jump straight out of his chest. Sweat poured off his forehead behind the mask, and his armpits lathered as his antiperspirant gave up trying to stem the flow.

Seeing movement behind the eyepiece in the center of the door, his attention riveted just as the door swung open and a surprised Shimdugger stared at him with a quizzical look on his face.

"May I help you?" Shimdugger asked.

Swiftly but smoothly, Matt released the balloons from his left hand and transferred his grip to include both hands on the handle of the bat whereupon he jabbed twice with all his might straight into Shimdugger's solar plexus. It was a move he had learned while in shore patrol and witnessed first hand as Sergeant Black had used it on him at Butler; it served him well now.

Stepping through the door, Matt quickly slammed the bat into Shimdugger's face, once from a right swing and then backhand from the left side, shattering his jaw on both sides.

Some people believe that before a man is truly a man, he must give of himself, deliberately and entirely in a single emotion, so much so that he is beyond his own control and feels nothing but the moment. If that is true, then at this moment in his life, Matthew Hightower truly became a man. Grunting from the exertion and sweating profusely inside his costume, he became like a man possessed. Collar bones, elbows, knees, leg bones, ribs, hands, ankles all broke like twigs under Matt's ferocious onslaught. Twice he took deliberate aim at the genitals and one of those blows was so great that he snapped the pelvic bone underneath.

While Shimdugger's clothes and shoes may have saved some few bones, most fell with the relentless fury of Matt's induction into manhood.

So far gone that the only sounds he heard were like the roaring of a giant fire, he was barely able to discern reality when he heard a woman's voice from far away. "Honey, who's there?"

With extreme effort, he snapped back into reality and seeing Shimdugger's wife approaching, he flung the bat with all his remaining energy at the tile wall beside her, making a loud crashing noise and eliciting a yelp and a jump back from the woman.

Turning quickly, he almost fell when the oversized shoes surprised him and he tripped, luckily recovering and moving out the door. Once outside, he walked fast and deliberately to his car, sat in the front seat and slipped off the shoes, swung behind the wheel and dropped it into reverse. As if he had rehearsed it a thousand times, he drove away. It only took him three house lengths to rip off the mask and unzip the front of the clown suit.

Apparently too concerned with her husband's fate, Shimdugger's wife had never come outside to view the car, so Matt was able to proceed slowly outside the subdivision without attracting any attention. Driving straight to the roadside park he had waited in before, he stripped the lower half of the suit off and dumped everything except the gloves in the dumpster. The clown suit was covered in blood, but it was not his and he wasn't worried. According to the sign, the dumpster would be emptied Monday morning, and after shifting rubbish over it, he did not expect it to be found. All weekend long, people would be piling trash on it and the authorities would have no clue that he had left it behind.

Ten minutes later he left the car in the same spot he had first picked it up, electing to take a chance that it had not been missed by its owner, the nurse, and his hunch paid off. As he slid behind the wheel of the Honda, he knew; he had pulled it off.

Looking down at his still soaked body, he rolled down the windows and let the fresh air start to do its work. He would have to shower when he got home. If any explanation was needed, he would say that the heavy operation machine had become stuck and he had worked for an hour to free it and return it to the van. There was no reason for Marilyn to believe otherwise.

Soon, the enormity of what he had done began to sink in, and suddenly he felt like a bird on the wing. Free: free of a major part of his mission. No more state attorney. No more Shimdugger. The man had to have hundreds of enemies with violent records and Matt was not one of them. His feelings of freedom turned euphoric, and he was humming and keeping time to an Otis Redding song, *Sitting On the Dock of the Bay*, absolute tears of joy running down his cheeks.

He would need no Viagra, and no excuses. Tonight he would make it up to Marilyn for his failure last night.

Sittin' on the dock of the bay,
Watchin' Shimdugger float away,
No-oo more tears to shed,
Since I took a baseball bat to his head.

* * * *

The *St. Pete Times* had the best story on what was now being called the work of a maniac. No photos of Shimdugger had been allowed and his address was being touted as a secret location.

Too late now, the horse is already out of the barn.

Reporters noted that no description of the assailant was available as Mrs. Shimdugger had been so engrossed in caring for her husband that all she saw was a nasty clown who threw a bat at her. The police were trying to track down the bat, but it was a common variety bat with no serial numbers and was available in sports stores and K-Marts across the nation. Unless something broke, they had little hope of catching the brutal thug who perpetrated the crime. However, like the good politician he was, the sheriff swore he would leave no stone unturned. He hinted at several recent divorce cases of Shimdugger's as being fertile ground for a qualified suspect. Doctors estimated several months and surgeries, along with lots of rehab before Shimdugger might walk and use his hands. He was currently expected to eat through a straw for at least three months.

Matt smiled as he finished reading the article, and then threw it in the trash. No souvenirs.

Only one more to go, and then my mission is over.

CHAPTER THIRTEEN

Before he could continue his mission, Matt had two priorities. Initially, he wanted to get rid of the Honda; it was no longer needed and eventually it might cause someone to question him. After that, he needed to take three or four months off and be a husband and father. Even though he had successfully finished with Shimdugger, he was shaken by the intensity and complete ruthlessness he had experienced during the beating. Never in his life had he been so totally out of control; hell, he had never believed it possible to lose himself to that kind of frenzy. It was almost as if he had been demonically controlled, a puppet whose body was being worked by some evil being.

You go through life thinking you know who you are and what you are about, then something happens and you realize you don't know yourself at all. And now, I want to top that off with murder! Yes, I need a little time.

Lost in his reverie, he drove to his office.

Time is what I need. But time won't erase the fact that one person is responsible for bringing out the devil in me. One Judge who even now continues to hurt others, destroying men and their families for political gain. One person who, because of her actions and lack of conscience and morality in her job is more evil than the evil she caused to come out in me. Judge Alice Dana!

Yes, Judge, you will die; I will be your executioner.

Even though he was physically taking time off from his mission, the real test had already been taken and passed. He was committed, even to the point of violating his Hippocratic Oath and taking life instead of saving it.

* * * *

Driving the Honda to Jacksonville seemed to be the best way of disposing of it. Mayport, part of the Jacksonville area, was duty station for a large contingent of sailors. They made the used car business a major sales industry covering several miles.

Once he arrived in Mayport, Matt took a cheap screwdriver and removed the stolen plate from the Honda and threw it and the screwdriver in a dumpster.

Within two blocks he came to a car lot advertising, *We Buy and Sell Used Cars. Cash for Your Car, Credit for Ours. Pay By the Week.* Using his phony I. D. and the temporary title and sales receipt he had received in Alabama, he sold the Honda for $1,100 cash. He probably could have shopped around and gotten more for the car, but disposal was all he wanted and this was now accomplished. A cab ride to the airport and a one way ticket was enough to send him back home, totally confident that no connection with the assault could ever be made.

Before he got out of the airport, however, an incident occurred that reinforced his belief in his mission.

"Afternoon, Your Honor."

"Afternoon, Judge. Nice day isn't it."

"How's the game, Your Honor? Haven't seen you on the course lately."

Although Matt did not recognize her, the lady in the seat across from him in the terminal was obviously a Judge. Tight lipped with a pinched face and short, mousy brown hair, she could never attract favorable attention from her obviously lacking physical feminine merits. The prim, business skirt and suit jacket were masculine; the knobby knees that just barely escaped confinement from the hem of the skirt should have been encased in a pair of slacks to prevent eyesore. There was nothing attractive about this woman, nor was her demeanor in any way friendly. She acted haughty, acknowledging her greetings as her due with an almost imperceptible nod. No smile ever dared attach itself to those lips. Matt had never seen Judge Allen out of her robes, but the similarity was otherwise uncomfortably close enough for him to generalize.

What the hell is it with our society? We treat these people like gods and they treat us like dirt. When they're lawyers, everybody hates them, but put a robe on them and they are suddenly idols to be respected and worshiped. We give them job security that takes an act of God to throw them out, and they take advantage of it and rule with an iron hand, leaving justice to fend for itself. 'Judge,' I never realized how foul that word is!

Three hours later he was back in Tampa, headed for his own car. He still relived the scene in the airport. He had been forced to sit there for 45 minutes and watch as people paid homage to a totally unappreciative bitch. He had almost decided not to take as much time off from his mission as earlier planned. Disgust filled his senses and hatred began to fill his belly. The fires, at low ebb since dealing with Shimdugger, were beginning to burn again and his thoughts were getting darker.

Only one more to go, then I can spend the rest of my life with my wife, watching the girls get married and playing with the grandkids as they come along. But first, the judge must die. My oath will be avenged and my word will be followed.

* * * *

He had toyed with the idea of adding Geno to his list, but that was not possible. Geno was serving a twenty-year sentence for a loan sharking conviction he picked up after he got out of prison for the incident with Matt. With Florida's new mandatory 85% sentencing requirements, it would be a long time before Geno would be out on the street, and Matt was not about to waste any more of his life pining on revenge.

My revenge will be finalized when the Judge is dead. Then, I can get on with my life.

* * * *

The next three months were good months for Matt and his family. Jenny, who was now in Medical school at USF, announced that she was going to get married upon graduation and that filled their lives with planning and dreams for the future couple. Marilyn immediately began making lists of everything that would be required, even though the wedding was many months away. He knew that many parents liked to plan well in advance, but he was unprepared and a little envious at Marilyn's immediate and positive response.

Carol had completed her Bachelor's degree and been accepted into law school at Florida State and they all made a trip to Tallahassee to check out the area for student housing, etc. It was a fun weekend and everyone was thrilled with the rolling hills and lush landscapes of the state's capital. Matt never allowed his mind to wander into the dark areas of Florida's criminal justice system when they all visited the First District Court of Appeals, just down the street from the law school. He was enjoying quality time with his family and the rest would come later.

Even though he and Marilyn enjoyed their time as parents, watching as the girls spread their wings, he and she became closer as husband and wife, lovers and friends. Weekends were prime time for family and closer union, and church had become a regular thing. At least three nights a week, he and Marilyn spent the evenings alone, dining, talking, making future plans and making love. Everything seemed to be ideal, but Matt knew that nothing could be ideal until his mission was finalized.

Three months had now passed and the fires in his belly were growing, unbidden but hotter every day. Hatred again began to fill his thoughts, especially when he lay awake at night after Marilyn had fallen asleep in his arms following a lovemaking session.

I think I must be insane. How can I lay here, totally sated and loved, and feel such hatred come over me? What has that Judge done to me to make me lose such control of my emotions? I'm a doctor, for God's sake.

Rhetorical questions never contain unknown answers, and he knew it. The only answer to the dilemma was to finalize his mission and end the problem once and for all.

Rising slowly and quietly from the bed without disturbing Marilyn, he crept to the garage and jammed a folding chair against the door. Turning on the light, he made his way over to the gun safe and opened it, surveying the contents to insure that everything he needed was there. He took out the 22 rifle and the scope along with 500 rounds of ammo, all 22 Stinger long rifle bullets, hollow point and deadly. A shot to the head would blow a hole as big as a Cuban cigar through flesh, brain and bone and out the other side.

He added a gun cleaning set and gun oil to the weapons and placed them all in the trunk of his car, tossing a throw rug over them to exclude them from unwanted eyes.

It begins now. Soon, the Judge will die and I will be free. God help me.

* * * *

Pulling the key out from inside his top desk drawer, Matt smiled. It opened a Yale lock, owned by a friend who had 200 acres of pine forests just below Manatee County. The property was completely enclosed in a chain link fence, a massive undertaking for no real purpose other than his friend's desire for privacy. That kind of security was what Matt needed now, as he left his office and headed to the woods. As a convicted felon, possession of firearms would land him in prison automatically. However, he needed to ensure that the rifle and scope were exactly on target. This forest was the only place he knew of where he could fire 500 rounds and not fear exposure.

Chains, fences and locks! How much of my life was wasted behind fences and walls.

An eerie sense came over Matt as he locked the gate behind himself and surveyed the area. The accumulated pine straw was evidence enough that no one had driven over the roadway anytime recently. The Continental and the well-dressed man standing beside it would look strangely out of place had there been anyone there to see them; that, however, was not going to happen. The gate he had just entered was two and a half miles from any paved road and the dirt road leading to the entry dead-ended where he now stood. Getting back in the car, he drove for another ten minutes until he came to a natural opening in the woods, with a cleared out sandy area measuring about two hundred yards across. Careful not to stray off the beaten roadway and onto the fine Florida sugar sand of the clearing, Matt pulled forward alongside the clearing until he came to a fallen group of trees. Probably a hurricane or tornado had downed the trees and they gave him what he needed.

A few minutes after he had gotten out of the car, he had gathered enough limbs for his target. Loading his arms with several branches, he paced off 100 yards from the roadway and erected his structure. Then, using thumbtacks, a note pad, a silver dollar and a quarter, he took eight sheets of paper and traced first the silver dollar and then inside the circle from it, he traced the quarter; each of these eight targets he then tacked to the makeshift pine holders. Satisfied, he walked back to the car and got the rifle and scope out.

Although basic alignment had been done at the Bausch and Lomb factory, precision shooting required additional sighting with the scope secured to the gun at the approximate distance intended for use. The fitting attachments were specifically designed to fit the scope on the Ruger and the only tools he needed were the quarter and a dime. In minutes he had the weapon assembled and ready for use. Popping in the clip, he pressed the final bullet to make sure that it was fully loaded: it was firmly in place, no slack or give when pressed. All fifteen bullets were ready to fire.

Spreading the throw rug on the ground alongside the front wheel of the Continental, he placed the gun and all the cartridges on it and sat down. After assuming the traditional military seated shooting stance with his back against the car wheel and his knees bent facing up, he picked up the gun, braced it on his knees and sighted down the scope at his target. His first shot was just outside the silver dollar circle. Firing the rest of the clip, he quickly deduced that the sights were off about two inches up and to the right at 100 yards.

Adjusting the scope as per the manufactures instructions, he used three more clips before he was hitting inside the center of the quarter with every shot. He continued to shoot until he had fired 200 rounds, and then he stopped and cleaned the gun.

Following the cleaning, he shot another 300 rounds and then cleaned the gun once more. He had experienced no jamming, even when firing rapidly, a remarkable feat accomplished only because of the quality of the new gun.

He found himself stroking the gun, almost as if it were a living being. It was as if the metal and wood combined to give him a feeling of powerful, living vibrations that penetrated his senses and sent them soaring, letting him know that with this weapon, he was poised to accomplish anything and everything he needed to right the wrongs heaped upon him by Judge Dana.

Satisfied with his shooting and the reliability of his weapon, he placed the gun back in the car, walked out into the clearing, and dismantled his target. After scattering the branches around, he burned the pages of the notebook paper, watching until they were completely finished before scattering sand over the ashes. It took him about five minutes to find and bag the spent shells which he would drop off in the nearest dumpster.

That night, as he placed the gun back in the safe, he began to plot out phase two of his final mission.

* * * *

Tuesday, Matt had an appointment in Orlando and while he was there, he went to a Home Depot and purchased a quality pair of heavy duty bolt cutters and a blue vinyl tarp, both of which he placed in the built in storage compartment behind the driver's seat in the rear of his company van.

On Friday, he waited until everyone had left the office and then stripped the van of his sales inventory, leaving only the bolt cutters and tarp in the otherwise empty van. The van itself was a plain white Dodge Caravan, with no extra windows and no company markings of any kind. Early on, the company had used logos on its fleet of vans; however, the expense of the mechanical devices they sold was well known and the markings made them easy prey for specialized theft. Now, their entire fleet of vans was just like Matt's, plain white and very nearly ugly.

Having already told Marilyn that he had an early appointment the next morning in Ocala, he headed out of town to spend the night there in preparation for his alleged meeting. Before reaching Ocala, however, he pulled off at the Brooksville exit and drove up to the Holiday Inn just off the interstate. This motel, seated back from the Hwy. 50 and I-75 intersection, was adjacent to the entrance of the Crooms State Park, a State owned facility that catered to off road cycling of all kinds; two wheelers, three wheelers and four wheelers were given specific areas to be tested by riders with varying degrees of skill. The weekends were especially crowded, with the park filling to capacity and often lines of eager motorists waited for others to finish before they could take their turns.

Because of the popularity of Crooms, many riders came from out of town and stayed the weekend, most rooming at the Holiday Inn. This was the reason he had chosen Friday night and this motel as his first stop. Checking in, he asked for and received a room at the back on the second floor overlooking the parking lot. Again using his phony ID card and a phony license number, he paid cash for the room. In less than ten minutes he had driven to the back, gone into and inspected the room and returned to his van and headed out toward Ocala.

In Ocala, he pulled off on State Road 200 and, one block away, he entered the Hilton lobby and went up to the check in desk. After securing a room in his real name, he retired to his bed and made several phone calls and ordered up room service, all on his company American

Express card. His final call was to Marilyn, about 10:30 that night. Everything was traceable and his whereabouts verifiable.

Hanging up the phone with Marilyn, he went to his van and then drove to Brooksville. Arriving at the Holiday Inn, he first drove around the back parking lot, choosing to park his van about three spaces from a pickup with an open motorcycle trailer and three motorcycles secured on it with heavy chains through the frames and wheels. He had found the bike he came for, a Yamaha 250 that appeared to be in excellent shape. From the looks of the nearly new truck and the well-kept trailer, he figured the bike would be equally well cared for.

Locking his van, he went to his room and stripped his clothes off, falling nude onto the bed and checking his watch against his travel alarm. Setting the alarm for 2:30 AM he covered up on the fresh starchy sheets and quickly fell asleep. His last thoughts were that he was once again about to commit a real felony.

It must have been a heavy thought indeed, for when the alarm awoke him, he bolted upright in bed, covered in sweat and sitting on sheets almost pooled in wetness. He couldn't even turn off the alarm clock, instead, listening as it wound down to a final, muted dinging. Shaking his head only produced a cascade of sweat and no other relief, so he jumped in the shower and turned the water on full force and cold. The shock brought him back to life and as he dressed, he began to feel the fire overcome the fear.

I have got to get a grip on myself. I cannot afford to lose it now. Not when I have almost achieved my goals. Not when the judge is so close to paying up. Not now, not this close. Get a grip, boy, get a grip!

Head cleared and concentration back, he surveyed the parking area for ten minutes.

Absolutely nothing moved. There were still several open spaces, but quite a crowd of bikers were staying there this night.

Matt walked to his van and sat in the driver's seat for another five minutes, watching for signs that anyone had noticed him.

Feeling unobserved, he climbed into the back of the van and grabbed the bolt cutters and the tarp out of the box. Dropping the cutters on the seat, he quickly spread the tarp over the floor of the van and then picked the cutters back up and exited the van through the back doors, shutting them only slightly.

Not rushed, but very deliberately, he walked to the trailer, snapped the chains in two, and followed up by cutting the bike straps that braced the bike on the trailer with his pocket knife. The Yamaha was still standing, leaning against the other bike, which still had its supporting straps intact.

Careful not to make any more noise than necessary, Matt placed the cutters on the edge of the trailer, jumped up on the flatbed, grabbed the bike by the front forks and the rear wheel and lifted it over the one foot raised sidewall and down to the parking lot. In seconds he was alongside the bike, cutters in hand, pushing the bike to the van. A few more seconds and the bike was in the van, lying on its side on the tarp, floor fully protected and no stand up chains necessary.

Driving slowly, Matt moved to a parking spot near to the stairway to the second floor. In his room once more, he checked to make sure he had no oil stains or other tell tale signs of his activities on himself or his clothing.

Satisfied, he combed his hair and took a towel and wiped down the room anywhere he might have left fingerprints. He even wiped the key, which he left on the end table where the maid would find it.

In less than 10 minutes he was back in the van and headed to Ocala.

As he lay in the bed at the Hilton, he couldn't help thinking how good he was getting at felonious activity. He also couldn't help thinking about how much his family would be aghast at his actions. His calculating mind, the one developed through hard science courses in pre-med, realized that no matter how much you plan and how good you might be at breaking the law, something will eventually come up (like in the Publix lot in Ocala) and break you. His luck was always running out; it was just a matter of time until it happened.

But his reasoning mind never had a chance against the mind that dwelt on the pain and deprivation associated with and resultant from Judge Alice Dana. He could see her, in her robed splendor, looking at him with utter contempt as she boosted her political standing. She had condemned him to all those years in prison all because she needed a few more points in the polls. She would pay, and the only payment worthy of her deeds was death.

I condemn you to an afterlife in Hell. I will be the instrument that gets you there early, but you have devised your own eternal damnation. Damn you to Hell, anyway.

* * * *

By 9:30 Saturday morning he had caught up on his sleep and returned to Tampa.

Stopping first at Mail Boxes Etcetera with his fake mustache and clear eyeglasses, he rented a box under his phony name and ID, using the non-existent address on the ID as his home. With an established address to send notices to and give as a reference, he then went to the U-Haul

Store East on 56th Street and rented a small unit, paying quarterly and in cash. The location was perfect, about 6 miles from the area where he believed Judge Dana resided.

After purchasing a lock from the storage manager and receiving the code number for 24 hour entry through the gate, he drove back to the unit and pulled up close. The side door of the van opened about a foot from the roll up door of the unit, making visibility nearly impossible for anyone who happened to be watching as he unloaded the Yamaha. At times like this, he often wondered if the minute precautions were even necessary. Who, after all, would think to link this bike with a non-reported stolen bike 100 miles away? And who would have any idea that the theft of the Yamaha would link up with a total of six serious crimes?

Whether they could or not is not the question. I will not return to prison; therefore, all precautions are necessary no matter how trivial they might appear.

D-16, the small unit he had rented, opened to the back of the storage lot and was completely out of sight from the sides and the front of the business. Straight behind the facility was a heavy wooded area bordering the 10-foot fence that surrounded the entire lot. Except for the strip behind the very back of the facility, he was completely invisible when he visited the unit. It was ideal for his purposes.

Before leaving, he cranked the Yamaha to test it, surprised that it fired up on the second kick and immediately leveled out: almost instantly it was running smoothly and responding easily to his throttle twists. It felt so good that he toyed with the idea of taking it out for a test spin, before rejecting the idea as an unnecessary risk. Even though Florida was a *choice* state for wearing helmets, he had no intention of ever riding the bike without his full visor and helmet.

Satisfied, he turned off the bike and stood it on its stand next to the rear wall. Stepping back into the van, he folded up the blue tarp and placed it against the storage wall for future use if necessary. He thought about taking the bolt cutters home to use in his garage, however, even a remote as the chances were, it could be possible to match the cutters with the chain he had cut to steal the bike.

He dropped the cutters in the dumpster by the par three golf course a block away as he drove the van back to his office.

Over the next week, Matt bought a five gallon gas can and filled it with the right fuel mixture for the bike; stole a tag from a similar bike at a mall in Orlando; ordered a grey, long haired wig from a mail order house, paid for it with a 7-11 money order and had it sent to his Mail Box Etcetera address; and bought an assortment of makeup and beards and handled them the same way. From a Wal-Mart he picked out a cheap pair of black riding boots and similarly colored nylon gloves. His final purchase was from a thrift store in Bradenton where he bought a pair of severely worn pants for 50 cents, a shirt for a quarter and a pair of tennis shoes with holes in the sides for another 50 cents. He did wash his 'new' clothing in a laundromat before placing them in the safe.

OK, Judge, it's your turn now.

* * * *

The Hillsborough County Courthouse was a divided legal complex. Civil trials were primarily handled in the older, main Courthouse. Criminal trials were handled in the Courthouse Annex, across the street. A block long, the Annex housed the main office of the State Attorney, as well as several courtrooms both upstairs and down. Each judge was assigned his or her own courtroom and all senior judges had parking spaces behind their respective offices. Judge Alice Dana was a senior Judge and a black Buick was parked in what Matt believed was her appropriate slot. However, he could not be sure and so he waited until the next morning and drove back in his Continental. It was before eight, so he parked in an open space two blocks away, walked to a nearby coffee shop and picked up a cup of coffee.

Coffee in hand, he was about half a block away when the Judge drove up in her black Buick and parked in her spot, the same one he had believed to be hers yesterday.

Got you.

Feeling excitement surge through his veins, he concentrated on masking his emotions as he walked slowly, but purposefully down the street and past the Judge's car. The Buick was spotless and the tag was no problem to read. Matt burned the number into his memory, as if he had taken a branding iron and seared it into his brain.

Noticing how much his breathing had quickened, he was surprised to find that he was almost hyperventilating.

Good Lord, this is almost like cocaine high. Hell, I better wear rubberized under shorts when I shoot her, or at this rate, I'll stain my pants.

When he returned to his car, he waited a full five minutes to start the engine as he sat and marveling at the tremendous surge of pleasure he had experienced at the sight of the Judge and her auto. The medical side of his brain deduced killing the Judge would not trigger the fear and disgustingly manic hatred he had assumed, but instead, he would feel happiness and relief at her demise. There was no other explanation for the reactions he had just experienced.

Damn, damn,
I'll soon be a happy man.

Damn, damn,
I'll soon be a happy man.

Drumming his fingers on the steering wheel, he drove away with his new, catchy little ditty running through his brain...*Damn, damn*...

* * * *

USF was already busy at 9:30 this morning, and all parking spaces were taken except those in the far outside areas of the lots. Matt didn't really care; he relished the walk as he made his way to the library and the computer that had revealed so many secrets to him in the past. One more secret was all he needed. One address and then his mission was over. He was smiling broadly as he entered the computer room and took his seat at a keyboard.

First a frown, then a grimace replaced the smile as he searched the state licensing records for Judge Dana's address. Apparently, the Judge had used the courthouse business address as her home address for the tag on her Buick. This would complicate things, but only for a while. He would do this in small increments, never pressing his luck until he had followed her to her home. After all, he was committed.

Knowing the general area in which she lived helped a lot. With a city map, he was able to ascertain that only three roads would lead into the section of country where she lived. In newspaper interviews and political speeches, she had noted several times over the years how much she liked her little house in the country. That, plus other references, gave Matt a good sense of where to look.

He was even luckier than he'd hoped, spotting her Buick on the first morning of his surveillance as he waited in his car at a convenience store on Fowler Avenue and 56th Street.

Attempting to further hone in on his final destination, he waited at an intersection near the I-75 interchange and Fowler that evening, and was just fortunate enough to spot her car as it turned south onto what appeared to be a frontage road along side I-75.

Driving west on Fowler, he saw her car vanish around a curve about half a mile down the frontage road.

Well now, I guess its time to put the Yamaha into use. Can't have the Continental being spotted around her house while I am looking for it.

On his way home that evening, he stopped at Eckerd's and picked up a makeup mirror with battery powered lighting on top. Later that night, he went to his garage and took the makeup materials, wigs and beards, etc. and placed them in his trunk; he added to that the old clothes and some jeans, a shirt, a jacket, the tennis shoes and his riding helmet, boots and gloves.

7:30 AM, and he was the only one in the storage facility.

After emptying the trunk into his unit, he parked the Continental with the back bumper against the rear fence so that no passers-by could identify the tag. The area was so remote that he didn't think anyone would ever see the car, much less the tag, but he was still taking no unnecessary chances.

Spreading his costume equipment around, he realized that he needed a small table and chair to use when the time came. He would take care of it later on. For now, the riding clothes, boots and helmet would be all he needed.

By 7:50, he was headed down the frontage road where he had seen the Judge the night before. Cruising along at about 35 mph, he was glad of the opportunity to be in the opposing traffic lane with no one in front or behind him to urge him faster. With one eye on the oncoming traffic, he swept the driveways and side roads to his right as he looked for her car. The area had few houses visible from the road, and as the road turned away from the interstate, the left side became wooded and dense. Some of the woods were thinner, reflecting a pasture that had overgrown many years ago, with old fencing that was fallen in more places than it was up.

Most of the homes were set back 50 to 75 yards from the highway, and many were older houses from the 1950's. Even in the early morning chill, he couldn't stop the sweaty, clammy feeling in his gloves and crotch as he searched for the Buick, his only identifiable connection to the Judge. Everything had gone smoothly up to this point, but panic was just beginning to set in as he realized it could take weeks to pinpoint the Judge's residence. By then, all pretense of cover would be blown.

Son of a bitch! Where the hell is she? Don't do this to me now; I've waited too long for the Judge to get away.

If he could have wiped his face with a hankie, he would have soaked it through and through. Behind the face guard, he could only blink away the sweat and feel it stinging in his eyes. Disappointed and agitated, he knew that it was over for today. He would take the next major thoroughfare to his right and work his way back to 56th Street.

After a few twists and turns, he came out at 56th Street, on the corner where the par three golf course and driving range sat. Looking over the area carefully, he realized that this would be good cover if he had to make too many trips to the storage lot. Each time he went there, it increased the odds of being recognized, and he was well aware that when the Judge went down, a real investigation would ensue, with no holds barred.

Once he had committed the entire scene to memory, it only took him 15 minutes to get to the storage unit, slip out of his riding garments and into his normal clothes. A minute later and he was out the gate and headed to his office, disappointed but not swayed from his mission.

I have a job to do, and I will not fail.

So intent was he in his reverie, that he failed to notice the slight tremors in his hands; the Tums that he automatically popped into his mouth and the beginnings of what was now a regular routine; near migraine headaches every evening since he had started on this final leg of his mission. He hadn't been able to have sex without Viagra in over two months, and he wasn't sure how much longer he could keep Marilyn in the dark. He was doing his best to cover his emotional reactions to the challenge he faced, but the wall was wearing thin and the cracks would soon become noticeable crevices.

Dear God, I've come this far; don't let me fail in my sworn duty...Jesus, I wonder what the minister would think about someone who prayed for help to kill a Judge. Maybe I really am losing it.

Matt wasn't losing his desire to finish his mission, but prison had been such a long time ago, seeming longer every day and the fires in his belly, although still burning fiercely at times, were inconsistent. More frequent was the acid indigestion and headaches as he subconsciously fought with the idea of becoming a murderer. Cold-blooded killing was alien to everything he had ever believed, and the subconscious acknowledgement of what he was doing was taking its toll on his conscience.

Headaches, night sweats, insomnia, sexual dysfunction, nervousness and occasional hyperventilation were now constantly part of him: even with his medical training, he couldn't shake a single one of them. But human resolve is stronger than conscience, and he was committed. He would win this battle. He would try to work things out with his God later.

* * * *

A little before 5:30 that evening, dressed in his biker clothes, he was slowly riding the Yamaha back past the golf course and on the road where he had last seen the Judge. Figuring that if anyone saw him, it would appear as if he was returning from his day's work; he planned on alternating directions morning and evening until he found her. After that, he would formulate his plan.

He might have traveled the road a hundred times before he sighted the Judge, but his luck held. Rounding the curve where both sides of the road were wooded, he noticed occasional driveways and homes to his left. Some were widely cleared areas, while others were merely openings in the woods barely large enough for the houses and any outbuildings. The woods to his right were dense for about 30 to 60 feet, and then thinned out to planted pines about eight to ten years old.

Almost snatching the handlebars too fast, he swerved uncontrollably for an instant as he spotted the descending garage door of the house that suddenly appeared on his left. In just a second or two, he had recognized the back end of the Judge's Buick before it was lost behind the descending door.

Regaining full control, Matt realized he had done it. He found her.

Hot damn, I did it! Damn, damn, I'm a happy man...

So excited was he with his discovery that he didn't even work on a plan on the way back to the storage unit.

I know where she lives. I can take her out any time now. License plates be damned, I found her. The Judge is mine.

It was only after he arrived at the storage unit that he realized he had wet his pants. Not a lot, but enough to sober him up. He still had a job to do and just finding her was not the end, but only the beginning of what had to be the perfect crime. He was not going back to prison. Period.

Later that evening he laid in bed next to Marilyn, listening to her light snoring and wondering about his deteriorating sexual abilities. He had been so preoccupied with his findings that he had forgotten to take his Viagra before bedtime. Marilyn, sensing something in him was in need, began to arouse him in preparation for a sweet, loving sexual encounter. Instead, she had aroused an insatiable demon who thrusted savagely and coldly with no love or tenderness in his body. Unable to ejaculate, he quit only when she became frightened and began to cry out in pain; her salty tears spilling from eyes straining in the dark, attempting to see what possessed the man she was beginning to think she no longer knew.

Lying there in shame, sweat pouring from his heaving body, Matt tried to comprehend what was happening to him that would allow him to hurt the woman who had become so dear to him. Turning slowly, he kissed her face, tasting her tears; feeling her body as it trembled with fear. For the first time in his life, he felt loathing for himself. Deep within, he was afraid of what he had become and sickened by the person within who could do this to the one person in the world who loved and trusted him completely.

Revulsion set in and almost before he could make it to the bathroom, he vomited, missing the commode with almost half of the vile, harsh liquid spewing from his mouth. He cleaned the mess, wiping it up with bath towels off the shower rack. It took two tries, as he experienced a bout of diarrhea while he was doing the cleaning.

When he came back to bed, he could see Marilyn in the semi-darkness, staring straight upward, eyes wide and wet and looking like a scared doe caught up in something she couldn't understand. No words were spoken, but after a while, she snuggled up to him and eventually, fell asleep.

As he watched her now, he felt more like a deranged animal than a medical doctor, husband or father. Feeling the pain that an honest man feels when he causes hurt to a loved one, he desperately tried to fight back his own tears. As he fought, the fire returned, searing his very soul. Judge Dana's face loomed up in his thoughts, as clearly as if he were standing in front of her in court.

You are the last thorn in my body and it is you, not my wife and family, who should suffer. Look closely at the man you tried to destroy. This man: me. I am the one who will bring you down. Mark my words, I am coming for you soon and you will die. You will hurt no one else in this lifetime!

Matthew Hightower finally fell asleep, dreaming of the Judge burning in Dante's Inferno.

* * * *

10:00 AM, and Matt was dressed in his finest Goodwill outfit, complete with filthy looking clothes and ratty sneakers. A full raggedy beard covered his countenance and over his shoulder hung a black garbage bag with holes punched in it to accommodate his arms while he scoured the side of the road for aluminum cans. The Yamaha was hidden in the bushes, completely out of site from the highway.

There actually were about a dozen cans in the bag, compliments of the dumpster at the back of his office. None would be added during this false treasure hunt; he was working on a plan and this was his disguise.

Half a mile from the Judge's house, he found a piece of what he was looking for: a break in the thick underbrush that adorned the old bob wire fence at the edge of the woods. He was looking on the side of the road across from the Judge's house, and working out the final pieces of the puzzle: *How to Kill a Judge.*

Actually, it wasn't so much how to kill her, but how to get away with it.

At the break in the woods, the fence was down and he saw what appeared to be a small trail used by animals, probably deer and opossums. After carefully assuring himself that no one was watching, he stepped through the fence and followed the barely discernable trail into the woods.

In a few moments, the trail turned and paralleled the road, keeping a steady distance of about thirty feet to the inside of the edge of the woods. Although no recent tracks appeared on the path, it was plainly a well-used route for animal travel.

Dropping the black plastic bag, he continued on the path.

Hands sweating and pulse racing, he finally saw what he came to find: he was directly across from the Judge's house. About four feet in front of him stood a tall, fully grown oak tree with branches the size of a grown man's leg sticking out in every direction, climbing as high as twenty feet before smaller branches took over.

Awe, pure awe is what Matt felt as he realized the potential of what he had uncovered.

Wiping his hands on his pants, he began to climb the limbs of the giant oak, searching for the perfect spot. He almost slipped and fell when he looked through the gap in the trees and over the road, straight onto the Judge's front door. With his practiced eye, he guestimated the range from his perch to the door at almost exactly 100 yards. Directly in front of him was another limb which, when he sat as he did now, was positioned in perfect alignment to be used as a gun mount.

I don't even think I'll need a brace. Dear God, this is a perfect spot. I couldn't have found it so soon and so easily without providential help. Thank you, God; thank you.

Totally unaware of the trembling that pulsed throughout his entire body, he eased down from his perch, confident that he had found the spot from which he would commit the perfect crime. The puzzle was almost complete. Only timing remained.

In many ways, the next week was the most dangerous time of his mission. If he was caught, it would not be for murder, it would be for stalking, still a serious felony for an ex-con. Every morning, Monday through Friday, he arrived at the break in the fence at 6:00 AM. After hiding the Yamaha, he left it and the helmet, and, with a cup of 7-11 coffee, he walked to and sat in what he now thought of as his *killing perch*.

Notes were not needed, as everything he observed was etched into his memory. Importance was the key to memorization and, in this case, only one thing remained important: timing. Although the Judge left home at different times depending on her schedule, she always opened the door to retrieve her morning paper at exactly the same time: 7:15.

7:15. The Killing Time. As the Good Book says, A time for all seasons. A time to live and a time to die. 7:15, Judge. That is your time to die. The Killing Time.

Matthew, a committed Knight, had finally found his Holy Grail: killing. He was completely convinced that only the Judge's death could cure his mounting mental and physical ailments and make him whole and worthy of respect. Nothing mortal had led him to this place of carnage, as it would soon be known. No, he had been led by divine inspiration and he accepted that as fact. Sitting in his killing perch, he reflected on the numerous doubts that had recently plagued him.

I know the difference between right and wrong. I know the difference between good and evil. I am not a prude nor a moralist, but I know. And yet, my doubts have almost cost me the most important persons in my life. My wife. My girls. I am weak, but I will be strong. I will overcome these inhibitions that—

Pop, pop, followed by an immediate *zing, zing,* was the sound of bullets as they passed close by. Matt slipped from his perch. An almost uncontrollable urge to hold his hands up and yell, "don't shoot" was tempered only by the fact that he vaguely realized he had done nothing here to warrant being shot at. Clutching at the mounting limb, he prevented his fall, which gave him time to figure out what was happening.

"Jimmy, you better not shoot that gun off any more. You know what daddy said. He's gonna bust your ass if we get caught."

"Shut up, you little chicken! You ain't got to worry about daddy now, you got to shut your mouth or worry about me. Daddy ain't gonna say shit if I bring back a string of doves shot with a 22 and you know it."

"Yeah, but you ain't shot nothing but leaves and sky, and that don't fill no frying pan. Sides, you shooting daddy's shells, not your own. I ain't gonna lie for you none. We got to be on the bus come 7:45 and I ain't gonna miss it. Be your own ass if you do."

"You little shit! You better not get on that bus alone, you hear me!"

Voices drifting off, the two young hunters slowly retreated from hearing range and out of Matt's immediate concern.

Turning carefully and deliberately, Matt placed his back against the mounting limb and re-positioned his feet on the other side of his seating limb. As he looked down at his legs, he could see the involuntary jerking as spasm after spasm of uncontrollable nervous waves rolled down his torso.

From euphoria to perdition in two seconds. It is time. If I don't do it soon, I won't last the race. The Judge has some sort of protective aura that has kept her alive after so many years of hurting people with unjust decisions. I have to burst that bubble, or die trying. So be it! The gauntlet is thrown. Long live the enforcer, little ol' me.

* * * *

Killing Judge Alice Dana would happen Monday morning, at 7:15. It was written in the stars, and Matt was the person chosen for the job. His weekend had not been pleasant with so much on his mind. He stunk so much from his Friday morning fright and sweat accumulated during that time that he had gone home to shower, a decision which raised questions from Marilyn. His lame excuse of unspecified car trouble had not been believed, and now she suspected his recent problems might have a female reason and the female was not her.

Going back to work that Friday morning and pretending to have to work on Saturday were the only ways he knew to cover for himself during the day. Nights at home consisted of cold leftovers and an even colder bed.

After attending church on Sunday with the family, he lay awake most of Sunday night, unable to sleep or get the picture of the Judge on her front porch out of his mind. Several times he could see her face as his bullet entered it, starting a small hole between her eyes and then blowing another hole the size of a navel orange out the back of her head.

In his mind's eye, he watched as the white front door turned crimson with splattered blood and brain matter. As her legs buckled, his pulse quickened and when she hit the porch floor he sat straight up in bed, soaked in rivers of sweat and smelling of a sweet, sickly, odor so rank that he was afraid Marilyn would become ill. At the very least, she must know he was having terrible thoughts.

Returning to bed after a shower, he knew Marilyn wanted to talk, but he pretended to fall asleep until she finally rolled away and drifted off into a restless sleep.

This had to be the last night of this madness. The Judge must die tomorrow. He would not lose his family again to her.

Leaving home in the early dawn, he kissed Marilyn and held her tight. He was afraid to say too much because he couldn't be sure that she wouldn't relate what he said this morning with the death of the Judge when it was aired later. So he left her after an almost wordless embrace and drove to the storage unit.

Leaden arms moved the rifle from the trunk to the room with the Yamaha. Although he thought his mind would be racing at this point, it was actually sluggish and his body was weak and clumsy. Wearing latex gloves, he wiped the rifle down for the last time, including the bullets and clip in his final prep. It was only when he slammed the clip into the rifle and chucked the top bullet into the chamber that he felt a surge of energy flow through his body.

Yes. Just a little while now and this mission will be complete. I can go on with my life. Only a little longer now, only a little longer.

He'd wrapped the rifle, with the pre-sighted scope and inserted clip, in a black garbage bag and taped it to the Yamaha before zipping through the cool breeze of early morning on his way to the Judge's house. It attracted no attention on the way, and offered no interference when he pulled off the road at the little path and shot into the woods.

Once hidden from the road, Matt continued on the bike all the way to the base of his tree. After removing his helmet and unwrapping the gun, he took a deep breath and began to climb up to his killing perch. He never even noticed that in the cool early morning air his clothes were already soaked.

He took his seat.

Sighting down the barrel, Matthew squinted into the scope, through the crosshairs onto the front door where he was certain the Judge would shortly appear: she always did.

7:10 AM. The door would open at exactly 7:15 AM and she would come out on the porch in her white terry-cloth robe, bend over and pick up her morning newspaper.

Pulse racing, he ignored it, focusing on his duties. Refusing to allow the wrong questions to enter his mind, concentrating only on the necessities of marksmanship. Still, his mind wandered, so he deliberated on what he was doing and how he had gotten to this point.

He adjusted his scope, a Bausch & Lomb Elite 4200 with a 6X36 Matte: an expensive one and very precise. His rifle of choice, a Ruger semi-automatic 22 with a single 15 round clip. Carrying no spare clips was natural for him. Just as with his last five victims, he brought only what was necessary to the crime scene. The one full clip he had was loaded with Stinger 22 long-rifle hollow point bullets. In reality, he knew that one bullet should be more than enough for his purpose.

Come on, Judge. Come and get it. I've waited ten years for this moment. Your time has come.

Appearing cool on the outside, inside his head was a cacophony of sound, a tremendous roaring, as if he were standing in a cave under a giant waterfall. Having waited far too long to be put off by imaginary noises, he shook his head, hoping to clear it and quiet the distractions. *Concentrate. Only a few moments to go. Almost there.*

All in all, Dr. Matthew Hightower was a man of many talents. During the last ten years of his life his talents had been honed, refined and conditioned by a searing hatred. His entire being had been focused on revenging the wrongs heaped upon him by six individuals.

Five were now history. Only one victim remained.

Uncharacteristically and totally against his will, his mind wandered to Marilyn and the girls. What would they think if they knew that he was a murderer? What kind of husband could kill a Judge? What kind of father could kill an unarmed woman in cold blood? They knew nothing of his other victims. What if the unthinkable happened and he got caught? No 18 years this time. Nope, this was old sparky, straight up.

My God, Matt, get your act together! She'll be out in a moment. Feel the fire in your guts. Put it out! There's no other way! For God's sake, get a grip!

Blinking the sweat from his eyes, he looked at his watch. 7:12 AM. Focusing on the mailbox under which the newspaper lay in the curled up arms of the black wrought iron holder, he knew the rifle sights were perfectly set; he had tweaked them himself, dead on target at 100 yards. Perched, about 10 feet off the ground in a seated position with a solid limb in front for a gun prop, he was situated almost exactly 100 yards from the Judge's porch. It was a clear shot from the perch to the Judge.

Cold and bruised from sitting on the hard bark of the limb, his ass hurt severely and his legs were totally numb from lack of circulation; still, he did not shift his position. No telltale motion would give him away before he completed his deadly task.

7:15 AM. Judge Alice Dana opened her door. As she did every morning, she stopped to smell the fresh air, breathing it in deeply as she looked around, absorbing the peace and tranquility of the country area she had chosen for her home.

No longer feeling the pain and numbness of his long wait, Matt blinked away the sweat from his eyes for the last time. All visions of Marilyn and the girls receded into the recesses of his mind to allow total focus on the job at hand. Shutting down all questions and concentrating only on the job at hand, his finger began to take up slack on the trigger. Taking a deep breath, he let out half of it, and gently squeezed. Through the scope he centered the crosshairs on a space at the top of her nose, precisely between Judge Dana's unsuspecting eyes.

* * * *

No. Just as his finger sent the bullet speeding through the air, a picture of Marilyn and the girls blasted into his conscious mind and Matt yanked the rifle upward. The deadly projectile whirled off into the sky, far above the Judge's head.

Holding his breath, Matt froze in place and waited for the Judge's reaction.

Judge Alice Dana looked around, curious but not frightened. Recognizing the sound for what it was, she assumed someone was hunting in the woods near her home. It wasn't the first time, and if it happened again, she would call the sheriff and have a deputy sent to check it out. Another deep breath and she shook her head and returned into her home, out of Matt's sight and out of his life, forever.

Unable to breathe, he watched her until she disappeared inside, into the darkness beyond her doorway. After a five minute wait, during which he scarcely allowed himself to blink, he climbed down from his perch and walked deeper into the woods until he came to the tree he wanted; a solid oak with two limbs about six inches thick and only inches apart. After removing the clip and ejecting the one bullet from the chamber, he jammed the gun barrel into the space between the two limbs and bent the barrel into a complete U-shape, ruining it forever. Taking the bent barrel with his hands, he smashed the scope and firing mechanisms against the tree, once again ensuring they were totally destroyed. Only then did he toss the worthless gun into the woods.

Patting the pocket with the clip in it, he walked back to his perch tree and stood there waiting, until the Judge drove off to work. He would get rid of the bike, the storage unit, the mailbox and the contents of his gun safe.

It was over.

He had been to the mountain; had held Judge Alice Dana's life in his hands. However, unlike the vicious, jaded political woman that threw his life into total chaos, he had chosen not to harm her. Not to kill, even in the throes of justified hatred and anger, was the ultimate power. He had unequivocally proven to himself that she no longer had any hold over him. She never again would.

Matthew

Hightower was finally a free man.

EPILOGUE

One year after his stand outside the Judge's home, Matt was granted total release from probation and two years after that, his license to practice medicine was reinstated. With Marilyn as his one and only life partner, he regained ownership of his flagship clinic and went on to become a prominent, respected and philanthropic citizen of Tampa.

Judge Alice Dana died, six months after her near murder, of inoperable ovarian cancer.

Rupert Shimdugger's wife left him and took over half of the $2,000,000 paid him by his partnership insurance. He lived the rest of his life a broken, mean, nasty old man using walkers and wheel chairs. He was picked up twice for soliciting prostitution: misdemeanors, which the local State Attorney declined to prosecute.

Sergeant Rufus Black regained partial use of his limbs, but was never able to be fitted for usable dentures due to the malformations of his jaw and upper palate after numerous unsuccessful reconstructive surgeries. His girlfriend continued to live with him in his trailer until his return from the hospital some seven months after his attack; she moved out the day he came home. He died alone three years later, a totally wasted man who hated everyone with whom he came into contact.

Officer Jhonus recovered from most of her injuries, albeit without the ability to speak plainly and with limited use of her legs, which required permanent knee braces, without which she could not stand. She became active in the newly formed Church of the Avenger, a branch of which was opened just a few miles from her home. Her husband left her and her kids shortly after her attack, and her kids each legally and vocally left as soon as they reached the age of 16. She lived to the ripe old age of 85, a bitter and hateful woman whose children never even sent her a Christmas card.

Officer Stony, permanently blinded and physically disabled, committed suicide two days after arriving back at his trailer.

Major Kelly recuperated for seven months and, after several surgeries, she was able to return to her beloved uniform and her job. However, she wore a colostomy bag and was officially declared unfit to command after two years at the prison. Dismissed with a 100 percent disability, she was able to find work with the County Sheriff's office as a dispatcher, the only job she could find that allowed her to wear a uniform. For three months after returning from her last surgery, she laid in her bed with her toys, looking at the massive mirrors and dreaming of what used to be. No longer having the ability to feel any type of sexual stimulation, eventually, she tossed the toys away.

Sergeant Lacy divorced when the scandal broke out. She did have a much better recovery than the Major, however, and soon regained full use of her body. Disgraced by the incident, she moved to Colorado and became a sales clerk at a ski resort gift shop. After working there for two years, she fell in love with an Indian spiritualist and became one of his numerous followers, panhandling for donations and serving him in any capacity he wished.

Matthew Hightower was a happy man, completely free of the demons that had haunted him for so long.

Matthew might not have been so happy if he had known that in the Sarasota County Sheriff's evidence room stood a carefully wrapped and preserved baseball bat out of sight and out of mind. No fingerprints had been found; however, unknown at the time the bat not only contained traces of human blood, Shimdugger's, but also traces of human sweat, Matthew Hightower's.

DNA was not yet a known acceptable scientific form of evidence.

Not yet.

www.ingramcontent.com/pod-product-compliance
Lightning Source LLC
Chambersburg PA
CBHW060106260626
47160CB00005B/1824